I0761898

NO WAY OUT

(A Carly See FBI Suspense Thriller —Book 1)

Rylie Dark

Rylie Dark

Debut author Rylie Dark is author of the SADIE PRICE FBI SUSPENSE THRILLER series, comprising six books (and counting); the MIA NORTH FBI SUSPENSE THRILLER series, comprising three books (and counting); and the CARLY SEE FBI SUSPENSE THRILLER, comprising three books (and counting).

An avid reader and lifelong fan of the mystery and thriller genres, Rylie loves to hear from you, so please feel free to visit www.ryliedark.com to learn more and stay in touch.

ISBN: 978-1-0943-9358-2

BOOKS BY RYLIE DARK

SADIE PRICE FBI SUSPENSE THRILLER
ONLY MURDER (Book #1)
ONLY RAGE (Book #2)
ONLY HIS (Book #3)
ONLY ONCE (Book #4)
ONLY SPITE (Book #5)
ONLY MADNESS (Book #6)

MIA NORTH FBI SUSPENSE THRILLER
SEE HER RUN (Book #1)
SEE HER HIDE (Book #2)
SEE HER SCREAM (Book #3)

CARLY SEE FBI SUSPENSE THRILLER
NO WAY OUT (Book #1)
NO WAY BACK (Book #2)
NO WAY HOME (Book #3)

PROLOGUE

Denise Holder shuddered with dread as fog billowed up around her feet until she couldn't even see the floor

I ought to be used to it by now, she thought.

But even after several performances, the effect of the fog machine still seemed weird to her. It gave her the feeling of dancing through a cloud that obscured something scary beneath the surface.

Denise was making her Act 3 entrance as one of the three witches in the Boundless Bounty Theatre Company's production of *Macbeth*—or as she and the other actors preferred to call it, "The Scottish Play."

Shakespeare's tragedy was said to be cursed.

It was considered to be very bad luck to even say the name of the play aloud in a theater except during rehearsals or performances. Much of the cast was always on edge about the curse, more than half-expecting something awful to happen on that gloomily-lit stage. But *Macbeth* was very popular with the company's supporters and therefore a necessity in their repertoire.

Accompanied by creepy music, Denise and the other two witches chanted and danced through the thick carpet of fog.

Poor Gentry, she thought glancing upward.

The actress playing Hecate, the queen of the witches, was about to descend from some 30 feet above the stage. Denise knew that Gentry Chapman was terribly afraid of heights, yet night after night she sat up there all alone until it was time for a stagehand to lower her in her throne. Of course, the technicians said that the fly system was absolutely safe, and that Gentry was in no danger of falling.

I wish I could believe that, Denise thought.

As she continued to dance, Denise felt something wet on the back of her extended hand—like a droplet of rain, except that it was warm instead of cold. Still dancing, she glanced at her hand and saw that the drop was bright red.

Blood? she thought.

Fake blood?

She glanced behind her and saw that the other two witches were now evading a few similar drops of the red liquid falling from high above them.

Like the others, Denise did her best to keep dancing and chanting and staying in character as the throne bearing the queen of the witches appeared overhead and floated downward.

But as the base of the throne neared the foggy floor, Denise saw that something seemed very wrong. The queen was slumped forward, not looking at her followers and not appearing ready to speak her lines.

Denise danced closer and had to stifle a gasp at what she saw next.

What appeared to be a dagger was protruding from Gentry's chest, and all around it her elaborate gown was stained red.

For just a moment Denise thought that this must be something else that the director had added without mentioning the change.

A fake knife? she wondered.

Fake blood?

Then the throne touched down on the stage with a gentle bump.

Gentry's head lolled to one side.

Denise clearly saw the open staring eyes, the gaping mouth.

She let out a piercing scream, which seemed to echo again and again.

But it wasn't really an echo.

The other two witches were screaming as well.

Gentry Chapman was dead.

CHAPTER ONE

Special Agent Carly See's eyes followed the crisscrossing beams of searching flashlights that glared across the rain-drenched brushy landscape. She could hear the deafening barking and yelping of the enormous bloodhounds as they dragged on their leashes, trying to catch some scent of the missing young woman.

Carly didn't know much about dogs, but she thought they sounded discouraged.

The circumstances were far from ideal for the hounds to do their job. This was the second night of rain, and 19-year-old Jean Bassman had been missing for more than 24 hours now. Any scent she might have left had probably been washed away.

Waving a flashlight of her own, Carly plunged on through the wet and heavy September fallen leaves into the rain and the deepening darkness. Carly's tall, lanky African-American partner, Special Agent Lyle Ramsey, was sweeping the area right beside her. Like Carly, Lyle was clad in lightweight rain gear.

They were searching at the southern flank of a team of local police and FBI agents from the nearest field office. One of the local agents had put in a request to Quantico for help from the Behavioral Analysis Unit. Carly and Lyle had been obvious choices because of their reputation for locating lost people—especially dead people. And there was reason to fear that the girl they were searching for might be dead.

Two years ago at about this time of year, Jean's older sister, Arlene, had been abducted and then found dead the next day in a creek bed. Her killer had never been caught. Now the distraught family was facing the possibility of another tragedy.

As she kept up a slogging pace alongside Lyle, Carly felt a familiar tingle of gratitude for having such a fine older partner. It had been sheer luck that she'd been assigned to him directly out of the academy.

Or was it luck?

She often wondered whether something more than luck had brought them together. Always sure-footed, self-confident, and ready for action, Lyle was both her mentor and her friend. He also seemed more like a father to her than her actual father had ever been—although she knew it would make Lyle uncomfortable if she told him that.

Confused though the hounds might be, they seemed to be leading the searchers toward the same location where Arlene's body had been found two years ago. Carly knew that it was all too likely that the team would find Jean's body in nearly the identical spot.

A gust of wet, early autumn wind blew past Carly's face, and the night suddenly grew uncannily darker. Even her flashlight seemed barely able to penetrate the darkness. She could only see spark-like arrows of raindrops darting swiftly in front of her.

Suddenly a flash of lightning lit up the whole landscape. For a split second, Carly saw a ramshackle house standing directly in the path ahead.

Then the darkness crashed down again.

Again, her flashlight beam revealed nothing ahead except raindrops and darkness.

"We should check that house," Carly said to Lyle.

"What house?" Lyle asked.

"The one I just saw up ahead of us," Carly said.

"There's no house up ahead of us," Lyle said.

"Sure there is. I just glimpsed it in the lightning."

"What lightning?" Lyle asked.

Carly was surprised by the question. Before she could reply, an even brighter flash engulfed the scene, again revealing the house a short distance in front of her. Then the darkness slammed down again, harder and darker than before.

"Didn't you see it?" Carly asked.

"What are you talking about?" Lyle said. "This isn't a thunderstorm. It's just a fall rain."

At that moment something occurred to Carly.

I don't hear any thunder.

And Lyle didn't see any lightning.

She knew perfectly well what that meant.

I'm the only one who's seeing it.

Which meant she was getting a message. But what did this message mean? Why was she seeing an old house that wasn't even there?

Then came another flash of weird, silent lightning, and the house appeared fleetingly before vanishing yet again.

Carly's confusion swept over her in a wave of dizziness. She staggered to the nearest tree and leaned against its trunk. Although she couldn't explain it to Lyle, she knew it was a bad sign that she was getting these impressions.

The night isn't going to end well, she thought.

After all, she didn't get messages like that from the living—only from the dead.

Lyle stopped in his tracks and stared at her.

"Hey, kid, what's wrong?" he asked with genuine concern.

Carly didn't know what to tell him. She gulped down a lungful of air to steady herself.

"Lyle, are there any houses near here?" she said. "Aside from the Bassmans' I mean?"

"None that I know of," Lyle said.

"Could we check a satellite image and make sure?"

Lyle gazed at her from under his cap, his dark eyes silently asking her, *"Why?"* But of course she knew Lyle wouldn't ask. Instead, he took out his cellphone and hunched over it so it wouldn't get drenched by rain.

Carly huddled next to him over the phone to look at the satellite image of their exact location. They certainly didn't see anything that looked like a house nearby.

"Scroll around a little," Carly said to Lyle.

Lyle scrolled across the map until something to the south of them caught Carly's eye.

"There!" she said. "Look!"

In the dense woods just a short distance away from them was what appeared to be the roof of a house in a small overgrown clearing.

"We should check there," Carly said.

Lyle hesitated for a moment, and Carly understood why. After all, their present course was taking them in a completely different direction. But then he nodded in agreement.

As they turned to walk away from the other searchers, a cop called out to them.

"Hey, where are you two going?"

"Just making sure we cover the whole area," Lyle replied.

"But the dogs are heading that way," the cop protested, pointing.

"Yeah, I know, but we just want to be thorough."

The cop shrugged and kept moving in the same direction as the team.

Carly and Lyle only went a short distance before their flashlights came upon a dense patch of rainswept woods. They plunged into the stand of trees and pushed their way through brambles and bushes until they came to the object of their search.

In front of them was a small house, a shack really, in what must have been a cleared area before kudzu and ivy and scrub brush had taken over.

"We need to go inside," Carly said.

"OK, but watch your step," Lyle said. "This place looks like it might fall down around our ears."

They climbed up onto a rickety stoop and passed through the front door, which hung open on broken hinges. Their flashlights revealed a desolate interior filled with cobwebs and emptied of furniture. Floor boards had collapsed here and there.

Lyle's right, Carly thought. *We'd better watch our step.*

They moved about the tiny interior, examining every corner with their flashlights.

"I don't see anything," Lyle commented.

Before Carly could reply, they heard a thump and a moan.

Carly and Lyle both looked straight up to where the sounds were coming from.

"An attic," Lyle said.

They shined their flashlights along the low ceiling until they found a trapdoor with a cord hanging from it. Lyle pulled on the cord, and the trapdoor dropped open. A ladder came rumbling down from above.

Carly followed Lyle up the ladder into a shallow attic under the sloping eaves. Sure enough, both of their flashlight beams fell upon a young blond woman bound with duct tape to a wooden post. Her mouth was gagged with a rag, and she stared at Lyle and Carly with pleading eyes.

Carly was swept by a wave of relief as she recognized the woman from photos.

Jean Bassman was alive.

And yet she wondered …

How did I get that vision if she's not dead?

"Don't be afraid," Lyle said, showing his badge as he crouched down to approach the moaning woman. "We're here to help you."

But when Lyle loosened the gag, the young woman let out a yelp of warning.

"He's here!"

A noise erupted behind Carly and Lyle. They whirled around just in time to glimpse a man dropping down through the open trapdoor. Then a loud thump and a clatter of footsteps made it clear that he was running.

Without hesitation, Carly dropped down through the trapdoor after him and Lyle was right behind her.

They tore out of the house, and their flashlight beams spotted the man pushing his way through the brush. He was about to disappear into the dark forest when he stumbled badly, and that was all the time the agents needed to catch up with him and take him down. Carly put him into cuffs while Lyle read him his rights. With his face in the mud, the man growled with humiliation and anger.

"I'll call for help with this guy," Lyle said, snapping out his cellphone. "You go back and take care of the girl."

As Carly made her way back toward the house, there came another flash of that mysterious lightning. For just a second, she saw a dark-haired woman standing in the front doorway. She was smiling at Carly with gratitude.

Then the darkness crashed down again.

Carly's flashlight illuminated an empty doorway. The woman was gone.

Suddenly Carly understood.

Her message hadn't come from Jean Bassman at all, but from her older sister Arlene—the one whose body had been found near here two years ago. Arlene had sent Carly the message that helped find her little sister.

"Thank you," Carly murmured aloud as she walked back into the house to free Jean Bassman.

The night itself seemed to reply, *"You're welcome."*

CHAPTER TWO

Later that night, Carly drew a breath of relief when she closed her apartment door behind her. She leaned against the door, waiting for her heart to slow down.

"She was still alive," she reminded herself.

That was what she'd been mentally telling and retelling herself ever since she'd helped Jean Bassman escape from her bindings in that ramshackle attic. Much of the truth had come out since then. The man they had captured—Jean's abductor and her sister's killer—was a local high school teacher murderously obsessed with the two girls. If she and Lyle hadn't stopped him when they did, Jean might well have been dead by now.

Again, Carly breathed a quiet "thank you" to Arlene's protective, life-saving spirit. Then she switched on the lights and glanced around at her small, neat one-bedroom apartment. She had chosen the simple furnishings for their nice clean lines, easy upkeep, and lack of distinguishing features.

It's nice to be home.

As she took off her muddy shoes and walked on inside, she tried to put today's whole ugly episode behind her.

A nice hot shower will help, she decided, heading for the bathroom.

She was right. The hot water had a healing effect, washing away not just the muck and dirt of the search, but also at least some of the stresses and anxieties of the day. She got out of the shower and put on a soft terry robe. She let down her long, straight black hair and looked in the mirror, studying her own gray eyes.

I look so normal, she thought. *Average even.*

Which was true as far as her height and weight and general features were concerned. Of course, at age 30 she was in much better than average physical shape, as FBI agents had to be.

Nobody would guess that her brain was weirdly wired to pick up hints and riddles from dead people. She was glad of that, and she made the most of her unexceptional appearance, tying her hair up daily so that she looked like some perfectly ordinary young professional.

But try as she might to seem normal, she still stirred up suspicions.

As she stood looking at herself in the mirror, she remembered the question that the search team asked her and Lyle near that house—a question that kept on echoing in Carly's mind.

"How did you happen to come looking here?"

After all, it had been a considerable detour from the path the searchers and their dogs had been following. What possible reason could Carly and her partner have had for coming here?

Fortunately, Lyle had said something vague about finding the house on GPS and getting curious about it and then going there. He was covering for Carly, of course. Lyle himself didn't understand Carly's unusual gift, and they never talked about it, but he always did whatever he could to tacitly support her. She was grateful for that, although it would be awkward to tell him so.

As soon as they'd gotten back to the Behavioral Analysis Unit, Lyle had told her he would make the official report, and that he wouldn't need her help.

"Go home," he'd said.

"You deserve some rest."

So she'd driven the 20-minute commute from Quantico to Glensted. And now here she was in the apartment where she lived all alone—and living alone suited her just fine.

After a day of braving the intrusive gazes of law enforcement professionals, it felt good to know that nobody in the sprawling five-story apartment complex knew exactly what she did for a living, much less that she possessed some sort of freakish mental quirk. Most of the people here seemed to be commuters like herself, and they minded their own business.

Not surprisingly, she was hungry, so she went to the refrigerator to look for something to eat. Living alone as she did, she hadn't gotten into the habit of preparing proper meals for herself. She survived mostly on frozen dinners and deliveries. Right away she saw a couple of slices of pepperoni pizza. She slapped one of the slices onto a plate and didn't even put it in the microwave, just took it to her dining area and sat down at the table and began to eat it cold. It tasted just fine that way.

As she ate, she glanced over at the bookcase on the nearby wall. One shelf was full of family and childhood memorabilia. There were photos, of course, of school events, vacations, and a portraits of family members.

It was all a reminder of a very different life in Currie, the small town in Illinois where she'd been born and raised. As she looked at a paired portrait of her parents taken for a wedding anniversary some years back, she felt a stab of guilt. She hadn't been back to Currie for at least a year and a half. She hadn't even called Mom and Dad for a couple of months.

Maybe I should call them now, she thought.

But no, she quickly decided against it. Her father, the town dentist, was a taciturn man who was just about impossible to talk to face to face, let alone on the phone. By contrast, Carly's mother, an English professor at the local community college, tended to be pushy and domineering. Carly wasn't in the mood to deal with either of them right now.

On the same shelf stood a colorful toy pinwheel, its slender dowel handle planted in a lump of clay.

I should get rid of that thing, she thought.

After all, it was just a silly toy she'd kept since she'd been seven years old. When her friend Tyler Glick had turned seven, he and his family had given out these cheap little pinwheels as birthday party treats. Carly had kept hers ever since.

She closed her eyes and flashed back through the years to after that party, when she and Tyler were both 12 years old and she still kept that silly pinwheel in her bedroom. Tyler left school one day, but never got home. A full day went by, then another, then another, and the whole town of Currie became frantic with alarm over the boy's disappearance. The local police were helpless to find any trace of him.

After Tyler had been missing for a week, Carly had a dream with that pinwheel in it. In her dream, the pinwheel had been enormous, towering over Tyler who was lying motionless on the ground nearby.

Then the pinwheel had changed shape, becoming a wind-powered water-pump with a whirling, multi-bladed wheel at the top of a tower. Carly had awakened from the dream in a panic and ran to her mother.

"Mom, I know where Tyler is," Carly had said.

"And where is that?" Mom had replied as she made breakfast.

"Right near the windmill on Sam Mercer's farm."

Mom's forehead had crinkled with her customary skepticism.

"What makes you think that?" she'd said.

That was the moment when Carly had first faced a dilemma that still kept confounding her. She'd felt with every cell in her body that she'd had some kind of connection with Tyler, and that she knew something that everybody desperately needed to know.

And yet she couldn't talk about it.

Mother would never have believed her—and why would she?

Nevertheless, Carly had been so insistent that Mom had conveyed her hunch to the police. Mercer's farm had lain outside the original search area, but a small group of searchers finally went there. Sure enough, they'd found Tyler's body in a shallow grave within sight of the windmill. He'd been abducted and brutally murdered.

Fortunately, Tyler's killer was soon found—a lone drifter who had passed through the area recently.

Carly had never told anybody how she'd gotten that hunch. Nevertheless, the experience had changed her life. Along with a fascination for the paranormal, it had whetted her interest in law enforcement. After she'd finished college in nearby Southey, she'd joined the police department in her own hometown.

Being a policewoman in Currie hadn't been very exciting or challenging.

Just a step above being a meter maid, she'd liked to joke.

So Carly had gone to the FBI Academy in Quantico and eventually joined the BAU. Tonight hadn't been the first time her strange gift had proven useful, nor was it the first time she'd been stymied to explain just how she did things.

Carly got up from the couch and walked over to the pinwheel and idly blew on it, making it turn around.

"I miss you, Tyler," she whispered. "I'm sorry about what happened to you. I wish I could have stopped it from happening. And now … well, I guess the only thing I can do is keep trying to make the world a little safer. I hope it helps."

She finished eating and took her plate to the island between her kitchen and living area. Then she stepped closer to the bookcase and looked directly at a frame. It was of herself at 19 and a younger girl at a carnival eating cotton candy together, smiling and laughing. More than 10 years had passed since the picture had been taken.

We both look so happy, Carly thought as a lump of emotion formed in her throat.

It was painful to remember that this was the last time she'd ever seen her sister.

"Where are you, Megan?" she whispered. "Am I ever going to see you again?"

Just then she was jolted by the sound of her cellphone ringing. She took the call, which was from Lyle.

"Hey, kid," her partner said, "I hope I didn't wake you up."
"No," Carly said.
"And I hope you haven't settled in for the night."
Carly chuckled. Of course Lyle knew better than that. And of course it wasn't the first time he'd called her at such a time. She'd long since gotten used to being ready for duty at all hours.
"Oh, no, of course not," she said with playful sarcasm. "It's not like I stripped out of those filthy clothes the minute I walked in the door and took a long hot shower and got into a warm comfy bathrobe and ate a delicious slice of cold pepperoni pizza and I'm just about ready for bed. It's not like that at all."
"I'm relieved to hear it," Lyle said, chuckling as well. "I'm still at Quantico and I just now got our marching orders. It looks like we've got more work to do tonight. How soon can I pick you up?"
"Give me 20 minutes," Carly said.
"I'll be there."
"Where are we going, anyway?"
"The Shaddon Center for the Arts."
Carly's eyes widened with mild surprise.
"Are we going to catch a play?" she asked.
Lyle scoffed and said, "I'm afraid we're going to be a little late to catch a performance of the Scottish Play. I'll explain when I pick you up."
Lyle ended the call, and Carly sat staring at the phone for a moment.
The Scottish Play? she wondered.
Oh, she realized. *He must mean* Macbeth.

CHAPTER THREE

Carly got off the elevator at the ground floor and headed out the front door of her apartment building just in time to see Lyle pull up in an SUV owned by the BAU.

She climbed into the passenger seat and saw that her partner looked refreshed. Although Lyle had a nice apartment off of the Quantico base, she knew that he kept a change of clothes ready at his office. With his dark suit and the touch of gray in his close-cropped hair, he looked quite ready for an evening at the theatre.

Carly had pulled her own hair back into a bun and donned a dark blue pants suit that she hoped was nice enough for those elegant surroundings.

"So what's going on at the Shaddon Center?" she asked as they got on Interstate 95 and headed for Washington.

Lyle said, "I guess maybe you heard that the Boundless Bounty Shakespeare Company opened a production of the Scottish Play there recently."

"Actually, no," Carly said.

She knew that Lyle tended to keep up with that kind of thing better than she did.

"Well, it's a pretty big deal, with Emery Hardwick starring as Mackers and Yvette Duryea as his lady. But the tonight's performance got cut a bit short—at the beginning of Act 3, Scene 5, to be precise."

"What happened?"

"The actress who played Hecate, Queen of the Witches, was dead when she made her entrance."

Carly squinted curiously.

"How could she make her entrance if she was dead?" she demanded.

Lyle shook his head, "You know, I kind of wonder that myself. I only know what the Chief Voss told me, which wasn't much. I guess we'll find out when we get there."

"Does it look like part of a serial case?" Carly asked.

"Not that I know of."

"Then why … ?" Carly began.

"Why are we getting called in? The boss didn't say, but I think I can guess. The murdered actress's name was Gentry Chapman. As it happens, she's the daughter of Sean Chapman, the congressman."

"So does somebody think her murder might have been politically motivated?"

Lyle said, "I guess that's one of the many things we're supposed to figure out. It's high-profile, anyway, and there's going to be lots of publicity. I'm sure it will look better if more than the D.C. police are investigating it."

He scoffed and added, "Too bad about the show, though. I was hoping to catch it. It's been a long time since I've seen a production of the Scottish Play."

Carly tilted her head and asked, "Um … why do you keep calling it that?"

"Calling it what?"

"The Scottish Play."

"Oh, that," Lyle said. "Just habit, I guess. I played Mackers myself once."

Carly's mouth dropped open.

"You mean you used to be an actor?" she said.

"Naw, it was just in high school, OK?" Lyle said with just a trace of defensiveness. "And I wasn't any good. Nobody else was either. High school kids aren't ready to tackle Shakespeare, believe me. And *please* don't ask me to show you any pictures. I was just a scrawny kid with a really big cardboard crown hanging down around my ears and a big wooden broadsword all covered with aluminum foil. I looked pretty ridiculous."

I'd love to see those pictures, Carly thought with a smile.

Lyle continued, "Anyway, I just got into the habit of saying the Scottish Tragedy and 'Mackers' instead of the actual title."

"You mean *Macbeth?"*

"Yeah, that's what I mean. Look, it's OK to say it here in the car, or pretty much any place except for a theater. But in a theater it's strictly forbidden, unless you're saying it as part of a production. So don't go saying that name to anybody at the Shaddon Center."

"Why not?" Carly asked.

Lyle darted her a glance of disbelief.

"You're kidding, right?" he said.

"No, I'm not kidding."

"You've never heard of the Mackers curse?"

"Nope."

Lyle shrugged and said, "Well, there's a legend that a coven of witches came to see the play back when Shakespeare first wrote it, and they weren't amused at how he used their authentic spells and incantations, like they thought it was plagiarism or something, so they put a curse on the play. Ever since then, there's been all sorts of bad luck associated with it. And you've got to be careful about saying the name of the play."

Carly's eyes widened with curiosity. Her partner was normally ultra-rational about everything.

She said, "I never took you to be …"

She hesitated at the next word, which always made her a bit uncomfortable, considering her own strange abilities.

Lyle finished her thought for her.

"To be what? Superstitious?"

Carly nodded.

"Well, I'm definitely not superstitious," Lyle said. "But we did have all kinds of bad luck with our high school production—falling spotlights, laryngitis, even broken bones. Oh, there was nothing supernatural. It's a psychological thing. When a group of people believes something like that, things start going wrong. They get careless, clumsy, accident-prone. The curse isn't real, but it might as well be, given how crazy people can get about it."

It seemed like a reasonable explanation to Carly. Of course, she knew that Lyle was good at reasonable explanations. He'd surely come up with lots of reasonable explanations for Carly's own peculiar ways.

*

Their drive into Washington took them to the Shaddon Center for Arts, just a few blocks away from the National Mall. Lyle pulled the car up to the curb in front of a gleaming, modern building with posters advertising the production of *Macbeth* with its two big name stars. Several police vehicles were already there, and several uniformed officers were standing on the sidewalk.

As they parked, Lyle said with a sigh, "It looks like we're expected."

Coming out through the glass doors was a plainclothes officer whom Carly and Lyle knew all too well—Detective Lance Brown of the Metropolitan Police Department.

As the two FBI agents got out of the car and walked toward the building, Brown kept his arms crossed, not offering so much as a handshake. His acne-scarred face, as always, seemed to be paralyzed into a permanent smirk, and he had the cynical expression of someone who thought he knew the world better than he probably really did.

"Wish I'd known sooner you'd be showing up," he growled. "I'd have hired a caterer."

Although Lyle didn't look amused, he quipped back mirthlessly, "Next time we'll plan further ahead."

Carly noticed that Brown, as usual, seemed barely to notice that she was there. That was just as well as far as she was concerned. She did better work when her colleagues weren't paying much attention to her.

She followed Lyle and Brown into the theater lobby, which was empty of people.

As they crossed the lobby, Brown said to Lyle, "This case is weird, but really, it looks like just a plain murder. I take it you Feds are here because the victim's dad is a congressman."

Lyle said, "Nobody explained it to me that way, but it seems likely."

Brown shook his head and added, "Let's face it, you're probably just window dressing, here to show the powers that be that somebody's taking the case seriously. But it sure doesn't look like anything we locals can't deal with. I'd appreciate it if you just smiled for the cameras and said smart-sounding BAU-type things to the press and left the real detective work to me and my guys."

"I'm not making any promises," Lyle replied.

"You never do," Brown grumbled back.

The three of them passed through one of the doors that led into the auditorium. As they walked past the rows of cushy padded seats, the first thing that caught Carly's eye was a throne in the middle of the stage, ominously decorated with carved goats' heads and topped off with an upside-down pentagram.

As they continued on down the aisle toward the stage, Brown explained, "That's where the body was found. She was playing some kind of a witch queen, and she got flown in sitting in that throne, but she was dead when she hit the stage."

So that's how a dead woman made an entrance, Carly realized.

Pointing, Brown said, "You can see blood on the throne and the floor."

Carly did indeed see the blood, especially the dark puddle on the floor. But she also saw that something important was missing from the crime scene—something that her partner noticed as well.

Lyle snapped at Brown, "Where the hell's the body?"

"The Medical Examiner's team has been here and gone already," Brown said.

"And you let them take the body?" Lyle complained.

Brown shrugged defensively.

"Hey, the cause of death was pretty obvious. She was stabbed straight through the heart. If you wanted us to keep the corpse around, you should have gotten here sooner. Anyway, I've got pictures, so what difference does it make?"

"Pictures," Lyle growled. "That's just great. What about the audience? I don't see any of them around. Did you just let all of them go too?"

"There were about thirteen hundred of them," Brown said. "What was I supposed to do, make them all stay until you got a chance to talk to them?"

Lyle sighed and shook his head.

"I just hope you didn't let the killer walk out the front door," he said. "What about the cast and crew?"

"They're still downstairs in the greenroom," Brown said. "They're getting pretty antsy, though."

"Well, they'll just have to be patient," Lyle said. "Show us those pictures."

Carly, Lyle, and Brown were standing at the edge of the stage now. Brown took out his cellphone and brought up a series of photos showing the elaborately costumed woman's body sitting on the throne, with her head hanging down and a knife in her chest. Lyle clicked through photos showing details, including the knife wound and the woman's hands.

Carly felt unanswered questions pile up in her brain. The stabbing must have taken place high above the stage.

But how? she wondered.

And who could have been the culprit?

And what possible motive could the killer have had?

Carly thought about what Brown had just called it:

"Just a plain murder."

Carly doubted that very much.

Suddenly the three of them heard a booming voice from the wings.

"When are you going to let my people go?"

Carly and her partner turned and saw a man dressed all in black and wearing a cape and a broad-rimmed fedora walking toward them.

Lyle nudged Brown and asked under his breath, "Who does this guy think he is, Moses or Dracula?"

Brown whispered back, "A bit of both, maybe."

Brown made introductions as the man walked toward them.

"This is Barry Coddington, the play director," he said to Carly and Lyle. "Mr. Coddington, these are Special Agents See and Ramsey of the BAU. They're here to help get to the bottom of what happened."

Coddington sneered angrily.

"You surely don't need to keep my entire company here to do that," he said. "They need to get home and get a good night's sleep. They've got a matinee tomorrow."

Carly's tilted her head with surprise.

"You're not stopping the run of the show?" she asked Coddington. "At least for the time being?"

Coddington scoffed, "Why would we? We're sold out for a month. It's bad enough that this performance got stopped in Act 3. That wasn't my call. My damned stage manager brought the whole thing to a grinding halt as soon as the actors saw that Gentry was dead."

Lyle looked as startled as Carly felt.

"What else was she supposed to do?" he asked.

"Keep the show going, of course," Coddington said. "All she had to do was give an order to the man on the fly system to fly the corpse right out again. Hecate's a flashy part, but a small one. Some scholars don't even think Shakespeare really wrote her lines. We could have skipped the whole scene, and also her appearance in Act 4, and the audience might not have even noticed—at least not most of them. But the stage manager panicked and ruined everything."

Carly and her partner exchanged puzzled looks. Detective Brown grumbled aloud what she was sure that she and Lyle were both thinking.

"That's carrying the whole 'the show must go on' thing a little far."

Ignoring the detective's comment, Lyle asked Coddington, "Do you have any idea who might have meant the girl any harm?"

"No idea at all," Coddington said. "She was a nobody as far as I was concerned. I didn't even know she was a congressman's daughter until one of the cops told me a little while ago ..."

As Coddington kept talking, Carly shifted her attention to the empty throne.

Should I touch it? she wondered.

If she did, maybe she could make some sort of connection with the victim. But it was risky to take that chance. Sometimes she could feel overwhelmed by impressions she received.

She gathered up her courage and cautiously reached out one hand as Brown eyed her uneasily. As her fingers barely made contact with the black, coagulating blood on the throne, she got a slight tingle.

Ducking her chin so others might not notice, Carly closed her eyes.

An image popped into her head.

It was one of the photos Brown had just shown them—a shot of the victim's hand with her fingers curled toward her palms.

But flickering in and out of that hand was something that hadn't appeared in the photo—a crumpled piece of paper.

Carly stifled a gasp of alarm.

The tingling and the image vanished as quickly as they'd come, but the dead woman had communicated something to her, all right.

There was a piece of paper in her hand when she died, Carly realized.

Someone removed it.

Someone took it out of her hand before the police even arrived.

CHAPTER FOUR

As Special Agent Lyle Ramsey listened to the irritating director talk about the murdered actress as just some "nobody," he managed to appear politely attentive. He found Coddington repulsive, but it would serve no purpose to let the man see an honest reaction.

Fortunately, Lyle had practiced his concerned expression over years of dealing with self-centered people to whom the loss of someone else's life was merely an inconvenience.

Even as he tried to stay focused, he became aware of Carly moving about off to one side.

What's she doing now? he wondered. He was accustomed to the wandering attention of his young partner, and he knew that her odd behaviors sometimes led to surprising conclusions.

Turning his head just slightly as the director rambled on, Lyle could see that Carly was touching the clotted blood on the throne with a tentative finger.

His curiosity sharpened as he saw her shiver deeply.

Lyle wondered—had she discovered something that others hadn't seen?

It wouldn't be the first time, he thought.

Then Carly seemed to collect herself.

She turned toward Coddington and asked him, "Did anybody remove anything from the crime scene?"

Lyle was struck by the odd fact that Carly was asking the director, not the police detective who was standing right there with them.

Coddington visibly winced at her words.

"How would I know?" he asked peevishly.

Carly made no reply, just locked eyes with the man.

Lyle smiled a little.

She can be pretty intimidating when she gives them that wide-eyed stare, he thought.

There was a moment's silence, then Coddington's face got a little paler. He reached into his pocket and pulled out what looked like a yellowed page that had been torn out of book. It was somewhat crumpled up.

"OK, there's this," Coddington said. "She was holding it when I first walked up to her … dead body."

Detective Brown's eyes widened with surprise.

"You mean you took something from a murder scene?" he said. "And you didn't even tell me about it?"

"I hadn't thought of it like that," Coddington said defensively, but also a little fearfully. "I didn't think it was anything important."

Brown scoffed angrily, "'Didn't think it was anything important'! Huh!"

Lyle, too, found that hard to believe. He wondered whether he and Carly had already found a suspect.

Lyle also wondered something else.

Had Carly somehow known that Coddington had taken something from the scene? Or had she seen something that made her guess at the possibility?

It was the sort of thing Lyle often wondered about her.

But over their four years working together, he'd gotten accustomed to her peculiar insights and didn't ask questions about them. For example, earlier tonight she'd uncannily led him to where Jean Bassman was being held captive. He hadn't asked how she'd done it, and he'd made up some kind of a vague explanation for the rest of the team.

I've sure learned to cover for her, he thought.

Lyle was aware of his paternal, protective feelings toward his young partner. She was a good agent—as good an agent as his previous partner, Dawn—in every ordinary way. He saw no point in pressuring her over her odd quirks, especially since they often proved helpful.

Besides, whenever he had pressed Carly for an explanation, it had only resulted in a strained distance between them. She always wound up seeming uncomfortable and evasive, as if she somehow couldn't explain herself.

Meanwhile, Lyle took hold of the piece of paper with a pair of tweezers, trying to keep this bit of evidence from getting more contaminated than it surely was already. He dropped it in a plastic sheath so that both he and Carly could look at it, and Brown and Carly both snapped some pictures of it. It was a short poem with the number 9 at the top. The first two lines read:

Is it for fear to wet a widow's eye
That thou consum'st thyself in single life?

Detective Brown said, "What's this? Poetry?"

"It's a Shakespeare sonnet," Coddington explained. "He wrote 154 of them."

Lyle had already figured that out it was a Shakespeare sonnet. He was fairly sure he'd read it at one time or another, but he wasn't very familiar with it.

He glanced at Carly. She was usually better at literary matters than he was, probably because her mother was an English professor at a community college in Illinois. But at the moment, Carly was leaving the discussion up to him.

Lyle turned the page over to show Sonnet 10, which began:

For shame, deny that thou bear'st love to any
Who for thyself are so unprovident.

But a line was drawn through this whole sonnet, as if to cross it out.

Coddington pointed to the page and explained, "These early sonnets are addressed to the so-called 'Fair Youth,' a handsome young man, probably a nobleman, whom the speaker of the poem believes should marry and beget an heir. The speaker also promises to immortalize him through his poems."

Lyle wished the director would skip the pedantry. He was much more concerned with why the victim had been holding the page in her hand than he was over whatever the sonnets were all about.

Lyle's thoughts were interrupted by a man's voice from the wings.

"Excuse me for interrupting …"

Lyle and the others turned and saw a slender but wiry-looking man wearing jeans and a t-shirt.

The man added cautiously, "The folks downstairs in the greenroom are getting kind of impatient. What can I tell them? How long are we all going to be here?"

"That will be up to our local police and these two from the FBI," Coddington replied sharply. He told Lyle, "This is Deke Puckett, one of our stagehands. He was running the fly system when Gentry's body came down to the stage."

Lyle felt a tingle of interest. This guy might have a useful perspective on the murder. He might be able to tell them how it could have happened. It also occurred to Lyle that this might be the killer himself. A stagehand might have had the best opportunity to commit the murder.

"I'm Special Agent Lyle Ramsey," he told the stagehand. "I'd like to have a word with you, Mr. Puckett."

"You two go ahead and talk," Carly said. She put the bagged page into her satchel, then told Coddington, "Meanwhile, I want you to take me down to the greenroom and introduce me to your company. Detective Brown, I'd like you to come with us. "

Coddington grumbled, "Just as long as you don't keep them here all night."

As Carly, Coddington, and Brown disappeared down a spiral stairway, Lyle said to Puckett, "I'd like you to talk me through everything that happened, from your own point of view."

"Where do you want me to start?" Puckett said.

Lyle thought for a moment, then said, "First of all, how does this theater's fly machinery work? How do you drop a witch queen out of the sky, so to speak?"

"Let me show you," Puckett said, leading Lyle into the wings.

Along the wall at the side of the stage was a system of pulleys and weights.

Puckett pointed to one of the ropes and said, "This is called the purchase line. This is what I used to raise Gentry up into the fly loft, then bring her down when her big scene came."

Lyle looked back and forth from the throne to the rope with surprise. With all its ornate decor, the throne looked awfully heavy to him.

"You mean you brought her in and out *by yourself?"* he asked. "No offense, but you're not the biggest guy in the world. This looks like a job for a bunch of real burly weightlifters."

"Not at all," Puckett said, pointing to a rack stacked with iron weights. "This is what's called the loading arbor. The weights are exactly equal to the amount of weight that has to fly in and out—the batten, plus the throne, plus Gentry's weight, costume and all. The whole system is balanced so that flying them in and out is no effort at all. Even a child could do it."

Lyle noticed a fleeting smile cross Puckett's face as he explained all this. Then his smile disappeared as he seemed to remember the terrible thing that had happened.

The reaction of an innocent man, maybe, Lyle thought.

But at this point, he couldn't be sure.

"Could you show me this thing in action?" Lyle said.

“Not with this line,” Puckett explained. “Remember, the total weight included Gentry herself. Without her sitting in the throne, the whole thing would be out of balance.”

Fingering an iron latch, Puckett added, “If I unlocked this, the throne will be too light, and it would go flying up all by itself, and both of us together might not be able to control it. But I’ll show you another purchase line that’s properly weighted with just a pipe batten.”

Puckett led him over to the next line and opened the latch.

“Here, try it yourself,” he said, indicating the line. “Move the rope upwards.”

Feeling a little nervous, Lyle took hold of the line and raised it. He was a bit surprised to realize Puckett was right—moving the line took no effort at all. He kept moving the rope upward until a horizontal pipe descended from high above them and stopped within a few feet of the stage.

“Now fly the pipe out,” Puckett said.

Lyle pulled the rope in the other direction, and it moved just as effortlessly as the pipe rose up again. When it reached its original location, Puckett locked the latch again. A new question came into Lyle’s mind.

“How did Gentry Chapman feel about all this flying around?” he asked.

Puckett shook his head with a sad smile.

“It scared her half to death, the poor girl. She was terrified of heights to begin with. I had to explain this whole system over and over again and promise her it was perfectly safe before she’d get into that throne. To make things worse, her costume was too bulky for her to climb the spiral stairway up the catwalk and get into the rig there. I had to raise her up with the fly system before every performance, before the house even opened. And she had to sit up there for the first three acts until it was time for her to make her entrance.”

Lyle’s brain clicked away as he tried to make sense of what he was hearing and what he knew. It appeared from the photos that the victim had been stabbed to death just a few moments before she’d been lowered to the stage. Which meant, of course, that someone else must have been high up in the fly loft near Gentry when she was murdered.

How is that possible? he wondered.

He could ask Puckett, of course, and the stagehand could probably explain it pretty clearly.

But if Puckett himself was the murderer ...

He decided it was time to ask Puckett an obvious question.

"Where were you during the time before you had to fly her in?"

Puckett squinted back at him uneasily.

"How much time are you talking about?" he asked.

"Oh, say, a half hour."

"I was standing right here waiting for my cue. I'm always at my post well ahead of schedule."

Puckett shuffled his feet and added, "I guess you want to know whether I might have been up in the fly loft with her when she was killed. I definitely wasn't. I was right here."

"Can anybody confirm that?" Lyle asked.

Puckett sighed and said, "I don't know. Maybe. I mean, I was standing in plain view, and people were coming and going. But it's pretty dark in these wings during a show. And besides, nobody pays any attention to stagehands while a performance is going on. We're practically invisible. Maybe somebody can say they saw me. Or maybe not. I just don't know."

Not the answer I wanted to hear, Lyle thought.

And he saw that Deke Puckett was looking very uneasy. Although Lyle's own intuitions weren't uncanny like Carly's, they were considerably sharper than average, even for a BAU agent. And right now he got the strong feeling that Puckett had something on his mind.

He asked Puckett, "Is there something you think you should tell me?"

Puckett's body tensed and his voice thickened.

"Yeah," he said. "Maybe there is."

CHAPTER FIVE

Lyle folded his arms and waited for Puckett to speak.

The stagehand slumped and said, "Look, this is … well, kind of hard for me to talk about, and I'm not sure why it even matters as far as you're concerned, but …"

Puckett fell silent for a moment, then continued.

"If you ask around the cast and crew, just about anybody will tell you … I had a huge crush on Gentry Chapman. I'm pretty sure everybody knew about it … except probably for Gentry."

"So you never told her?" Lyle asked.

"Oh, no, absolutely not. Look, she was an actress and I'm just a lowly stagehand. Besides, she was a congressman's daughter. She was completely out of my league. But there was something … I don't know, kind of romantic about how I was so responsible for her safety. At least it felt that way to me. She probably didn't even give it a thought. Still, I kept trying to get up the nerve to invite her out for a drink or a cup of coffee or something …"

Lyle studied Puckett's face as the stagehand avoided his gaze.

Puckett added, "Anyway, what happened to her … I guess it's going to take a while for the reality to sink in. I just wish … I feel like I should have been able to … protect her, I guess."

"It's good that you told me," Lyle said.

The stagehand nodded mutely. Lyle thought the guy certainly seemed sincere enough. But that was hardly the same as having an airtight alibi. Puckett hadn't even claimed that he could prove where he was at the time of the murder.

And if the guy was obsessed with her …

There might be all kinds of issues at play, especially if the girl had been seeing another man. Lyle knew that a true psychopath could fake exactly the distress Puckett was showing.

Meanwhile, he still needed to get some idea of what had happened at the moment of the stabbing. He pointed to the spiral stairway that extended both below the stage and high up into the fly loft.

"Could you take me up to where she was killed?" he said to Puckett.

"Sure," Puckett said. "Come with me."

Lyle followed Puckett up the narrow, winding stairway. The steps were made of steel grating, so Lyle could see all the way down to the stage below his feet as he climbed.

He felt bumps rise up on his skin. He wasn't normally afraid of heights, but something about this particular staircase made him distinctly nervous. It wasn't very wide, and all the openings in the grating made them look fragile, although of course they were quite sturdy.

Finally they arrived at a steel landing some 35 or so feet from the stage floor.

Lyle could see that they had reached the level where the battens were raised when they weren't in use. They were suspended from cables that reached up into a gridded platform directly above them, which extended in all directions.

A short distance below the battens, a catwalk stretched from the landing where they stood across the stage.

Lyle pointed and asked Puckett, "How close could somebody have gotten to her on that catwalk?"

"Right behind her," Puckett said. "Let me show you."

Lyle felt somewhat queasy as he followed Puckett out onto the catwalk. Through the grating, he could see the throne far down on the stage, looking very small from this height.

Puckett pointed just over the catwalk rail.

"When the throne was raised, it hung right here, just inches away," he said.

Lyle now found it easy to imagine how the crime might have been committed. The killer might have crept out onto this catwalk without Gentry noticing it. He or she could have stood right behind the throne, reached around her with a knife, and stabbed her in the chest.

But how did he get here in the first place? Lyle wondered.

He asked Puckett, "Did you see anybody climb up here while she was waiting for her cue to descend?"

Puckett shook his head.

"No, I think I would have noticed that," he said.

And how did he get away? Lyle also wondered.

Lyle looked back toward the spiral staircase, which wound its way beyond them toward the ceiling.

"What do those stairs lead up to?" he asked Puckett.

"The roof."

"Show me," Lyle said.

Puckett led him back to the stairway, and the two of them climbed upward past the gridded platform, where the top pulleys for the fly system were anchored. Finally they arrived at a landing with metal door marked by an EXIT sign.

Lyle's eyes immediately fell on a small square of dented cardboard lying on the floor in front of the door. A tingle up his back signaled to him that things were about to make a whole lot more sense.

He picked up the piece of cardboard and pushed the bar that opened the door. A gush of cool night air poured in from outside.

As Lyle started to step outside, Puckett warned, "If we both go out on the roof, we'll get locked out. The door will lock behind us."

"No, it won't," Lyle said.

Then he did exactly what he was sure the killer had done—he put the piece of cardboard against the door latch so it would stay loose even with the door closed. Carefully shutting the door behind him, Lyle walked with Puckett out onto the roof.

Lyle's eyes immediately fell upon the curved top of a fire escape ladder. He walked over to the ladder and saw that the metal structure led almost all the way down to an alley below.

He asked Puckett, "How is the security inside the building? During the day, I mean?"

Puckett shrugged and said, "Well, the building itself is usually wide open. But some areas are locked up when they're not in use. The tool cage, the costume shop, the prop room, the sound and light booth—any area where there's something that might get stolen."

"What about the theater itself?" Lyle asked. "I mean, could just anybody waltz in here and come all the way up the stairs and out onto this roof?"

"I suppose," Puckett said. "If they could avoid our security guy, which might not be hard to do. And we don't have any security cameras."

Things were coming clearer to Lyle by the second. At some time during the day, the killer might have simply walked into the building and headed up the spiral stairway and blocked the door latch with the piece of cardboard and come out onto the roof. He could easily have stayed hidden up here until it came time to commit the murder.

Then he could have reentered the building, climbed down to the landing and out onto the catwalk, and committed the murder. After that he could have hurried back up to the roof and then down the fire escape. If he was careful, he might never be seen.

Or at least that's how it could have happened, Lyle thought.

For all he knew, the crime could have been committed by someone in the cast or crew—including Deke Puckett. It might even have been committed by someone in the audience.

In any case, Lyle had learned as much from Puckett as he could expect to for the time being.

"Come on," he said. "Let's head down to the greenroom."

*

Down in the crowded greenroom, Carly was asking the cast and crewmembers questions and jotting down notes on her notepad.

Standing near the doorway, Barry Coddington grumbled yet again, "I've directed *Macbeth* a half dozen times. I've never had this kind of trouble. Certainly nobody ever got killed before."

Carly noticed a few of the actors squirming with superstitious discomfort. This wasn't the first time since the meeting had started that Coddington had spoken the name of the "Scottish Tragedy" aloud. He always did so with a gloating grin, as if he took satisfaction in provoking unease among some of the actors.

A bit of a sadist, Carly figured.

Personally, Carly thought the man looked rather comical in his black outfit, complete with a cape and a broad-rimmed fedora. But he was also arrogant and charismatic, and Carly sensed a palpable dislike of him among the actors—something close to fear.

Carly felt as though the greenroom was getting hotter and stuffier and more crowded by the minute. Actually, the number of people here was the same as when she'd first walked in a little while ago. But this was normally a place for members of the cast to take breaks and relax between scenes. Right now the whole production company was crammed in here—costume and set changers, makeup artists, prop people, and the technicians who ran the lights and sound.

Overall, there were some 35 people in this normally laid-back, comfortable space, and not a single one of them looked happy to be here. Carly hardly found it an ideal situation for asking questions, but right now, there was nothing else to be done.

Of course so far, Carly had been asking the group all the usual questions—including whether they knew of anyone who might have meant Gentry Chapman any harm, or knew of any threats to anybody else in the company, or if they'd seen any strange or suspicious people during the performance. So far the answers hadn't been very informative.

Carly had actually been gleaning more information from watching people's faces and body language. The celebrity leads who were playing Macbeth and Lady Macbeth, Emery Hardwick and Yvette Duryea, stood apart from the others—and also from each other.

Carly didn't know a lot of celebrity gossip, but she'd seen both actors in movies and on TV, and she knew that they had been married to each other and divorced two or three times, and it was pretty obvious that they weren't on good terms right now. They were sitting on opposite sides of the greenroom and studiously ignoring each other.

Carly wondered how their palpable mutual hostility played itself out in their scenes together.

I guess the tension could be pretty electric, she thought.

As Carly studied Yvette Duryea's posture, she was startled when the actress abruptly made eye contact with her. It was the first time their eyes had met since this meeting had started. Then, just as quickly, the woman's eyes darted away.

That quick glance stirred a memory in Carly's mind.

Earlier, when she'd seen that dark pool of coagulating blood on the throne, felt its unpleasant stickiness when she'd touched it, she had glimpsed the sonnet that had been left with the body. As she flashed back to it now, she heard a woman speaking in a soft voice.

Out, damned spot! Out, I say!

Carly recognized the words immediately. They were from Lady Macbeth's famous "sleepwalking scene" late in the play.

But the voice she heard was definitely not that of Yvette Duryea.

The voice was higher and more youthful.

A hunch started to form in Carly's brain. But she knew she'd better be careful what questions she asked next—and of whom she asked them.

She turned to the actor who had been playing Macbeth and asked, "Mr. Hardwick, do you happen to have an understudy?"

"Of course I do," Hardwick said, indicating a young man seated nearby. "It's Bart Unger here. He normally plays one of the murderers."

Slapping him on the shoulder, Hardwick added, "He's got a lot of promise."

As Carly turned her eyes back toward Yvette Duryea, the tension in the room got suddenly thicker.

"What about you, Ms. Duryea?" she asked the actress.

Yvette Duryea's face twitched.

"As a matter of fact," she said in a tight voice, "my understudy was Gentry Chapman."

Carly was hardly surprised. But she was far from pleased that no one had told her this until just now. She glanced over at Detective Brown, who glanced back at her with an embarrassed expression and shrugged his shoulders. Obviously, this was the first time he'd heard that the murder victim had been understudying the part of Lady Macbeth.

Why didn't Barry Coddington at least mention it? she wondered.

Carly looked around for him, almost on the verge of asking him. But to her surprise, she saw no trace of him, although he'd been standing there on the edge of the group just a few moments before.

Had he slipped out without being noticed?

Why would he do that? Carly wondered. Surely the police had warned everybody not to leave.

Meanwhile, Yvette Duryea crossed her arms and spoke with a forced, scoffing laugh.

"Surely that doesn't make me a suspect. In situations like this—or so I'm told—it's the understudy who kills the leading lady, not the other way around."

Carly couldn't disagree with this little attempt at dark humor. It was hard to imagine why Yvette Duryea would have killed Gentry Chapman. Having her as an understudy didn't seem like a plausible motive.

But where is Coddington? she wondered.

At that moment, Lyle pushed his way into the room with the stagehand, Deke Puckett, at his side. Carly was glad to see Lyle, even though the room now felt packed to the point of exploding. She hoped he'd had more success at finding evidence than she had.

Now that he was here, it seemed like a good time to bring this meeting to a close. Carly looked out over the faces in the greenroom.

"I've got one more question," she said. "Does Shakespeare's Sonnet 9 have any special significance to anybody?"

She skimmed the faces rapidly, trying to gauge every single reaction. As she expected, most of the people in the group seemed mildly surprised. They were surely wondering what a Shakespeare sonnet could possibly have to do with the case at hand. Also as she expected, some of the others looked utterly indifferent to her question.

What she was looking for was a different sort of expression—she wasn't sure what it might be, except that it might hint at somebody's guilt.

But none of the expressions she saw seemed the least bit suspicious.

She looked at Lyle and silently mouthed the words, "I think I'm done here."

Lyle nodded with approval.

"Thanks for your time," Carly said to the group. "My partner and I are terribly sorry for the ordeal you are going through. You may go now. But please call us if you think of anything that might help us find Gentry Chapman's killer."

Carly recited a phone number, and the group began to break up and head on out of the greenroom, either to finish taking off their costumes and makeup or to leave the building.

Carly was a little uneasy about having no choice except to let everyone go. But keeping everybody here wasn't going to reveal the killer, even if he was still in the group. On the other hand, if someone in the company didn't show up on schedule tomorrow, that might give them a viable suspect.

Carly, Lyle, and Detective Brown approached each other.

"So what do you think?" Brown asked both Lyle and Carly. "Did either of you find out anything?"

With a sigh, Lyle said, "Well, I've got a pretty good idea of *how.* But I still don't know *who.*"

Then he turned to Carly and asked, "How about you?"

Carly squinted and said, "I'm not sure. Did you see Barry Coddington while you were looking around the theater?"

Lyle's eyes widened with surprise.

"You mean he wasn't here with your group?" he asked Carly.

"He was at first, but he slipped away without my noticing it," Carly said.

Lyle scratched his chin and said, "No, I didn't see him anywhere."

"I don't like the sound of that," Detective Brown grumbled.

Carly didn't like the sound of it either, and she was sure her partner felt the same way. Meanwhile, it seemed that their business at the theater was finished, at least for the moment.

As she and Lyle stepped out of the greenroom, a young woman

approached them in the hallway. Judging from what remained of her makeup, Carly guessed that she'd played one of the three witches. She seemed agitated and anxious as she kept glancing around and over her shoulder.

She asked Carly and her colleagues, "Is Barry Coddington still around?"

"He doesn't seem to be, no," Carly said.

The actress inhaled sharply.

"There are some things … I guess … you might want to know," she said.

CHAPTER SIX

When Carly and Lyle and the police detective stopped to hear what she had to say, the young woman just stood there, her eyes darting fearfully around the hallway. The remains of the witch makeup didn't suggest any supernatural power to Carly. In fact, she looked rather small and fragile.

"Maybe—maybe this isn't a good idea," she stammered. "It's nothing important anyway. I'm sorry I bothered you."

She turned away, but Carly stopped her from leaving with a gentle touch on the shoulder.

"Not yet, please," Carly told her. "What's your name?"

"Denise Holder."

"And you played one of the three witches?"

"That's right. I'm the one who first noticed that Gentry was … you know."

Detective Brown growled ominously, "Young lady, if you have any information about Gentry Chapman's murder, you'd better spill it right away. It's against the law to withhold information from the police, and—"

Carly silenced him with a sharp, disapproving look. Tough cop talk was the last thing they needed at the moment.

Lyle broke in gently. "Maybe you'd like to talk with my partner alone," he suggested.

Denise let out a gasp of relief.

"Oh, yes, I would like that better, thanks," she said.

Carly mouthed a silent "thank you" to her partner as she and Denise headed back into the greenroom. Lyle was always good with witnesses, particularly at figuring out the best approach to each one. She appreciated his sensitivity in this case. The actress was clearly more comfortable talking with another woman.

She and Denise found an empty makeup room and sat down.

"Just relax and tell me what you think I should know," Carly said, taking out her pad and pencil again. "I promise it will be OK."

Denise rolled her eyes.

"Oh, I don't see how you can promise that," she said. "You've got no idea how powerful Barry Coddington is in the American theater. He can make or break just about anybody. That's why nobody else spoke up just now. They're scared to death of him."

A silence fell between the two women.

Don't push her, Carly thought. *Just let her talk in her own good time.*

Finally Denise said, "Something happened between Barry and Gentry yesterday. Something bad. I caught them alone backstage. Barry had backed her into a corner and it sure looked like he was threatening her. I just stayed as still as I could. Then I caught part of what he was saying … and he definitely was threatening."

"Can you remember his exact words?" Carly asked.

"Pretty nearly," Denise said. "It was something like, 'If you think ruining your career is the worst thing I can do to you, you'd better think again. I can do much worse than that, believe me.'"

Carly felt a small jolt as she jotted down the words. If Coddington wasn't in fact the killer, he nevertheless struck her as a pretty terrible human being—and capable of some really terrible behavior.

Carly asked, "Did either Barry or Gentry notice you were there?"

"No, and I slipped away before they saw me."

"Do you have any idea what he might have meant?" Carly asked.

Denise shuddered deeply.

"I just got the feeling it was something really ugly," she said. "And now that she's been killed I can't help wonder …"

Her voice faded and she lowered her head and muttered, "I mean, it's probably nothing."

"Maybe," Carly replied. "But it could be really important. Tell me more about Barry Coddington. Why is everybody so afraid of him?"

"It's mostly the women who are afraid of him," Denise said. "I think he hates women. He's always abusive and insulting, especially toward the actresses. I haven't seen him do anything physically violent, but … well, there have been rumors of groping and forced kissing and such. And he's always putting the moves on some actress, and he really doesn't like to hear the word 'no.'"

"Do you think maybe something like this happened between Gentry and Coddington?" Carly asked. "I mean, maybe she turned down his advances?"

"I don't know. Gentry was awfully jittery after that happened. I asked her what was wrong, but she got kind of defensive and wouldn't talk about it, like she didn't think it was any of my business."

Denise lowered her eyes regretfully.

"I guess I should have asked … well, I guess I should have been more insistent. Maybe if I'd pushed her more about it …"

Her voice faded. But Carly immediately understood the thoughts that were starting to creep into Denise's mind.

She reached over and touched the young woman's arm. "It's really important that you not blame yourself," Carly told her. "What happened to Gentry was not your fault. Not in any way. And right now you're trying to help, which is the most anyone can expect you to do."

Carly knew that what Denise had told her about the director and women was likely to be common knowledge, but none of the others had brought it up. She added, "It's more than some others have done."

Denise nodded silently.

Carly thumped her eraser against her notepad and thought for a moment.

Finally she asked, "Was Gentry romantically involved with anybody?"

"Not that I know of. She told me she was interested in one guy, though. It was the stagehand who came into the greenroom with your partner. Deke Puckett is his name. A nice guy, but I don't think he had any idea she had a crush on him. I kept telling her she should just haul off and ask him out. But she was just too shy, I guess."

Denise shrugged and added, "And anyway, they came from really separate worlds. Her dad's a congressman, you know. Her family would probably totally freak out if she'd dated a working-class guy like Deke."

The Deke Puckett story didn't sound to Carly like it included a possible motive for murder. But Barry Coddington struck her as a likely suspect. It was too bad he'd disappeared without warning. Of course, he could have had an urgent reason to leave, but he hadn't bothered to mention that to anybody.

She asked Denise, "Does Coddington live here in D.C.?"

"No, he lives in Manhattan. Actually, I think he has a nice place in London, too. He's just been staying in Washington to direct the play. I've heard that he's staying at the Verdana Hotel over in Georgetown."

Lyle and I had better have a word with him, Carly thought.

Pocketing her notepad, Carly said, "Thank you for your time, Denise. You've been a great help."

Denise's eyes were darting around again.

"Um … I hope we can keep this conversation … between

ourselves," she said.

"Nobody has to know about it," Carly replied, handing Denise her personal contact card. "But if anything else occurs to you that we should know, please get in touch with me directly."

"I'll do that."

When Carly and Denise left the makeup room and exited the greenroom, Lyle and Detective Brown were still waiting patiently in the hallway.

After watching Denise disappear up the stairs, Lyle asked, "Did you find out anything?"

"I think we need to pay Coddington a visit over in Georgetown."

"Coddington, eh?" Lyle said. "Does he look like a possible suspect?"

"Maybe," Carly said. "Just maybe. Let's head for the car. I'll tell you all about it as we drive."

Detective Brown asked, "Where are you going in Georgetown?"

"The Verdana Hotel," Carly said. "That's where Coddington is staying."

Brown said, "Don't you think we should call first to find out if he's there right now?"

Lyle let out a grunt of annoyance.

"Brilliant idea, Brown," Lyle said. "That way we can alert him to be prepared for us." Taking out his cellphone, he added, "It might be a good idea to check with the hotel desk, though."

As they all headed out of the building, Lyle called the hotel desk and found out that Barry Coddington was, indeed, in his room.

"I'll meet you at the hotel," Brown said, walking briskly away toward his car.

Carly and Lyle exchanged irritated glances as they headed toward their own vehicle. Carly wasn't fond of Detective Brown, and she could see that Lyle was even less so. The cop wasn't the sort of company either of them would choose.

But Carly also figured Brown might be helpful to have on hand if they wound up making an arrest. After all, they had no idea what they might be in for.

*

Lyle frowned sharply as he drove toward Georgetown listening to Carly relate the details of her interview with Denise.

He shook his head and said, "This director sounds like a real sweetheart. Of course, I got that impression the minute I met him."

"Yeah, he's a jerk, all right," Carly replied.

"Let's not get our hopes up that he's our man, though," Lyle said. "I hear that 99 percent of all jerks aren't murderers."

"Even the male jerks?" Carly asked with a smile.

"Well, the stats might be just a little higher for them," Lyle said with a chuckle. "Did the actress tell you anything else of interest?"

Carly thought for a moment, then said, "I take it you had a little talk with the stagehand, Deke Puckett."

"Yeah, he showed me the ropes—*literally.* He demonstrated how the victim got flown in and out for her scenes as Hecate, the queen of the witches. He also showed me where the murderer must have been when he stabbed her to death. He did it from a catwalk some 35 feet above the stage."

Carly said, "Well, not that it probably matters, but the victim had a crush on Puckett."

Lyle's eyes widened with surprise.

"No kidding? Puckett told me he had a crush on her. Never dared go anywhere near her, though. He thought she was out of his league."

"That's sad," Carly said. "She couldn't get up the nerve to approach him either."

"So neither one of them had any idea how the other felt," Lyle said with a shake of his head. "That *is* sad. I wonder if it would have made any difference …"

Lyle's voice faded, but Carly understood what he was thinking. In their line of work, it was impossible not to think about hypotheticals.

"What if" this, "What if" that?

If two young people had simply gotten up the nerve to tell each other they liked each other, might that have changed events? Might one of them have not gotten killed?

Of course the question was pointless, but somehow Carly found it hard to drive it out of her mind. She knew that Lyle was probably wondering the same thing.

One of the hazards of our work, I guess.

Lyle asked, "What about Yvette Duryea? Does it bother you that she didn't say upfront that Gentry Chapman had been her understudy?"

"Maybe a little," Carly said. "But then, nobody else said anything about it either. And it wasn't exactly a secret."

"True," Lyle said. "Besides, Duryea was onstage at the time of the murder. That's about as good an alibi as anyone could hope to have."

The two of them fell silent as they drove into upper-class Georgetown. Carly found herself wondering what her partner was thinking.

She knew that some of her actions tonight had stirred his longstanding questions about her, starting with how she'd found Jean Bassman earlier. She was sure he'd also been struck by how she'd picked up on the sonnet page Barry Coddington had snatched out of the victim's hand.

What about the way she'd gotten Yvette Duryea to admit the murdered woman had been her understudy? Had that also piqued his interest? Or had he just chalked it up to solid detective work?

She figured it didn't matter. Lyle seemed perfectly used to her odd ways.

Besides, now isn't the time to worry about that, she told herself.

They had a murderer to catch.

CHAPTER SEVEN

The man sat fingering the now-empty leather sheath.

It's too bad I had to leave the dagger behind, he thought.

He'd stolen the weapon from a theater props cage some years ago, and he'd become rather attached to it. With its stainless steel hilt and blade and carved wooden handle, it was quite handsome. It would have made a nice keepsake, a reminder of the marvelous act he had just committed.

But of course, leaving the blade in the woman's body had been an essential part of the spectacle. It looked like the sort of knife that would appear in a production of *Macbeth.* That was part of its …

What was the word he was looking for?

Charm, I suppose, he thought.

Yes, there was something quaint about making this murder appear at first glance like it might be part of the play. It was as if he were rewriting Shakespeare to suit his own ends.

And in a way, that was exactly what he was doing.

He knew all the plays extremely well, and of course there were many kinds of deaths in them—he'd counted some 74, and almost half of those were stabbings of one kind or another. There were eight of those in *Macbeth* alone, although some—like the stabbing of King Duncan—took place offstage.

In Shakespeare's bloody world, men were routinely armed with such weapons, and they killed with them at the drop of a hat. People didn't live or die that way anymore.

The man smiled and thought, *Which makes me an innovator.*

That was to be expected, of course, considering his pedigree and creative promise. Although his power of words had been taken away from him, his sense of drama was dangerously, fatally keen. And as of tonight, he was bringing his violent vision to life—to *real* life.

He wondered—had Shakespeare himself ever stabbed someone?

Did he have any idea how it felt?

If not, the man couldn't help considering it a bit lazy of him to dramatize so many such acts without bothering to murder anybody himself and really get the feel of it.

For his part, the man had found it to be a surprising and exhilarating experience. He relished the memory of creeping out along the catwalk high above the stage while Macbeth was reeling with horror from the apparition of the murdered Banquo's ghost.

Hence, horrible shadow!
Unreal mock'ry, hence!

The actor's powerful, resonant voice had covered any noise the man might have made during his approach behind the throne where Hecate, queen of the witches, sat suspended and waiting for her descent to the stage.

The man had gripped the knife handle tightly and reached around in front of the throne. The woman had let out a gasp of bewildered horror at the sight of the blade, but he had plunged it deep into her flesh before she could fend it off.

And how easy that part had been!

He'd been mentally prepared for struggle and difficulty. He'd heard that it was hard to stab someone, especially in the chest, where the blade was likely to get stuck between ribs before it could reach any vital organs. But he'd struck a softer spot below the ribcage and plunged the blade in effortlessly at an upward angle. His victim had let out a ghastly groan, far too quiet to be heard by anyone below. Then she had slumped and died.

It couldn't have gone better.

It seemed a shame that he had to hurry away and miss the magical moment when the throne actually descended to the stage, and his *tableau vivant*—his real-life picture—appeared in full view of a horrified cast and audience. But he knew the effect had been quite phenomenal.

And then there was the matter of the sonnets, which were so fundamental to his creative acts. He picked up the page he was going to leave with the next victim—Sonnet 19—and read the first two lines aloud, savoring the ominous words as he spoke them.

Devouring Time, blunt thou the lion's paws,
And make the earth devour her own sweet brood ...

Of course there was no way anybody could guess the significance of the torn-out pages—not yet, anyway. Perhaps after he'd finished his series of murders, someone might discover the pattern. If so, it would add a final dash of *denouement* to his dramatic masterpiece.

At this point, there wasn't much room for improvisation or surprise. The drama seemed to be writing itself, with the victims sealing their own fates in advance, as seemed appropriate for a tragedy-in-the-making.

But he felt a tingle of fear in the midst of his exhilaration, which of course was exactly as it should be. The tragedy of Macbeth was marked by the title character's long descent into apprehension and paranoia.

He remembered Macbeth's dread at a certain sound at his castle door.

Whence is that knocking?
How is't with me when every noise appalls me?

Glancing toward his own door, he wondered …

What if someone came knocking here right now?

He'd conceal the sheath, of course. Then he might even allow the visitor to enter. But could he keep his wits about him under someone's suspicious eyes and prying questions?

Of course he could. After all, he was as fine an actor as he was a playwright and a poet. He would never let himself get so swept away by anxiety and nerves that he might lose control of his own drama. Consummate artist as he was, he needed to be the master of every moment.

Meanwhile, it was very late, and he planned to claim his next victim tomorrow morning. Would he get any sleep between now and then? Probably not, but he didn't feel as though he needed it, not with the energy and excitement now coursing through his body.

It's all so thrilling, he thought with a smile.

And the play was just getting started!

CHAPTER EIGHT

Carly tried not to get her hopes up as Lyle pulled the car to the curb in front of the Verdana Hotel. While Barry Coddington might well be the murderer, she knew it would be an extraordinary stroke of luck to wrap up the case so quickly.

The Verdana Hotel was a majestic, palatial Victorian building that dominated the area, complete with battlements and turret roofs. As Carly and Lyle got out of the car, Detective Brown parked right behind them. He jumped out of his car and walked with them toward the arched entryway.

"I've got a feeling this is it," Brown said, rubbing his hands together eagerly. "We're going to catch our killer. I got suspicious of Barry Coddington the minute I laid eyes on him."

Carly and Lyle glanced at each other as the three of them continued on into the vast hotel lobby. If Coddington really was their killer, Brown was likely to take as much credit as possible for solving the case.

That's OK, I guess, she thought.

The important thing was getting it done.

All three of them stopped at the front desk, where they produced their badges and showed them to the butler-clad man at the desk.

Lyle said, "I'm Special Agent Ramsey of the BAU, and this is my partner, Special Agent Carly See."

"And I'm Detective Lance Brown, MPD," their colleague added.

Brown added, "We're here to see one of your guests—Barry Coddington."

The clerk looked around uneasily, obviously anxious about the effect of these visitors on clientele within earshot.

"Certainly," the clerk said, picking up a telephone. "Let me just give his room a ring and—"

Lyle interrupted, "We'd rather you didn't do that. Just tell us where we can find him."

The clerk's eyes widened with concern.

"Mr. Coddington is staying in room 348," the man said. "If you like, I can have somebody show you the way."

"That would be helpful, thanks," Lyle said.

A uniformed bellhop led them to an elevator with engraved brass doors, then upstairs to the third floor. They followed him down an elegantly carpeted hall lined with wall sconces to the room they were looking for.

Then the bellhop stood expectedly for a moment until Carly gave him a tip and waved him on his way. She didn't know what was about to happen next, but neither she nor her colleagues wanted a civilian standing around. The bellhop tipped his hat and headed back toward the elevator.

Lyle rapped on the door.

At first there was no reply.

Carly, Lyle, and Brown looked at each other worriedly.

Did he slip out on us? Carly wondered.

Lyle knocked on the door again, and this time they heard a reply.

"Who is it?"

"You met us all a while ago," Lyle said. "We're with the BAU and the MPD."

A brief silence fell.

"I told you everything I had to say," Coddington replied.

"Maybe so, and we're sorry to trouble you," Lyle said with calculated politeness. "We'd just like to tie up a few loose ends."

"This is not a good time," Coddington said.

"I'm afraid we must insist," Lyle said.

"Open up and let us in," Brown added.

After another silence, the door opened, and Carly and her colleagues walked inside. The room was every bit as luxurious as Carly could have expected. She wondered whether the Boundless Bounty Shakespeare was paying for Coddington's stay here as well as his doubtless considerable salary.

The director was dressed more casually than he'd been at the theater. On the bed lay an enormous open suitcase surrounded and partially packed with expensive clothes.

Looks like we got here just in time, Carly thought.

It sure looked to Carly as though Barry Coddington had not only skipped out on the meeting at the theater, but was about to skip town altogether.

Scratching his chin, Lyle commented, "Looks like you're about to go on a trip."

"As if it's any of your business," Coddington said defiantly. "I'm catching the next flight from Reagan International to JFK in New York."

"Kind of an odd time, isn't it?" Lyle asked. "I mean, with your show just beginning its run."

"Not at all," Coddington said. "I've seen it all the through rehearsals and previews, and it has opened to rapturous reviews and full houses. My work as director is done, and I'm ready to take a break before I embark on my next project."

Lyle said to him, "A while ago you sure sounded like you were still pretty attached to this show. You were really anxious that it keep running tomorrow. Now you act like you can't wait to get away from it."

"And besides," Detective Brown added, "I told the entire cast and crew not to leave the theater until we were done."

"Did you?" Coddington said. "Oh, yes, I suppose you did. Well, I didn't expect you to take so bloody long about it. And I had a plane to catch. Did I really require your permission? I can't imagine what else I might say that could be of interest to you."

"We'll see about that," Lyle said, crossing his arms. "Have a seat, Mr. Coddington."

"But if I miss my flight—"

"We'll deal with that if it happens," Lyle said. "Make yourself comfortable."

"Now really—" Coddington began to protest.

Detective Brown opened his jacket to reveal his service weapon.

"Agent Ramsey just told you to have a seat."

Carly stifled a groan of disapproval as Coddington obediently sat down in a chair. She didn't think that Brown's blunt-edged behavior would be helpful, but at least Coddington wasn't leaving now.

Lyle said, "Tell us where you were when the murder took place."

It was exactly the question Carly expected Lyle to ask. But the director's answer surprised her.

"I was out taking a walk," Coddington said.

Lyle squinted curiously.

"You mean you weren't in the audience or backstage watching your own show?"

Coddington smiled and said, "No, I was out enjoying the night air. Once a show opens, I don't give it much of my attention. In fact, it makes me nervous to watch it and know whatever happens is out of my hands. I prefer to get out of the building and relax."

"Can anyone confirm that you were out walking?" Lyle asked.

"Nobody that I know of," Coddington said.

Lyle exchanged glances with Carly. She knew that she and her partner were thinking the same thing.

He's got no alibi.

Then Lyle said, "Tell us about your relationship with the murder victim."

"Didn't I do that that earlier?" Coddington said, sounding noticeably on edge.

"We didn't really discuss it earlier," Brown put in.

"Well, why are you bringing it up now?" the director snapped.

Lyle just stood there looking stern, waiting for an answer.

Coddington shrugged nervously.

"Well, there's nothing much to tell," he said. "It was purely professional. Hecate is a small part—kind of disposable, really. She just gets flown in and out twice, gives a couple of pretty speeches. So I didn't spend much time working with the girl—Gentry was her name, wasn't it?"

Carly spotted the feigned uncertainty about the name.

Lyle squinted at Coddington skeptically.

"You told us she was just some nobody," he said.

"And so she was," Coddington replied. "I barely remember her name."

Not true, Carly thought.

"You didn't tell us she was understudying the part of Lady Macbeth," Lyle added.

"So what? An understudy's not exactly a star. I didn't spend any time actually directing her for Lady Macbeth. The stage manager talked her through all the blocking."

A silence fell in the room. A twitch of Coddington's cheek told Carly that the pause was having its intended effect. The man was surely wondering—did the detectives know about his altercation with the murder victim? Should he admit it outright?

"I really don't know what to tell you," Coddington finally said.

"The truth will do," Lyle commented flatly.

Detective Brown clumsily flashed his gun again and added, "Remember—it's a crime to lie or withhold information from the police."

Again, Carly stifled a grunt of annoyance.

Coddington stared at the floor for a moment.

Then he smirked and chuckled a little.

"Well, I guess the truth can't hurt," he said.

He drew himself up and crossed his arms.

"First you need to understand—theater is half art, half commerce, and all relationships. And it's just about the most transactional business there is. People give, people take, and some people wind up getting what they want, and some people wind up getting the screws put to them."

"We'd appreciate some specifics," Lyle said in an ironic tone.

"And I'll be glad to comply, but first …"

He paused, then nodded at Carly and said to Lyle, "I'm not sure it's an appropriate topic with a lady present."

Lyle couldn't help scoffing aloud. Carly felt her own face grow warm. She remembered what Denise had told her about the director back at the theater.

"I think he hates women."

Lyle glanced at her with a grin, as if to say, *"You take it from here."*

Carly felt glad to do that. Since the man was obviously a misogynist, she might have a better chance of flustering him.

She said to him, "First of all, tell me about that page you took out of the victim's hand. Why did you do that?"

Coddington shrugged and said, "I guess I just wanted to see what it was. My curiosity got the best of me. It was an impulse."

"But you concealed it from us," Carly said. "Or at least you didn't give it to us until we asked about it."

Coddington shifted his weight a little.

"It's like I told you at the time," he said. "I didn't think it was important."

Carly studied his face for a moment, then said, "Tell me about people getting the screws put to them. How exactly do you mean that?"

"How do you think I mean it?" Coddington snorted.

"That's what I'd like to hear," Carly replied.

Coddington chuckled and eyed Carly in an unsavory matter.

"Oh, I think you know all about it," he said. "You're not a bad-looking girl, even if you're not exactly shapely and your face could use some makeup and you're not my type."

Carly had to squelch a giggle. She didn't give a damn whether he found her attractive or not.

Just let him dig himself into a hole, she thought.

"Go ahead," she said with a wide-eyed smile.

Coddington said, "You've had some success in a man's game—law enforcement. Don't try to tell me you've accomplished that on merit alone. A woman just isn't built for the kind of work you do—not mentally or physically. You've done some things that you wouldn't brag about to get where you are."

He winked at Lyle and added, "And I'll bet you know all about that."

Lyle growled and stepped toward him.

Carly deterred him a subtle wave.

As Lyle backed away, Carly said to Coddington, "I guess you're implying something similar about Gentry Chapman."

Coddington snickered and said, "Let me put it this way. She was a talented girl. And pretty. But that's not enough to get you ahead in the performing arts. She auditioned and got the part of Hecate on her own. But she knew she was going to need an extra boost to get to the next level."

Carly looked at him closely and said, "And that's where things got … transactional."

Coddington chuckled again and said, "You're catching on. I knew the minute I saw you, you understood how these things work. She came to me and said she wanted more than just the part of Hecate."

Carly nodded and said, "So … she slept with you so she could be Yvette Duryea's understudy."

Coddington's roar of laughter took Carly completely by surprise. The man was striking her as more loathsome by the very second. In fact, he was practically flaunting it.

What that might mean, she wasn't sure. She had to ask herself—if he were really the killer, wouldn't he be making some effort to come across as an acceptable human being?

Coddington said, "Well … I'd prefer not to go into the rest of it."

"Just tell me," Carly said.

Coddington glanced at the ceiling wistfully.

"Let's just say promises were made. I kept my promise. She got to be the understudy for Lady Macbeth. But she didn't keep her promise. To put it delicately, she stood me up."

He shook his head and smiled bitterly.

"I'm normally an excellent judge of aspiring actresses, but I've got to hand it to her; she completely bamboozled me. She let me go ahead and publicly announce that she'd been chosen as understudy, then she just acted like there was nothing between us."

Coddington shrugged and added, "Well, the theater's like that. Like I said, my instincts are normally pretty good when it comes to females of the acting species. But she was more talented than I took her for. Damn, but she could have gone far."

There was just a trace of self-deprecation in his voice that Carly hadn't expected. She definitely got the feeling that he'd been telling the truth—at least up to this point. But she was sure that there was more to that story.

Coddington let out a sigh and told Carly, "So about people getting the screws put to them —well, in this situation, it happened to me, not to her."

Detective Brown grumbled, "You're forgetting the part where she got killed."

"True," Coddington said nonchalantly. "Maybe it was karma. It's not nice to go back on your promises."

"I'm not a big believer in karma," Lyle put in.

Carly asked the director, "So how did you react when she … bamboozled you like that?"

Coddington locked eyes with her and squinted.

"Are you asking if I killed her?"

Carly shrugged, "I'm just asking what you did."

They gazed at each other for a long moment. Carly could see that the director must be a good poker player. He was trying to figure out just how far he could bluff her and get away with it.

Finally Coddington said, "I get the feeling you know something about it already."

Carly didn't reply, but she did remember Denise's account.

"Something happened between Barry and Gentry yesterday," she'd said. *"Something bad."*

Carly silently waited for Coddington to lie or come clean.

CHAPTER NINE

As Carly watched the director closely, he finally took a long slow breath and spoke.

"I didn't take it gracefully," Coddington said, "what she'd done to me, I mean. I may have … said a few things that maybe I shouldn't have said."

Carly remained silent. She saw Lyle gesture to Detective Brown to do the same.

"I may have threatened her," Coddington admitted.

"Really?" Carly said, cocking an eyebrow. "I'd like to hear your exact words."

Coddington tried to hold her gaze without blinking, but then he looked abruptly away.

I've called his bluff, Carly saw with satisfaction.

She was pretty sure he'd guessed at least part of the truth—that someone had witnessed his altercation with Gentry and had already told her about it. He realized that lying would get him in deeper trouble.

"My … threat might have been pretty strong," Coddington said with a cowed expression. "I may have said … I could make things really bad for her."

Carly smiled slightly and nodded.

Now I can play my hand.

She said, "I believe you told her you could do much worse things to her than just ruin her career."

Coddington's lips twisted into an ugly sneer.

"That's right," he said, "and I would have made good on that threat. I would have done everything I could to poison every relationship she had, made it impossible for her to have friends or lovers, much less any kind of marriage or family. I've done worse, believe me."

He leaned toward Carly and added in a snarling whisper, "But I've never murdered anybody. I've found better ways to get revenge. All of them are nasty—but none of them are illegal. Which means they're none of your business."

Carly was startled by the sudden intensity of his words. For the first time, she wasn't sure whether he was telling the truth or not.

He leaned back and crossed his arms and laughed.

"So the three of you have been wasting your time, I'm afraid," he said. "And I've got a plane to catch. So if you'll excuse me …"

Lyle stepped in front of him as he started to stand up.

"Not so fast," Lyle said. "You're not going anywhere, at least not tonight."

"No?" Coddington said. "Then who's going to pay for my wasted flight reservation?"

Detective Brown looked around at the luxurious quarters and rolled his eyes and said, "It looks to me like you can afford it."

Carly realized that their poker game wasn't quite over. There was another bluff for her to call.

She held out her hand and said to Coddington, "Show me this flight reservation of yours."

Coddington winced slightly.

"I haven't printed it out," he said.

"Then bring it up for me on your cellphone or laptop or something. Make it fast, I know you're on a tight schedule …"

She smiled mock-politely and added, "And I don't want to inconvenience you more than we already have."

Coddington looked trapped and flustered. Of course Carly knew that he'd made no such plane reservation. He hadn't planned that far ahead. As soon as he'd realized he was a likely murder suspect, he'd slipped out of the theater, and his only plan was to head straight to Reagan International and catch the first plane he could catch. He didn't much care whether it took him to New York. For all she knew, he might have wound up in South America if they hadn't gotten to him in time.

Detective Brown chuckled with glee.

"So you don't even have a plane reservation? Coddington, you sure do look guilty."

He seems desperate, all right, Carly thought.

But she still knew better than to jump to conclusions.

Lyle put his hands in his pockets and spoke a faux-hospitable manner.

"You should stay in D.C. a few days longer. I'm sure getting a cursed play on the boards is a pretty consuming, round-the-clock sort of job, and you've had precious little time to enjoy our fair city. Have you been to the Washington Monument? Wonderful view from the top."

Detective Brown added, "What about the Capitol Building?"

"Hey, that's right," Lyle said with a tilt of his head. "You can sit in a gallery and watch the workings of a well-oiled, smooth-running democracy."

Lyle glanced at his watch.

"But look at the time!" he said. "It's been nice chatting with you, Mr. Coddington, but we've got to get going."

Carly and Detective Brown followed as Lyle walked toward the door.

"Anyway, let's stay in touch," Lyle said. Wagging a finger at the director, he added, "And don't think of leaving town, do you hear? That really wouldn't be a good idea under the circumstances."

Coddington had been standing there, silently cowed. But he spoke up just as Carly and her colleagues were about to leave the room.

"Agent Ramsey, I really do hope you catch Gentry's killer soon. I sincerely mean that. It was a terrible thing to happen to such a promising young talent. Please let me know when you get him."

Lyle said, "One way or the other, we'll make sure you're the first to know."

Carly and her two colleagues exited into the quiet, carpeted hallway.

Detective Brown muttered, "I sure as hell wish we could have taken him into custody. He still might try to skip town on us."

Lyle said to Brown, "That's why you're going to call in plainclothes cops to keep watch on him here at the hotel. But give him some freedom. If he leaves the hotel, just have your guys trail him for a while. He might give himself away."

He added with a shrug, "That is, if Coddington's really our killer."

Brown let out a noisy scoff.

"Is there any doubt?" he asked. "Why else would he have been trying to run?"

Neither Carly nor Lyle answered the question. But Carly knew they were thinking the same thing. Even innocents sometimes panicked when faced with possible arrest and false charges. And this one was obviously a coward as well as a bully.

As for whether he might be a killer, Carly still had no feeling one way or the other. All she knew was that the man thoroughly disgusted her.

During the elevator ride down to the lobby, Detective Brown phoned in the request for extra personnel to watch Barry Coddington. As they stepped out into the lobby, he let out a weary sigh.

"Well, I don't know about you two, but I've had it for today," he said. "I'm going home to catch some sleep."

Carly and Lyle watched the tired-looking detective go on out through the hotel's revolving doors. Carly knew from experience that she and Lyle were not about to quit.

This is going to be an all-nighter, she thought.

When they got back to the SUV, Lyle said, "I'm thinking maybe we should head over to Quantico and report in and make some plans for tomorrow. Of course tomorrow's technically here. What do you think?"

Carly took a deep breath. She had another stop in mind.

"I wish they hadn't taken the body away before we got there," she told Lyle as she got into the passenger seat.

As Lyle climbed into the driver's seat, he replied tiredly, "I wasn't crazy about that either. But the local cops were eager to clean up that scene in a hurry. We kind of got called in as an afterthought."

I guess I'd better just come out and say it, Carly thought.

"I think we should head over to the Medical Examiner's building now and have a look at the body," she said.

"What good would that do?" Lyle replied. "We saw the photos. The cause of death was obvious. She was stabbed. We even have a pretty good idea of where and how it happened. The coroner's report will tell us everything else we need to know."

Carly hesitated. Her partner sounded exhausted, and she was too. They'd spent much of yesterday hunting for a missing young woman in the Virginia woods. It was now the small hours of the next morning, and there hadn't been any letup. Here they were working on a murder case, and they weren't even sure why they'd been called in for it.

And Lyle was right, the photos were good. But Carly kept thinking about that moment when she'd touched the bloodstain on the throne and had caught a fleeting glimpse of the page that Barry Coddington had taken out of the victim's hand. There was a chance that the body itself would reveal more to her.

Lyle just sat there in the driver's seat and stared for a moment.

Finally he heaved a sigh and said, "Well, I guess it's as good an idea as anything I can think of. Let me send a text message and see who's in charge there at the moment."

Carly patiently waited while Lyle exchanged messages on his cellphone.

"We're in luck," he said to Carly. "Freda herself is there. She's just this minute finishing up the autopsy on Gentry Chapman's body. She'll be waiting for us. Come on, let's get going."

Carly knew that Dr. Freda Smith was D.C.'s Chief Medical Examiner, and she was glad she was on hand to meet them. Lyle started their vehicle and drove them south through Foggy Bottom past the Kennedy Center, then through the National Mall to the Medical Examiner's building.

They went on inside and headed straight to the spacious, state-of-the-art autopsy room with its icy white overhead lighting and its elaborate stainless steel dissecting tables. The sudden plunge into chilly, formaldehyde-scented air made Carly shiver.

Three of the tables had bodies on them, all of them covered with white sheets. Standing over one of the bodies was a tall, gray-haired, hawk-nosed woman who was wearing a bloodstained white apron and taking off a pair of bloodstained rubber gloves.

"You got here just at the right time," Dr. Freda Smith said to Carly and Lyle. "I just finished stitching her back up."

With her horn-rimmed reading glasses hanging by a beaded chain, Dr. Smith reminded Carly of Mrs. Busbee, the lady pharmacist at the drugstore back in Currie. All the kids in Currie were intimidated by her—especially the adolescent boys when they bought condoms under her disapproving gaze.

"Keeping pretty strange hours, aren't you?" Lyle said to the M.E.

"I could say the same for you," Dr. Smith replied with a frown.

"Haven't you got assistants who … ?" Lyle began.

"Who can work the 'graveyard shift' for me?" Dr. Smith interrupted in a coolly ironic tone. "Sure, but I just can't seem to be able to stay away from the murder victims. If I don't carve them up myself, I just can't sleep right somehow. They always worry me."

"Let's have a look," Lyle said.

Freda nodded and pulled back the sheet to reveal the body from the waist up. The dead young woman's skin had that waxy, unnatural bluish tint that Carly could never quite get used to seeing in corpses. Her eyes were closed, and her mouth was hanging slightly open. It looked to Carly as though she were snoring.

Forming a huge, ugly forked shape was a hideous autopsy scar that extended from each shoulder toward the center of the chest, then downward over the rest of the abdomen. As usual, Carly noticed that the stitches were wide and large and ugly.

Lyle said to the Medical Examiner, "You seem to have gone to a fair amount of trouble. It was pretty simple stabbing case, you know."

"I know, but I like to be thorough," Dr. Smith said. "I'm also waiting for a blood workup, not that I expect anything unusual in that department. How do you think she was attacked? It looks like it might have been from straight on."

Lyle explained, "Probably not. The killer probably sneaked up behind her while she was sitting in … uh, a throne."

"Yeah, I heard about the throne part," Dr. Smith said. "She was playing some kind of a witch in that new production of *Macbeth.* Pretty wild costume she still had on when she got here."

"What can you tell us about the stabbing itself?" Carly asked.

Dr. Smith pointed to an inflamed-looking mound-shaped wound in the center of the abdomen and gestured as she explained.

"Well, if the killer stabbed her from behind, he was either skillful or lucky or both—in his aim, I mean. The knife entered just below the base of the sternum, right in the solar plexus, so the blade didn't meet any bone on its way into the body, just glided in with very little effort. The blade was thrust in to the hilt, right up through the pericardium into the left ventricle. As stabbings go, it was very easy."

"Did the victim experience much pain?" Carly asked.

"I don't know," Dr. Smith said with a wry curl of her lips. "You'd have to ask her, I guess."

Exactly what I want to do, Carly thought.

She wasn't getting any information from just looking. She needed to actually touch the body.

There was no real rule against that.

It wasn't as if a mere touch was likely to destroy any forensic evidence.

But this wasn't the busy scene of a murder, where touching a body might not be noticeable. This was an autopsy room, under the eyes the chief M.E. herself. It would certainly seem like a weird, morbid gesture, and Dr. Smith would surely ask her why she did it.

And what would I tell her? Carly thought.

Meanwhile, Dr. Smith continued her answer to Carly's question.

"It was only a small puncture in the left ventricle, which was why the murder scene wasn't bloodier. Even so, she must have lost consciousness pretty quickly. She may not have felt any pain to speak of. But she might have been scared."

Dr. Smith shook her head and added, "I guess it must be a serial killer, or the two of you wouldn't have gotten called in for it."

Carly and Lyle exchanged glances. So far they hadn't even

discussed that issue.

"We don't know yet," Lyle said.

Dr. Smith peered over her reading glasses disapprovingly.

"What you mean, you don't know yet?" she said. "You're BAU. You wouldn't have gotten called in for a one-off."

Before either Carly or Lyle could start to explain, Dr. Smith rolled her eyes with annoyance.

"Oh, it's because her father's a congressman, isn't it?" she grumbled. "That's just the way everything works these days. The rich and powerful get all the care and attention, while ordinary people get left in the lurch. If it were one of my grandkids, there sure wouldn't be any BAU agents looking into it."

Dr. Smith clucked her tongue and added, "Not that I'm blaming you two. You don't make these choices. You've got to go wherever you're kicked by the powers-that-be. You're pawns just like the rest of us. It's just the way things are in this rotten world."

Lyle and Carly's eyes met while Dr. Smith was complaining. She knew that her partner was used to the way she always moved close to the body of a victim, and he had never asked why.

Now Lyle put his hands in his pockets and stepped away from the autopsy table.

"So how *are* your grandchildren these days, Freda?" he asked.

Dr. Smith turned toward Lyle—and also away from Carly and the corpse.

"Oh, they're fine," Dr. Smith said. "They're old enough now that their parents can't keep me from seeing them. I wish I could have skipped having children and gone straight to grandchildren. They're much easier to get along with …"

As Dr. Smith droned on about her family, Carly found herself completely unobserved. It seemed clear that Lyle was deliberately resetting the scene for her. She felt a twinge of gratitude toward her partner. Somehow he always seemed to know—and respect—her need for such moments to herself.

This was her chance.

But she wondered—as tired as she was, would she even get any impressions from this body?

There was only one way to find out.

Carly reached out with her right hand and placed a finger on each of the eyelids.

She felt a jolt like an electric shock.

CHAPTER TEN

The sudden flash of steel almost made Carly jerk her hand away from the dead woman's eyelids.

Steady, she told herself, as she struggled with the whirl of images churning through her head.

Stay calm.

Stay on your feet.

Try to bring it under control.

Just a moment before, she'd been afraid she was too tired to make a strong connection. But it was precisely because she was so tired that her conscious mind was weakened and unwary.

Something deeper than ordinary consciousness was coming over her.

She took a long, slow breath and closed her eyes and gathered her wits about her.

Then it came to her—that flash of steel was a knife blade directly in front of her chest. She was reliving the murder as Gentry had experienced it, first with surprise and incomprehension …

Before her brain had time to register true fear, the blade plunged deep into her abdomen, and the pain was positively searing. She felt a column of air rise out of her throat and burst through her lips with an agonized groan. Then she slouched forward and found herself staring down, down, the full 35 feet to the stage floor.

The victim flashed back to all the fear she'd been feeling about the ascent and descent in the throne.

But now, as her life started to slip through her fingers ...

I'm not afraid of the height now.

The irony was almost amusing as blackness enveloped her ...

Carly began to panic.

No! she wanted to cry out. *Don't go yet!*

Her contact with the dead woman was viscerally powerful, but it didn't tell her a single thing that she and Lyle didn't know already.

Don't go without telling me more!

As if in response to her unspoken plea, another vision came over Carly.

She was surrounded by a vast whiteness.

In the midst of that whiteness, a small, open hardback book fluttered near her like a moth. As the pages flipped by, a torn page fell out of the book and fluttered away through the air, then another, then another, then another …

Suddenly Carly's eyes snapped open, and she found herself in the autopsy room with her fingers on the dead woman's eyelids.

The torn page! she thought. *It's important.*

And so were the other pages she'd just seen fluttering out of that book.

Then she heard Dr. Smith speaking in a disturbed voice.

"Are you all right?"

Carly turned to see the Medical Examiner standing right next to her, staring at her over those reading glasses with concern. Lyle was also standing nearby, looking very anxious.

For a moment, Carly didn't know what to say.

Dr. Smith gently removed Carly's fingers from the corpse's eyelids.

"We seemed to kind of lose you there for a moment," the Medical Examiner said. "What happened, anyway?"

Carly still couldn't think of anything to say. Fortunately, her partner spoke up.

"The poor kid has had a long day. She needs to get some sleep. For that matter, so do I. Fat chance of that happening soon, though."

Dr. Smith smiled slightly.

"I know just how you feel," she said. "And this place can get the better of your imagination if you're not used to it—especially if you're tired."

Carly smiled weakly and said, "Yeah, I guess so."

Lyle said to the Medical Examiner, "Thanks for the help. We'd better get going now."

Dr. Smith shrugged and said, "I can't imagine I told you anything very helpful."

Maybe not, Carly thought.

But maybe she'd at least gotten some sort of insight from her fleeting vision.

Then Dr. Smith said, "Please tell me you've already got a suspect."

Lyle tilted his head noncommittally and said, "Maybe not a suspect, but a person of interest anyway."

"Well, I hope you close this case soon," Dr. Smith said. "I hate murders. I prefer it when people die in a natural manner."

Covering the corpse with the sheet again, she added with a sigh, "These kinds of deaths give me nightmares. You'd think I'd be used to them by now, but I'm not."

Then Dr. Smith yawned deeply.

"Well, if it's all the same to you, I'd like to call it a night. I'll get somebody to roll this body into the fridge and close up shop here and head on home and try to get some sleep. Good luck finding the killer."

"Thanks," Carly said.

"And thanks again for your time," Lyle added.

Lyle and Carly left the autopsy room and headed for the elevator. During the ride down to the ground floor, Lyle looked at Carly with concern.

"How are you doing?" he said.

"OK, I guess," Carly said, not wanting to admit how shaken she still was by her encounter with the body. "It's like you said, it's been a long day."

Lyle looked at his watch and said, "Jeez, look at the time. I guess we can forget about sleeping tonight."

"Do you think maybe we should head on over to Quantico?" Carly asked.

"Yeah, but not just yet," Lyle said. "I don't know about you, but I'm starving, and if I don't have a cup of strong coffee I'm liable to drop dead. What do you say we head on over to Fillmore's Pancakes?"

"That sounds like a good idea," Carly said.

Lyle and Carly left the building and got into the SUV. As Lyle drove them north back through the National Mall toward the all-night breakfast joint near Ford's Theatre, Carly looked around at the eerily empty streets. Although it was hard to be sure because of the streetlights, she thought she could glimpse a hint of morning light in the sky.

Lyle glanced over at Carly as he drove.

"So," he said in a tentative voice, "how are you doing?"

"I'm OK, thanks," she said. "And you?"

Lyle didn't reply. The two of them remained silent during the rest of the drive. When Lyle parked in front of Fillmore's Pancakes, he turned off the engine, but neither one of them got out of the car.

Finally he said, "Have you got any, uh, theories?"

Of course, Carly realized, Lyle had seen her get close to bodies and blood often enough to realize that she wanted to touch that body for a reason. He'd apparently accepted that this kind of intense focus helped her make intuitive leaps. He didn't know she was looking for a message from the dead, but he knew how she worked and he often helped her with it. Instead of pushing for an explanation, this was his roundabout way of asking about it.

And his question deserved an answer.

Carly flashed back to that image of the book fluttering about, and four pages falling out of it. The message of that image was starting to become somewhat clearer.

The victim had been holding the torn-out page with Shakespeare's Sonnet 9—a page Carly was still carrying in her satchel. Carly guessed that the killer probably put that page in her hand immediately after killing her. If she'd been holding it before the stabbing, she'd probably have dropped it. Carly's vision had shown her more loose pages, presumably with other sonnets.

And that can only mean one thing, she thought.

She said to Lyle, "I think we've got a serial killer. I think he's just getting started."

Lyle simply nodded.

They got out of the car and walked into the jarringly well-lighted all-night restaurant with its fluorescent overhead bulbs and plastic surfaces. There wasn't another customer in the place, which suited their purposes well.

They sat down, and a short-skirted, white-clad female server quickly came over to take their orders. Lyle ordered a Mexican omelet, and Carly ordered a plate of waffles with link sausages. Both of them asked for black coffee.

As they waited Lyle said, "Show me that poem again."

Carly reached into her satchel and pulled out the bagged-up page with Shakespeare's Sonnet 9 on one side and Sonnet 10 crossed out on the other. She handed it across the table to Lyle, who skimmed over Sonnet 9 and scratched his head and passed it back to Carly.

"You know these poems better than I do," he said. "What can you tell me about this one?"

Carly stifled a sigh.

Yeah, I know these sonnets, all right.

She remembered too well how her mother had made her read all 154 of them at the age of eleven. English professor that she was, Mom had demanded that Carly interpret each and every one of them. As was usual in such situations, Mom tore apart every single idea Carly could come up with, telling her over and over again that she was wrong before finally telling her what each poem "really meant."

Although it had been an unpleasant experience, some solid information had stayed in Carly's mind.

She read the opening lines aloud.

Is it for fear to wet a widow's eye
That thou consum'st thyself in single life?

Then she explained to Lyle, "Like Coddington said, the early sonnets are addressed to a 'Fair Youth' whom the poet seems to be rather obsessed with. In poems like this one, he complains that the Fair Youth hasn't gotten married so he can have children. He takes the youth bitterly to task about that. He thinks it's extremely selfish of the youth not to pass on his beauty to an heir."

"Do you see any clues in the poem?" Lyle asked. "Any hidden meanings?"

Carly cringed at that phrase—*"hidden meanings."*

She'd heard Mom say those words much too often, treating every great piece of literature as if it were a riddle that only very clever people like herself could hope to solve. Carly sometimes found it amazing that Mom hadn't destroyed her deep love of reading.

Carly read the poem carefully to herself, then shook her head.

"I don't know, Lyle," she said. "The words 'beauty's waste hath in the world an end' might refer to the murder itself. But I think that's kind of a stretch."

The server returned with their orders. The coffee wasn't much good, but at least it seemed reasonably fresh, which was all that really mattered to Carly and her partner at this time in the morning. Carly smothered her waffles with butter and maple syrup, hoping for a burst of caloric energy to sharpen her mind.

Lyle asked as they began to eat, "Why do you think Coddington snatched this page out of the victim's hand and tried to hide it from us? That seems kind of suspicious to me."

Carly thought back to Coddington's lame explanation for why he'd concealed the poem from the police.

"I didn't think it was important."

Carly said, "Maybe it's not so suspicious. If Coddington really was the killer, does it make sense that he'd put the poem in the victim's hand only to remove it later on? What would be the point of that?"

"How do you explain his behavior then?" Lyle said.

Carly thought for a moment, then said, "Maybe, when he first saw the body, he grabbed the poem in a fit of curiosity just to have a look at it. It was just some stupid impulse, but he's used to following his urges. Then maybe he realized he'd done something very wrong and probably illegal."

Lyle nodded in agreement with Carly's scenario and said, "So what could he do next? Put it back in the victim's hand? That might only make the situation worse for him."

Carly added, "So he maybe panicked and stuck it in his pocket, hoping no one would ask about it."

Lyle grunted, "It's lucky you *did* ask about it."

Probably not just luck, Carly thought, remembering the intuitive jolt she'd gotten by touching the blood on the throne. *Not if the victim wanted to make sure we found it.*

"I guess what we're saying makes sense," Lyle added. "But we're still a long way from eliminating Coddington as a potential suspect."

"I agree," Carly said, taking another bite of her waffles.

Just then Lyle's phone rang and he answered it. In reply to the caller, Lyle said, "Yes, this is Special Agent Lyle Ramsey. What can I do for you?"

Even from across the table, Carly could hear the voice of the caller almost shouting.

"Slow down, calm down," Lyle said into the phone. "Who is this, anyway?"

Lyle's eyes widened at whatever the caller said in reply.

Then he said to the caller, "I'm putting this call on speaker so my partner, Special Agent See, can take part in the conversation."

Covering the phone with his hand while he switched to speaker, Lyle said to Carly, "It's Congressmen Sean Chapman."

The victim's father! Carly realized with a gasp.

Carly said, "Congressman, my partner and I are terribly sorry for your loss, and we want to assure you—"

Chapman interrupted, sounding strident and angry.

"Skip the sympathy crap. Where are the two of you? What are you doing?"

Carly and Lyle exchanged worried glances.

"We are working on the case even as we speak," Lyle said.

Carly didn't add that they were sitting in a pancake house near

Ford's Theatre. There was nothing inappropriate about it, of course, but the irate caller might not be pleased to hear it.

"Have you found my daughter's killer?" Chapman asked.

"No, but we're doing everything we can," Lyle said.

"That's not good enough. Are you in D.C. right now?"

"Yes," Lyle said.

"Then come to my office in the Capitol immediately. We need to talk."

"May I ask what this is about?" Lyle said.

"I know who the next intended victim is," Chapman said.

Lyle stared at Carly. He looked as thunderstruck as Carly felt.

"Who is it?" Lyle said.

"Me," Chapman snapped. "Now get your asses over here."

The congressman ended the call without another word.

Lyle and Carly sat looking at each other for a stunned moment. Then Lyle waved for the server to bring over the check.

"Breakfast is over," he said to Carly. "We've got to be going."

CHAPTER ELEVEN

Caffeine, Bianca Voigts thought.

Must have caffeine.

And lots of it.

The cup she'd downed with a skimpy breakfast back in her apartment was definitely not enough to see her through the important seminar she had this morning.

Fortunately, she was in the right place. The coffee shop in the Cheswick College student center was open even at this ungodly hour for those unfortunates with very early classes. Cheerful and well-lit, the shop was already pretty busy and buzzing with muted conversations among students who weren't yet fully awake.

Bianca made her way to the front of the line and ordered a Cold Detonator, a notoriously jolting drink that boasted some 275 milligrams of caffeine, and which she had learned to rely on to get her through any early morning challenges. She paid for the drink and left a generous tip in the tip jar, then sought out an empty table to do some last-minute reading while she waited for her order. But as soon as she sat down and pulled a book out of her bag, her phone buzzed.

Glancing at the phone, Bianca shook her head with a bit of annoyance. She needed to be alert and even brilliant for the upcoming seminar. The email referred to an entirely different arena of her life, a sexting app called RacyChat that she'd recently joined.

She'd been having fun there with a fellow RacyChat patron who called himself Rod O'Horn. Bianca had no idea what his real name was, or for that matter anything at all about his non-virtual life, which suited her just fine.

Although the sender's name was slightly suggestive, the email was innocent enough:

Hi Lisa. Wanna play?

Her own sexting alter ego was Lisa Lascivia. She enjoyed the sheer escapism of putting on an anonymous persona for these online erotic adventures, but she wasn't in the mood for such activities right now.

This was a serious morning, with no time for play.

She typed back:

Sorry Rod. Evenings work better for me.

The reply came quickly:

OK. Later.

Whoever he is, at least he isn't pushy, she thought.

Bianca closed the email, set down her cellphone and opened up a copy of *The Duchess of Malfi,* an exceptionally violent tragedy by William Shakespeare's younger contemporary, John Webster. Today's seminar was going to deal with lycanthropes—werewolves—in Renaissance thought.

Bianca's eyes lighted on a passage in which a doctor describes men who "imagine / Themselves to be transformed into wolves," and who dig dead bodies out of churchyards. According to the doctor, such a man imagined no difference between himself and a wolf, except that "a wolf's skin was hairy on the outside, / His on the inside …"

Bianca shivered at the delicious creepiness of the speech, which had been preceded in the play by the strangulations of the title character and her maid and her three children. Bianca was familiar with the play, which culminated in a whole string of murders. Her personal favorite was a fatal kiss of a poisoned Bible.

I guess I've got morbid tastes, she thought.

She certainly found it to be an entertaining seminar, but it also meant a lot more to her than that. It was taught by the famous Renaissance scholar Neal Redfield, author of *Jacobean Phantasms,* and not just any English grad student could get into it. It had really helped that Bianca was a recent recipient of the Strabane Foundation's Renaissance Studies Prize.

In fact, she was already considered one of the most promising young English Renaissance scholars on the rise. Studying with Professor Redfield, and impressing him, would give her an extra edge toward being accepted into an excellent PhD program after she completed her masters here at Cheswick College.

So far, so good, she thought.

Not only had she hit it off with Professor Redfield, he'd invited her to his home to spend time with his family.

As she lost herself in Webster's gruesome tragedy, Bianca barely listened to the customers' names being called out from the pickup station. But when she finally did hear her own name, she dropped the book on the table, walked over to the station, and picked up her drink.

Just as she was sitting down again, a man approached her with an identical cup.

"Excuse me," he said, "but I believe we picked up each other's orders."

Bianca squinted at him, seized by a sudden craving for the caffeine boost she held in her hand.

"How do you know?" she asked.

The man shrugged and said, "Well, I just took a look under the lid. I'd asked that mine not have any foam on it, but I saw that this one does. It isn't mine, so it must be yours. They got switched, I guess."

That makes sense, I guess, Bianca thought, exchanging her cup for his.

She turned away from him and took a sip of the brewed coffee topped with sweet, slightly fruity-tasting cascara foam. The bracing, icy taste made her feel more alert right away. She picked up her book and started to read, but then she noticed that the man hadn't walked away from her table. He just stood there looking at her with his hands in his pockets.

Bianca tried to ignore him, but he didn't leave.

Finally she looked up at him with an inquisitive expression.

He smiled ever so slightly and said, "I guess you don't recognize me."

Feeling a bit embarrassed, Bianca peered at him closely. His face struck her as almost remarkably nondescript. He was neither bad-looking nor good-looking, and nothing about him seemed the least bit familiar.

"I'm afraid not," she said. "I'm, uh, sorry. Do we … know each other?"

The man's smile widened a little.

"Oh, excuse me," he said. "My mistake. I could have sworn I knew you from somewhere, but I was wrong. My apologies."

Bianca felt a flicker of relief as the man walked away from the table with his own drink in hand. Then she glanced at her watch and realized the time was later than she'd realized. She wasn't yet late for class, but she liked to be early so she could chat with Professor Redfield. After all, she would probably want a recommendation from him for her next step into the academic world.

I'd better get going, she thought. *I'll drink this on the way.*

She put her book in her handbag and walked out of the coffee shop, then out of the student center onto the campus. The briskness of the fall air made her almost wish she'd ordered something hot instead of the Cold Detonator.

On the other hand, the chill in the air was just the thing to get her wide awake. Besides, she loved the campus at this time of day, with its grand stone buildings glowing in the morning light.

I'm so lucky to be here, she thought.

But then, she knew luck wasn't all there was to it. She'd put in a lot of hard work to get here, and she had a lot more hard work to do to succeed academically in the competitive atmosphere of Cheswick's English Department.

As Bianca approached the building where her seminar was to take place, a strange sensation came over her.

She felt dizzy and confused, and the whole world began to swim around her.

She heard a male voice say, "Are you all right?"

She turned and saw the same man she had encountered back at the coffee shop. She felt a bit wary and didn't know what to say to him.

"Here, let me take this or you'll spill it," the man told her, gently taking the cup out of her hands. "Let's find a place for you to sit down."

Growing more disoriented by the second, Bianca felt a flash of gratitude for his attention. Then she quickly found herself sitting on a bench, and the whole campus seemed to be revolving around her.

It was a relief to get off her feet. She opened her mouth to thank the man who had helped her. But she looked all around for him in vain.

Where did he go? she wondered.

She felt something in her hand—a piece of paper, she thought.

How did it get there? she wondered.

As she began to lift it up to look at it, the world suddenly went dark, and she thought nothing at all.

CHAPTER TWELVE

How can he know? Carly wondered as Lyle drove the short distance between the Medical Examiner's quarters to the Cannon House Office Building.

Congressman Chapman's cryptic words over the phone had been riveting.

"I know who the next intended victim is."

"Me."

But then he had demanded that they come to his office and had hung up without explanation.

She asked Lyle, "Do you think he really knows something about the killer?"

Lyle shook his head. "Hard to tell," he replied. "People come up with some pretty strange ideas when they're grieving. His daughter was just murdered, so he could be in some kind of shock."

"I guess they could have been very close," Carly said.

"I've never met Chapman," Lyle told her. "But I'm sure he's the reason we're on this case. And that makes me uncomfortable."

"I understand he's influential," Carly said.

"Yeah, so they say."

Lyle drew a tired sigh. He parked the car, then added, "Politicians always make a case more complicated. And sometimes they make real trouble."

As they walked toward the congressional office building, Carly felt a bit daunted by the aura of power it seemed to exude. Of course it wasn't as overwhelming as the Capitol itself, which sprawled mightily a short distance away across Southwest Independence Avenue. But the stately Cannon Building, with its 30-some columns and its facade of marble and limestone, was quite majestic.

Inside, they introduced themselves to the guard at the security desk as BAU agents.

Lyle explained, "Congressman Sean Chapman is expecting us in his office."

The security guard eyed their badges carefully.

"Are you carrying any firearms?" he asked.

It struck Carly as an odd question, considering that she and her partner were BAU agents and required to be armed. But they said yes and placed their service weapons on the security desk.

"You'll have to leave those here during your visit," the guard said.

He scanned Lyle and Carly with a security wand, told them the way to Chapman's office, and sent them through a metal detector for good measure.

"Well, he's thorough, I'll give him that," Lyle said. "And I guess I can't blame him."

The corridors of power, Carly thought as they walked on into the lofty and elegant Cannon Rotunda and then down the hallway that led to Chapman's office. Inside the open office door, a secretary greeted them with a professional smile.

"May I help you?" she asked.

Again Carly and Lyle showed their badges.

"Congressman Chapman is expecting us," Lyle repeated.

The secretary's smile faded and she shook her head with dismay.

"Oh, this is about his daughter, isn't it?" she said. "Such a terrible thing, although I never really knew her. He's with somebody at the moment, but I'll let him know you're here. Make yourselves comfortable."

Lyle and Carly sat down in the leather-upholstered chairs, and the secretary announced the visitors over the intercom. In a few moments, the door to the main office opened, and two men came out.

Carly recognized Congressman Chapman right away from having seen him on television, although he wasn't as tall as she had expected. He was broad-shouldered, with angular, assertive features that hinted at some cosmetic work over the years, and he wore an expensive hairpiece that perfectly matched the steely gray in his hair.

An absolutely classic politician, she thought.

She didn't recognize the other man, who looked about the same age as Chapman and was similarly well-groomed.

"I appreciate your understanding, Logan," Chapman said as they came through the door. "I'm sorry we can't finish our business right now. We'll take it up at a later time."

"There's no rush," the man named Logan said in a sympathetic voice. "I'm terribly sorry for your loss. Gentry was a sweet girl."

"Yes, she was," Chapman agreed.

"If there's anything I can do … anything at all …"

Chapman put his hand on the other man's shoulder.

"Thanks, Logan," he said. "I can't tell you how grateful I am for your support. You've always been a good friend."

"And you as well," the other man said, then continued on his way out into the hall.

Then, in a markedly more curt voice, Chapman said to Carly and Lyle, "Come on in."

Chapman's office was spacious and well-furnished for small conferences. There were dozens of framed documents and photographs on the wall. Among them were pictures of the congressman with family, friends, and politicians, including two U.S. presidents.

"Sit," Chapman said, gesturing toward a pair of armchairs facing the wide desk at the far end of the room. He strode over and sat behind his desk, where he was picturesquely flanked from behind by a U.S. flag and an Ohio state flag.

The two agents took their seats and Lyle got out a pad and pencil, ready to take notes.

The congressman crossed his arms and told them, "Let's get right down to it and not waste any time. You two are going to want to know exactly where I was and what I was doing at the time of my daughter's death."

Carly shivered a little at the congressman's icy brusqueness. Of course he was right. As a matter of procedure, they did want to know that, and they would have tried to broach that question in as delicate a manner as possible. But Chapman was unexpectedly blunt.

As usual, her senior partner's face didn't reveal his reaction.

Chapman continued, "I was at home in Columbus, Ohio, when I got the news. My butler can confirm that. And any number of people can confirm that I caught the first flight I could to Reagan International."

Chapman leaned toward them and said, "But before I did anything else, I got on the phone and pulled strings to get FBI agents on the case. That's why you're here. And believe me, I expect prompt results."

"We'll do our very best, sir," Lyle said, returning Chapman's gaze.

Chapman leaned back in his chair again and said, "You won't find it a very challenging case. In fact, I expect you to crack it before the day is over."

Carly and Lyle exchanged uneasy glances.

"You told us over the phone—" Carly began.

Chapman interrupted, "Yes, I told you I was the next intended victim. And so I am."

The congressman took out his cellphone and brought up a photo and pushed it across his desk. Carly was startled to see that it showed the torn-out page that had been found on Gentry Chapman's body. She remembered Detective Brown snapping pictures of the page back at the murder scene. Chapman must have acquired it from Brown.

"I take it the two of you have seen this piece of evidence," Chapman said. "The D.C. police are keeping me up to the minute about the case, sending me every new scrap of information as it comes in. This looks like some sort of an old poem ..."

"It's a sonnet by Shakespeare," Carly said.

"Be that as it may. Someone killed my daughter to get my attention. And they're using this poem to send me a clear message."

Chapman read a phrase from the sonnet aloud.

"'The world will be thy widow.'"

He set the phone on the desk and pushed it toward Lyle and Carly.

"That means me, of course," he said. "I hope you don't mind my pointing out that I'm an important man, and I'm beloved by my constituents. And my political expectations are very high. I've got promise. The world will truly be my widow if I'm killed. I'll be mourned by people I don't even know."

Carly avoided Lyle's eyes, and she was sure he was avoiding hers. It was a dumbfounding theory, but they didn't dare show the least sign of skepticism.

Lyle asked calmly, "Do you have any idea who ... might want you killed?"

A flicker of a smirk crossed Chapman's face.

"The man who walked out of here just now," he said.

Carly managed to keep her mouth from dropping open. She flashed back to the words of friendship the two men had exchanged just a few minutes ago.

"You've always been a good friend," Chapman had said.

"And you as well," the man had said.

Carly's mind boggled as she tried to make sense of it.

Chapman continued, "His name is Logan Headly. He's a lobbyist from my home district. We've known each other since we were students together at Harvard. He's the kind of man who can shake hands with you and stab you in the back at the same time. But I hadn't figured him to be a killer until we talked just now."

"I—I'm not sure I understand," Lyle said.

"He's got his eye on my House seat," Chapman said. "I'm up for reelection in November. I expect to win easily. But if anything were to happen to me, Logan is the obvious choice to be nominated in my place. And by playing the 'grieving old friend' card, he'd get lots of voter sympathy and win hands down."

Carly began, "But how do you know … ?"

"I've got excellent instincts," Chapman said, interrupting again. "I can read people. That's why I'm so good at what I do. And I could see it in his face when we were talking just now—his fake surprise and shock when I told him what had happened to Gentry. I could see right through him."

A tense silence fell among the three people.

Finally Lyle said, "Respectfully, sir … we'll need more for an investigation."

Chapman's eyes narrowed sullenly.

"To the contrary, I expect you to find it very easy to prove. I'm practically handing your case to you on a silver platter. All you need to do is follow through on what I'm telling you."

Lyle thumped his eraser against his notepad.

"I—I understand what you're saying, sir," he said. "Perhaps you could help us prove your theory … by answering a few questions."

"Such as?"

"To start with, what can you tell us about your relationship with your daughter?"

Chapman looked a bit surprised at the question.

"What's that got to do with anything?" he asked.

Lyle shifted in his seat and said, "Just bear with me, please. Were you very close?"

Chapman's expression darkened. For a moment, Carly was afraid he might demand that they leave. But after a long, slow breath, he spoke in a calm, controlled voice.

"You're not reporters, so maybe I can be honest with you. I'm not very good at expressing my emotions. A hazard of my work, I guess. I'm a political animal, right down to my bones."

Chapman swiveled back and forth in his chair and continued, "Starting all the way back at the beginning, I've planned every move of my life to further my political career. I married the right woman from a rich political family, good-looking with a great smile and great instincts for always saying all the right things on the right occasions. As you might know, Andrea died of cancer a few years back …"

Before Carly or Lyle could say something sympathetic, Chapman silenced them with a wave of his hand and continued, "But she was exactly what I needed, especially early on—a great political partner, I couldn't have gotten where I am without her."

Carly tried not to look shocked by what she was hearing.

He doesn't talk about her as if she were a wife at all, she thought. *Or actually a person.*

He made her sound more like an ornament or fashion accessory.

Chapman steepled his fingers together and said, "And then there were the kids. You can't have a political family without kids. Our first one, Swain, was everything I could have hoped for. He's already a topnotch lawyer and I expect he'll follow in my political footsteps. But Gentry … well, Gentry …"

He clucked his tongue and shook his head.

"Gentry had no use for this kind of life, not from the time she was a little kid. Always into the arts, especially acting."

Chapman smiled wistfully, the first hint of sentiment Carly had noticed out of him so far.

But is it sincere? she wondered.

Chapman continued, "I was disappointed, of course, but I always gave her my support and my blessings. Even so, we drifted apart … or rather, she drifted away from me; I can't say why. We haven't been in touch at all for a couple of years. I didn't feel that I knew her anymore. So I guess it's taking a while for grief to kick in …"

His voice faded.

At that moment, Lyle's cellphone buzzed.

"It's Quantico," Lyle said, looking at the phone. "Excuse me, I've got to take this. I'll be just a moment."

Lyle stepped out of the office into the anteroom.

Carly's eyes fell on the single awkwardly-shaped object in the whole room. Right in front of her on the desk was a crudely crafted ashtray made out of glazed clay, with the word "Daddy" scrawled in it, surrounded by little hearts.

Carly asked, "Did your daughter make this?"

Chapman nodded and said, "Yes, when she was in first or second grade, I think, for my birthday. Isn't it cute? I was very proud of her. It's a wonderful memento of … well, better times."

Carly eyed the ashtray carefully. As far as she could tell, it might well be the only object in the room that the murder victim had ever actually touched. She wondered—could she find out anything from it?

Carly reached toward the ashtray and asked, "Could I … have a closer look at it?"

Chapman squinted curiously.

"If you like," he said.

As Carly reached over and picked up the ashtray, she immediately felt that familiar cold tingle. Careful not to close her eyes lest she draw too much attention to her reaction, she nevertheless got a fleeting sense of Gentry's girlish pride and delight when she'd handed the wrapped present to her father those many years ago.

Carly also glimpsed the sour, disapproving expression on her father's face when he'd seen what the present was.

"You know I quit smoking," he'd growled, then shoved the ashtray aside.

Jolted by this impression, Carly put the ashtray back on the desk. She locked gazes with Chapman for a fraction of a second, then looked hastily away.

The dead woman had delivered Carly a message, all right—that her father had been lying about being proud of the ashtray. In fact, the poor girl had found it just about impossible to please her father in any way.

The congressman kept the ashtray situated so prominently on his desk for the same reason he had family pictures hanging on the walls.

It helped make him look like a good family man.

And that was good politics.

Lyle suddenly came back into the office, looking rattled and alarmed.

He said to Chapman, "I hope you'll excuse us, congressman. My partner and I have to leave immediately."

"Have you got some sort of lead?" Chapman asked.

"We'll—we'll see," Lyle said. "Before we go, I just want to say that my partner and I are both sorry for your loss."

Carly had to quicken her pace to keep with Lyle as he hurried out of the office and into the hallway.

"What's going on?" she asked her partner breathlessly.

"I can tell you one thing for sure," Lyle said. "The congressman is not our killer's next victim."

"How do you know?" Carly asked.

"Because there's already been another one. We need to get to the crime scene right now."

CHAPTER THIRTEEN

"Another murder?" Carly asked as she and Lyle hurried out of the Cannon House Office Building toward their SUV.

"Yep," Lyle replied tersely. "That call was Detective Brown."

"And it's the same?" Carly asked.

"So it would seem," Lyle said. "The girl's body was found with a Shakespeare sonnet in her hand. This time at Cheswick College in Foggy Bottom."

Carly stifled a sigh of despair. She wished she was more surprised. She remembered the vision she'd had at the morgue of several pages falling out of a book and fluttering away. She'd had the strong feeling then that more sonnets would be found, which meant more deaths.

A lot of good those feelings are doing me, she thought.

She asked, "Do we happen to know which sonnet it is this time?"

Lyle smiled at her and said, "What, did you think I'd forget to ask? This is *Lyle,* kid. I don't overlook details like that. Brown says it's Sonnet 19. Does that mean anything to. you?"

It didn't mean anything to Carly off the top of her head. She took out her cellphone, did a search, and quickly found the text. She read the first two lines aloud to Lyle.

"'Devouring Time, blunt thou the lion's paws, / And make the earth devour her own sweet brood …'"

Lyle grunted and said, "Sounds ominous. Do you think it means anything?"

"I'm still trying to figure out whether the previous one, Sonnet 9, means anything," Carly told him.

"Let me know if anything occurs to you," Lyle said. "The only thing we can assume so far—we're dealing with a killer who likes poetry."

Or maybe has some awful connection with this particular poetry, Carly thought. But she wasn't sure enough of that notion to comment.

Carly scanned the rest of the poem, which included images of tigers and phoenixes and warnings about mortality.

Ominous is right, she thought.

But she couldn't begin to guess whether some specific deadly message was lurking in its lines.

Soon Lyle was driving them back across the National Mall toward Foggy Bottom. Carly found herself replaying parts of the peculiar conversation they'd just had back at the Cannon House Office Building—especially how eager the congressman had been to clear up his whereabouts at the time of the murder.

"What did you make of Congressman Chapman?" she asked Lyle.

"What do *you* make of him?" Lyle replied.

Carly chuckled under her breath.

There he goes, being Socratic again, she thought.

As her mentor as well as her partner, Lyle sometimes got into a particular mode where he insisted on asking the questions, challenging Carly to come up with her own answers. She'd found it did help sometimes to go through the simplest of steps in considering a case.

"Well, to state the obvious, he isn't the killer in either case," she said. "He was far away yesterday, then on a plane this morning. Of course, I suppose he could have hired someone …"

"Go on," Lyle said as Carly's voice faded.

"And we know he wasn't the killer's *next* intended victim, because someone else has already been murdered. But does that necessarily mean the killer doesn't still have him in his sights?"

"I dunno," Lyle said with a sidewise glance at her. "You tell me."

Carly thought for a moment, then shook her head and said, "I just couldn't make any sense of what he said. He was so hung up on that one line in the poem, 'The world will be thy widow.' He thought it definitely referred to him."

"Is that what you think?" Lyle said.

"No, I don't," Carly replied. "In fact, I think it was a weird idea. I could hardly believe he even meant it, like maybe he was making it up just to blow smoke in our eyes. But why would he want to do that? Doesn't he want us to solve his daughter's murder?"

Lyle shrugged and said nothing, waiting for Carly to think some more.

Carly thought back to how Congressman Chapman flat-out accused his longtime lobbyist "friend" of planning to kill him. Chapman hadn't offered the slightest bit of evidence for his suspicions, except for a supposed telltale expression on the lobbyist's face.

"I've got excellent instincts," Chapman had said. *"I can read people. That's why I'm so good at what I do."*

Things started coming clearer in Carly's mind.

"He's paranoid, isn't he?" she said to Lyle.

"Bingo," Lyle said. "What else?"

Carly thought about how coldly and impersonally he'd spoken about his dead wife. She also remembered that glimpse she'd gotten of his reaction to his little girl giving him a handcrafted ashtray for his birthday.

"You know I quit smoking."

Carly said, "He's also narcissistic. And a sociopath. It's like other people don't even really exist for him."

"Now you're catching on," Lyle said with a chuckle. "I'd add 'delusional' to the mix. Give him a line of poetry that was written more than 400 years ago, and he'll think it has to be about him and him alone. He lives in a twisted fantasy world."

Carly stammered, "But how—how did he get to be so … ?"

"Powerful?" Lyle said, completing her thought. "Narcissism and paranoia are pretty much the rule among successful politicians, especially the alpha males. That's one of the reasons I don't like it when politics gets mixed into investigations. Too many psychopaths. It gets hard to tell the innocent from the guilty."

The thought made Carly feel queasy. In her experience, tracking down a psychopathic killer was always a challenge. Now she was reminded that the world was full of psychopaths who weren't necessarily killers but couldn't be trusted.

And yet we still have to deal with them, she thought.

Soon they drove onto the Cheswick College campus, with its eclectic mix of old and new buildings. Up ahead they saw Detective Brown standing on a corner looking out for them. Brown flagged them down, and they pulled up at the crime scene.

"Damn it, what a mess," Lyle said as he parked.

Carly could see exactly what he meant. The immediate area of the murder was surrounded by a hastily-constructed privacy shield, a fence made of heavy-duty blue fabric mounted on aluminum poles.

Surrounding the barrier were dozens of gawking onlookers. Carly knew the crime scene must have gotten badly contaminated well before the cops arrived and put up that barrier.

Also parked nearby were several police cars and the Medical Examiner's van.

As Lyle and Carly got out of their vehicle, Detective Brown walked toward them looking remarkably fresh and alert.

"Hope the two of you got some sleep since we last saw each other,"

Brown said to Lyle and Carly. "I went home and managed to catch a few hours."

"Yeah, I can see that," Lyle grumbled.

"Hey, you both look like hell," Brown said.

"Thanks," Lyle replied.

Carly felt a wave of exhaustion pass over her at the mere mention of sleep. She and Lyle hadn't gotten any rest all night.

"So tell us what's going on," Lyle said to Detective Brown.

Brown put his hands in his pockets and said, "The victim is Bianca Voigts, a graduate student here. We've got somebody calling to notify her family over in Oregon. And this time, I've made sure that the M.E.'s people haven't hauled the body away just yet, so it's still behind the barrier for you to see."

He added with a smirk, "You're welcome."

"So I take it we've got a serial killer," Lyle said, ignoring the detective's sarcasm.

"I'm not jumping to any conclusions," Brown said. "It could be a copycat."

"Get real, Brown," Lyle said with a scoff. "Gentry Chapman's murder has barely made the news yet. It's way too soon for a copycat to get any ideas, much less act on them. What about the poem you said was in the victim's hand?"

"I've got it right here," Brown said, opening a small folder and taking out the crumpled page that was in a protective plastic sheath. As he handed it to Lyle, Carly could see that it was the same sonnet she had read during the drive here.

As Lyle held it in his hand, Carly took the poem from the previous murder out of her satchel and held it up to compare the two.

Carly said, "It sure looks to me like the two pages were torn out of the same book."

"Yeah, it looks like that to me, too," Lyle said.

Lyle flipped the new page over to reveal a poem that had been crossed out, the same as before.

He told Carly, "We need to get these to Quantico for analysis in the crime lab there."

She reached out and took the new page, as though she wanted to get a good look at the two of them together. Actually, she wanted to monitor her response to holding the new one in her hand.

Maybe a slight tingle, she thought.

But she didn't get any useful information.

Lyle commented, “Let’s give both of these pages to Brown, so one of his guys can drive them to Quantico.”

Brown growled, “Hey, what do you think we are, a messenger service?”

Lyle replied, “Don’t gripe, Brown. I’m sure you can spare one measly guy.”

Carly took a moment to get a photo of each sonnet with her cell phone, and then handed them to Brown.

Lyle said, “This was definitely no copycat.”

“If you say so,” Detective Brown grumbled. “But it wasn’t a stabbing this time.”

“What was it then?” Carly asked.

“I don’t know,” Brown replied. “Maybe the forensic technicians can tell you. Let’s go have a look.”

As Carly and her two colleagues walked toward the barrier, Detective Brown pointed out a disconsolate-looking middle-aged man standing among the onlookers. He wore thick-lensed glasses and was wearing a corduroy jacket with patches on the elbows.

Brown said, “That guy’s name is Neal Redfield—*Professor* Neal Redfield. He was teaching the seminar the girl was supposed to join this morning. He canceled his class and came over here as soon as he heard the news. The poor guy’s pretty broken up about this.”

Carly was well aware that the grieving professor or any of the other people crowding the area could be the killer. Some murderers did like to hang around and watch. But she neither saw nor felt any sign. It didn’t seem likely that she and her colleagues were going to catch this one before the morning was over

Then Detective Brown pointed out a young African-American woman sitting on a different bench. She was crying and being comforted by a female cop, who seemed to be doing a good job of keeping her friends away.

Brown said, “That’s the girl who found the body—or at least who realized she was dead. Her name is Tina Hart. She’s been crying nonstop since we got here.”

Carly said, “I trust you’ve told both the girl and the professor to stay here until we’ve had a chance to talk to them.”

“I have,” Brown replied.

Then Carly followed Lyle and Detective Brown through an opening in the barrier into a secluded area where a couple of forensic technicians were examining the body.

The dead girl lay sprawled on her back on a wide concrete bench, her arms and legs hanging every which way. That familiar, bluish waxy skin tone was just starting to come over the corpse.

Carly got the same uncanny feeling she always got when she saw a murdered body—a feeling that something worse even than cruelty or viciousness had to be at work. There always seemed to be an element of mockery as well—the expression of a mind who felt reverence for absolutely nothing, not even human life.

"How did she get into this position?" Carly asked.

"It's hard to say exactly," Brown said. "The girl who found her gave her a nudge or two before she guessed what was wrong. A couple of the girl's friends came around and checked her pulse and even attempted some CPR. So a lot of people have been in contact with the body."

Indeed, Carly could see plenty of scuffmarks on the ground where a group of well-meaning people had doubtless done everything they could to revive the victim. Unfortunately, they hadn't made things any easier for the forensic team or for the investigators.

The scene contrasted sharply with the one at the theater in one important way.

No blood, Carly observed.

She asked one of the white-clad technicians, "Any theories on how she died?"

The technician shrugged and said, "It doesn't look like strangulation. Dr. Smith will want to do an autopsy and a blood workup. My guess is it was an overdose of barbiturates—and since there seems to be a connection to the previous murder, it was probably deliberate and not accidental."

Poisoning, Carly thought.

She found it striking that the killer hadn't settled on a particular mode of killing. Was that somehow significant?

She edged closer, looking for some graceful way to physically touch the dead girl—or at least something belonging to her. Her eyes lighted on a gold locket hanging from a gold chain around her neck.

"Has anybody looked to see what's in the locket?" she asked.

"Not yet," Brown said.

The locket offered just the excuse Carly was looking for. She pulled out her plastic gloves, which she'd found didn't necessarily block any sensations from whatever she touched. When she put them on and took the necklace between her fingers, she felt a slight tingle all over her skin.

Then there was a vague, fleeting glimpse from the victim's point of view.

Bianca had been walking along dazedly in a deepening fog when a man had come up to her.

"Are you all right?" the man asked.

What happened next was hazy, but Carly thought that the man had taken a coffee cup out of Bianca's hand and helped her sit down on this bench and …

That was all. She got no further impression from the locket.

Carly held back a discouraged sigh. Bianca seemed to have nothing useful to communicate, except that a man had offered her help when she'd been succumbing to the drug. Carly hadn't even gotten a clear view of the man's face, just a sort of blur. The face apparently hadn't made much of an impression on the victim. He was just the last thing she'd seen.

Had anybody witnessed that moment?

If so, could they identify the man?

And even if they could, does it matter? Carly wondered.

For all Carly knew, he was just some helpful bystander.

Carly abruptly realized that the people around her were waiting for her to snap the locket open. She surely looked strange, holding the thing between her fingers and just staring at it.

She opened the locket expecting to find a picture, maybe of a boyfriend or a relative. Instead, there was just a folded-up piece of paper inside, and she felt no renewed tingle as she opened it up.

Two numbers were written on the paper—a four-digit number, and another ten-digit number broken up by dashes.

"The second one looks like a phone number," Carly observed, holding it up for her colleagues to see.

"I'll try calling it," Detective Brown said, taking out his own cellphone.

Carly glanced at Lyle as if to silently ask, *"Is that such a good idea?"*

Lyle shrugged as if to say he didn't think it would do any harm.

Brown punched the numbers into his cellphone. Everybody in the group jumped a little when they heard a phone ringing nearby.

"It's coming from her purse," Lyle said.

He pulled the ringing cellphone out of her purse, and Detective Brown ended his attempted phone call.

"It's her own phone number," Brown said, shaking his head. "Why would she be carrying around her own phone number in her locket?"

Carly couldn't help but smile a little. She didn't need any extrasensory intuitions to answer Brown's question.

She said, "My bet it it's a brand new cellphone, and she was having trouble remembering her own number. Haven't you ever had that kind of problem? Maybe she had a lousy memory for numbers. A lot of people do. A locket would have been a good place to keep it tucked out of sight."

"But what about the other number?" Brown said.

Carly chuckled slightly and said, "If I'm right, we're in luck. It's her cellphone passcode. We might be able to find out if she was communicating with anyone just before she died."

"Let me have a look," Brown said, abruptly snatching the cellphone away from Lyle.

Lyle crossed his arms irritably as Brown punched the four-digit number into the cellphone.

"Hey, it works!" he said. "I'm in! What do you think I should look for first?"

Lyle said, "Does she have any new calls or text messages?"

"It doesn't look like it," Brown replied.

"What about recent emails?" Carly asked.

Brown moved his fingers over the screen.

Then the detective's eyes widened.

"Holy smoke!" he cried.

CHAPTER FOURTEEN

Carly peered over Detective Brown's shoulders to read the words on the victim's cellphone:

Hi Lisa. Wanna play?

That was just the first in a string of three short emails. The reply was:

Sorry Rod. Evenings work better for me.

The final one said *OK. Later.*

That was all. But those brief lines held the attention of all three investigators.

Pointing out the times of the emails, Lyle commented, "These were exchanged about an hour ago."

"Right about when the girl was murdered," Brown said. "This has gotta mean something. But what about the name—Lisa instead of Bianca?"

"I don't think these were sent from either of their regular email accounts," Carly observed. "Look at the names on the addresses."

The name on the two emails Bianca had received was "rodohorn." And the name on the one she had sent was certainly not Bianca's own name. Instead it was "lisalascivia."

"Sure sounds kind of porny to me," Brown remarked.

"Uh-huh," Carly agreed.

In fact, she thought the emails suggested some kind of roleplaying activity.

"Maybe we're onto something here," Lyle said, taking back the cellphone. "All we have to do is find out who 'rodohorn' really is."

"That might take some time," Detective Brown said.

"Not at all," Lyle said, tapping something on the cellphone screen. "I'll just forward these along to our I.T. guys at Quantico. Email addresses contain metadata they can use to trace the original sender. It should only take a few minutes."

Just then, one of the forensic technicians approached them and asked, "What about the girl's body?"

Carly glanced at Lyle, and they shared a nod of agreement.

"You can take it away now," Carly said.

As the forensic technicians prepared a body bag for the corpse, Lyle got out his cellphone and called Quantico's I.T. department.

While her partner was taking care of that request, Carly took out her notepad and stepped outside the barrier. She glanced around the growing crowd for the two people she considered most urgent to interview—Professor Redfield, who had been expecting Bianca to attend his seminar that morning, and Tina Hart, the African-American student who had first realized that Bianca was dead.

Better talk to the girl first, Carly decided.

But as she headed toward the bench where Tina Hart was seated with a female police officer, Carly wasn't pleased to see Detective Brown tagging along beside her. So far, Brown hadn't impressed Carly with his finesse at interviews—and finesse was needed with this traumatized witness.

Carly frowned at her colleague and began, "Detective Brown, if you don't mind …"

She let her words fade, hoping Brown would get her message.

"What?" he replied.

Carly stifled a sigh and told him, "I'd like to conduct my interviews privately."

Brown scoffed and said, "Have it your way—although privacy might be a little hard to come by in this crowd."

Carly asked, "Have you and your team interviewed all the bystanders—found out who might have known Bianca, and whether she had any enemies? Also what they were doing at the time of the murder?"

"Yeah, but more people keep showing up," Brown grumbled.

"Well, have your people check them out too," Carly told him.

"But—"

"It's important," Carly insisted. "Just do it."

Without further comment, Brown ducked his chin and trudged away.

Carly wasn't actually sure just how productive such interviews might be, but this was the kind of thing that needed to be done. And at least it would keep Brown away from her for a little while. She approached the bench and introduced herself, showing her badge to the policewoman whose nameplate identified her as Heidi Unger. Tina Hart was just staring silently into space, although her face was still wet with tears and she was clutching a handful of tissues.

Carly silently beckoned the officer off the bench and spoke to her quietly.

"How is she doing?" Carly asked.

"Not good," Officer Unger said with a shake of her head.

"I want to talk to her," Carly said. "Do you think that would be OK?"

Unger raised her eyebrows in slight surprise. Carly guessed that she hadn't expected a BAU agent to ask for her opinion, and that she was even rather pleased about it.

"I think maybe so," Unger said. "Just go easy on her."

"OK," Carly agreed.

Unger tactfully stepped aside, and Carly sat down on the bench next to Tina Hart,

Carly patted the young woman on the shoulder and said, "I'm terribly sorry about what you're going through."

Tina nodded and coughed up a stray sob. She dabbed at her eyes with a tissue.

"Did you know the victim?" Carly asked.

"No," Tina said. "I mean, I saw her around, but we never actually met. I didn't even know her name. We didn't have any classes together, and I don't think we had any friends in common. Maybe if we'd gotten to know each other … Maybe this whole thing wouldn't have … I don't know …"

Carly stifled a sympathetic sigh.

It's like Gentry's friend back at the theater, she thought.

Another poor girl was racked with guilt over something that wasn't her fault in any way.

"There was nothing you could have done to stop this from happening," Carly said.

"I guess … that must be true."

Carly paused from her notetaking. She'd seen this kind of irrational guilt dozens of times. It always got under her skin, and she always felt tempted to play a trauma counselor.

That's not my job, she reminded herself sternly.

"Can you tell me exactly what happened?" Carly asked instead.

Tina nodded.

"I was sitting here reading my psych text when she showed up," she said, patting an enormous book beside her. "I saw her walk by and sit down on the bench across the path over there and …"

The young woman paused. She seemed to be slipping back into shock. Carly worried that she might start crying again.

I've got to keep her focused, she thought.

Carly flashed back to her brief and not very helpful glimpse of what had happened from the victim's point of view. She knew—or thought she knew—what Tina had skipped over and was trying to remember. But she also knew she had to be careful not to ask questions that were too leading.

Carly asked, "Was she alone when you first noticed her?"

"No, a guy was with her, helping her walk along because she seemed very wobbly. He …"

Tina squinted thoughtfully.

"She was carrying a coffee cup, and he took it away from her."

Carly felt a twinge of excitement as she remembered seeing exactly that same thing in her fleeting vision.

"Are you sure?" Carly asked.

"Yes. I think he was afraid she might spill it. He helped her sit down on the bench and …"

Tina's voice faded.

Carly asked, "Could you describe this man?"

Tina shook her head slowly.

"He just looked—ordinary. Medium height, I guess. Sandy hair, or maybe brown. His clothes were … kind of plain. A brown jacket, maybe. And maybe jeans. I'm not sure. I wasn't really watching them all that closely."

"What about his face?" Carly asked.

Tina stammered, "I—I'm sorry, I really have no idea."

"Do you mean you didn't get a look at his face?" Carly asked.

Tina shrugged slightly and said, "I guess not. Or maybe it was just that … I don't know, nothing about his face stuck with me. He was completely … ordinary."

Carly remembered her own impression of the man's face as Bianca may have seen it—as somehow utterly unremarkable. Whoever the man was, he lacked any distinguishing characteristics.

But did he have anything to do with Bianca's death?

Carly had no idea. But because the victim may have been drugged, Carly was certainly curious about that cup the man had taken out of her hand.

She said to Tina, "This cup of coffee you mentioned—do you have any idea where the victim might have bought it?"

Tina pointed to a building and said, "Probably over there in the student center. There's a coffee shop there where everybody goes."

Carly jotted down this information and said, "What happened to the young man?"

Tina said, "He went away, I think. The next time I looked up from my book, she was sitting there alone. I read a bit more, and then I looked again, and her head was slumped forward."

Tina shrugged and said, "Well, I didn't think anything of that, really. At that hour of the morning, just about everybody on campus is struggling to stay awake. So I read some more until I saw that it was just about time for me to get to my own class. When I got up to leave, I noticed that she was slumped a lot more, like she might fall off the bench. So I walked over to her and gave her a little nudge to wake her up and …"

Tina shuddered deeply.

"She toppled right over on her side on the bench, completely limp, and I knew something was really wrong, and I guess I screamed, because in a second there was a whole crowd of people around us. And one guy tried to give her CPR while I called 911, and …"

Tina paused and said, "I guess I kind of went into shock after that. Everything else is kind of a blur."

Carly patted her on the shoulder again.

"Thank you, Tina. You're being very helpful."

Then Carly signaled for Officer Unger to come back over to the bench. She said to the policewoman, "I need for you to talk to Tina some more. See if she can remember exactly which of the people still standing around here went near the victim. Then interview as many of them as you can."

Officer Unger nodded. "Anything else?"

"Yes. I need for you or another officer to go to the coffee shop in the student center. The victim probably ordered something there, and we need to know what it was. Then go around checking the trash receptacles and see if you can find the cup she was drinking from. Take it into evidence—very carefully, of course, and keep any contents that might be in the cup."

"I'll do it," Unger said.

As the policewoman sat down next to the young woman and began to talk to her in a gentle voice, Carly walked over to the other person she needed most to talk to—Professor Redfield. The man was standing by himself with his hands in his pockets, his mouth hanging open as he watched the technicians wheel the body away on a gurney. He didn't seem to have budged an inch since she'd first seen him.

Carly produced her badge again and said to the man, "Professor Redfield, I'm Agent Carly See with the FBI's Behavioral Analysis Unit. I'd like to talk to you for a few moments, if that's OK."

The man nodded mutely, still staring through his thick-lensed glasses.

Carly said to him, "Would you like to go somewhere and sit down?"

Seeming to snap out of a deep reverie, Redfield said, "Huh? Oh, yes. Of course. That would be fine."

Then his eyes glazed over again and he stood there without moving.

Apparently he hadn't really understood what she'd said. He seemed to be as deeply shaken as the girl Carly had just talked to.

I guess we'll keep standing, Carly thought.

With her pencil and notebook ready, Carly said, "Professor Redfield, could you tell me exactly how you found out what had happened to Bianca Voigts?"

"Huh?" the professor said again.

Then his mind seemed to clear a bit and he said, "Oh, yes, you want to talk to me about Bianca. It's all so terrible. I'll be glad to tell you whatever I can. Could we maybe … go and sit down somewhere?"

"Certainly," Carly said, relieved that he seemed to be becoming more coherent. The two of them found the nearest bench and sat down together.

Carly got her pencil and notepad ready.

Professor Redfield shook himself a bit, as if trying to wake himself up from a nightmare.

"I still can't believe this has happened," he said.

Carly waited for him to speak some more.

"I was in my seminar room, getting ready to meet with the group she was in. I expected her to show up early. She always did. We often talked about the day's topic together before the other students arrived. We were supposed to talk about … a Jacobean play called *The Duchess of Malfi.*"

He stared ahead for a moment, then said, "It came time for the seminar to start, and my other students arrived, but not Bianca. I got worried. Then one of the students glanced out the window and said something seemed to be wrong outside, and police were arriving, and I …"

He shivered and said, "It wasn't rational, I guess, but I *knew* something had happened to her. I hurried out of the building, and ran all the way here, just in time to see her lying on the bench before the cops put up that barrier …"

He turned and looked at Carly with a pleading expression.

"They say she's dead," he murmured. "Is that true?"

"I'm afraid so," Carly said.

"But how … ?"

His eyes glazed again, and Carly was afraid he might slip back into shock.

If it really is *shock,* she thought.

For all she knew, his apparent horror might be completely feigned.

"That's what I'm trying to find out," Carly said. "And I need your help. Do you know anyone who might have meant her any harm?"

Professor Redfield was jolted alert again.

"What do you mean?" he said, his voice getting tight and hoarse. "Do you think she may have been … ?"

His voice faded away. Carly knew from experience that it was more important for her to keep asking her own questions than to try to answer his.

She didn't need to ask the most routine question of all, which was where the man had been at the time of the apparent murder. He'd already said he'd been in his seminar room, and he wasn't likely to change his story. Carly made a note to have the police ask his students to confirm his alibi. But she did have to ask a question that tended to make even innocent people uncomfortable and defensive.

"What was your relationship with the deceased—aside from being her professor, I mean?"

To Carly's surprise, the man's face lit up with a trace of eagerness, as if he had no idea she was still considering him as a potential suspect and was actually pleased to answer the question.

"Oh … I thought she was just wonderful. She was so promising, the kind of brilliant young scholar who comes along just once in a very long time. She came here after winning the Strabane Foundation's Renaissance Studies Prize, which is a really big deal in academia."

"Go on," Carly said, taking notes.

"She was my protégé, and I was just getting ready to ask her to co-author a paper with me. But she was more than that to me. She was a friend, and she was almost family. My wife and I had her over to dinner often, and she was always a pleasure to have around, and she even got along great with my children."

His lips had shaped themselves into a smile, but suddenly his face saddened as a renewed wave of awful realization seemed to come over him.

For a moment, Carly wasn't sure what to say. His apparent guilelessness had taken her aback. Although she knew better than to eliminate him as a suspect with so little to go on, she found it impossible to believe that this man could have killed Bianca Voigts.

Instead, she wondered whether he might actually be able to help with the case. After all, he was a Renaissance scholar. Maybe, she thought, he could help her determine if those two sonnets that were left with the victims had any particular significance.

But before she could ask anything about it, Lyle caught her attention with a wave.

"Excuse me for a moment," she said to Professor Redfield.

She walked over toward Lyle, who definitely looked happier than he had a few moments ago.

"What's going on?" she asked Lyle.

Lyle's face broke into a grin.

"A lead, anyway," he said. "And with some luck, maybe even our killer."

CHAPTER FIFTEEN

Carly gasped aloud at Lyle's announcement.

"You think?" she almost yelled. "Tell me!"

"I said maybe," Lyle replied. "But the tech guys at Quantico worked their magic in record time. They've found out who 'rodohorn' is."

"Great!" Carly exclaimed. "Who?"

She glanced around to make sure she wasn't attracting any attention with her enthusiasm. This was still speculation, after all. But the police on the site were still methodically going about their work, and Professor Redfield was sitting on his bench, staring glumly into space.

"Turns out it's a philosophy professor right here at Cheswick College. His name is Bruce Clancy. And judging from those weird email addresses and fake names, our philosophy professor and a brilliant grad student were doing some sexting. Then Lisa, or lisalascivia, who was actually Bianca, became a murder victim. Sound suspicious to you?"

"We'd better have a chat with Professor Clancy," Carly said.

"Agreed," Lyle said. "I just called the philosophy department to see if he was on campus, but he's apparently still at home this morning. He lives right near here. Let's go pay him a visit."

"I'll be right with you," Carly said.

She hurried back to the seminar leader and told him, "Professor Redfield, thank you for your help." She handed him a card with her contact information. "I have to go, but I might be back in touch. Please call me if you think of anything I should know."

"I'll do that," Redfield said, looking a little startled at Carly's abrupt departure. "And please call me if you think I can help in any way."

Carly assured him that she would, then turned and trotted after Lyle, who was already on his way to their SUV. But en route, they were approached by a group of seven or eight people with notebooks and cameras and waving cell phones.

Press, Carly realized with dread.

Sure enough, the group surged around them, blocking their

progress.

One reporter shouted, "You two are FBI agents, aren't you?"

"Why are you asking?" Lyle growled evasively, elbowing another reporter out of the way.

The elbowed man replied, "Because that's what Detective Brown just told us."

Yet another said, "He told us that you're Agents Ramsey and See of the BAU."

Carly and Lyle exchanged annoyed glances.

"Well, I guess he answered all your questions, didn't he?" Lyle snapped.

As the press of bodies tightened around them, Carly looked back toward the crime scene and saw Detective Brown quietly standing with his hands in his pockets, watching and listening while Officer Unger interviewed a witness.

Then Brown glanced over at Carly and Lyle with a self-satisfied smirk.

Brown told him who we are just to get them off his back, Carly realized.

It really was a mean trick. And Carly knew that it was liable to have consequences that Brown hadn't really thought through.

Sure enough, the reporters took up a line of questioning they had hoped to avoid.

"Why is the Behavioral Analysis Unit looking into a campus death?" a woman demanded, waving her cell phone in front of their faces.

Another stated loudly, "Since you're FBI, you must be here to investigate a serial case."

And there it was, just as she'd expected. Brown had inadvertently tipped the reporters off that a serial killer was on the loose, which was the last thing they wanted the public to know at the moment.

Carly groaned aloud with frustration.

"No comment," Lyle said, trying to push a path among the bodies.

But the reporters were firing questions faster now.

Another asked, "Does this morning's murder have anything to do with the actress who was killed at the Shaddon Center last night?"

"No comment," Lyle repeated, more sharply than before.

They've already connected the dots, Carly thought.

She and Lyle broke away from the pack and got into their vehicle. The reporters finally backed away when Lyle started the engine.

“What a pain in the ass,” he grumbled as he pulled away from the curb. “I should have warned Brown to keep his mouth shut. Not that it would probably do any good.”

Carly said, “At least the reporters don’t seem to know about the sonnets that were left with the bodies.”

“Not yet, anyway,” Lyle said. “And anyway, maybe it won’t matter all that much even if it does get out. With some luck, we’re on our way to apprehend the killer right now.”

He clucked his tongue as he continued driving and said, “I’m trying not to get too far ahead of myself. I know that we’ve still got to cover all our bases. I’ve already gotten the second victim’s address, in case we need to go there. And I gave Detective Brown and his team a slew of instructions.”

Carly asked, “You put them to work interviewing Bianca’s friends and classmates and her other professors?”

“Sure did,” Lyle replied. “So the cops have got plenty to keep them busy. Not that Brown was particularly happy about that. But he’s efficient enough. They’ll get it done.”

They drove a few blocks, passing elegant homes in an expensive-looking neighborhood. Several blocks later, they entered a street lined with newer two-story townhouses. All of these were identical, with the same molding and window shutters and raised front stoops, but they were painted various lively colors to make them distinct from one another.

Lyle parked at the address they’d been given. This particular townhouse was an unobtrusive beige, as though to make it a bit more dignified than the others. Together Carly and Lyle walked up the steps and knocked on the door.

A worried-looking, casually-dressed middle-aged woman answered the door. She stared at them for a moment, then finally asked a bit curtly, “Can I help you?”

Carly and Lyle produced their badges and introduced themselves.

“Is this the home of Bruce Clancy?” Lyle asked.

“Yes, I’m his wife, Betty,” the woman said.

His wife, Carly thought.

A sour taste rose up into her mouth. Of course she’d had no reason to think Bruce Clancy wasn’t married. But he also visited online sex sites. Carly doubted that Betty Clancy had any idea of such activities.

I’m not going to like this guy, she thought.

“Could we come in and talk with your husband?” Carly asked.

Betty Clancy's eyes darted about nervously and she hesitated before replying.

Just behind her, a flight of wooden stairs led up to the second floor, and Carly could hear a door opening up there and then some footsteps.

"May I ask what this is all about?" Betty asked.

Before Carly or Lyle could reply, a man's voice called down from upstairs.

"Who is it, Betty?"

Betty called back upstairs, repeating the agents' names. She added, "They're Special Agents with the FBI."

After a pause, the man's voice called down, "Send them up."

Then there were more footsteps and the sound of a door closing upstairs.

Betty turned toward Carly and Lyle with a perplexed expression and said, "I'll take you to him."

She let them in the front door and closed it behind them. Carly could see that the narrow residence seemed to be snugly fitted between two other apparently identical townhouses. She could see past the kitchen area to an attractive living room with French doors leading to what was apparently a small patio. It looked like the kind of home a reasonably well-off couple would move into after their children were grown and space was no longer of the essence.

Looking distraught, Betty Clancy said "Please follow me" and headed up the stairs.

Carly felt sorry for the wife, who seemed to have been upset even before their arrival.

There's something wrong in this house, she thought.

Betty led them up the stairs and knocked on a heavy wooden door.

The man's voice called from inside, "Come in."

When Betty opened the door, Carly and Lyle stepped into a small, neatly-kept library/office with dark wood paneling and shelves filled with hardback books. A man was sitting at a large, heavy desk.

"Leave us alone, Betty," the man said.

The wife seemed on the verge of panicking now.

She stammered, "But—but Bruce, could you just please tell me—?"

"Not now," the man said sternly but not unkindly. "Please. Leave us alone."

Betty nodded, exited, and closed the door behind her.

Carly and her partner found themselves alone with a hefty, slouching man in a jogging suit who was clutching a whiskey glass in his hand. He was staring at a mostly-empty bottle of liquor on the desk in front of him. Without a glance at them, he took a swallow of whiskey, almost as if he were unaware that anyone else was in the room.

Carly and Lyle stood awkwardly for a moment, then took the liberty of sitting down in a pair of straight-back chairs in front of the desk. Carly's mind clicked away rapidly, trying to relate this man to the one Tina Hart had mentioned—the nondescript, almost singularly bland-looking man who had relieved Bianca Voigts of her coffee cup and had helped her sit down on the outdoor bench. Carly had also gotten a vague image of him in her vision and knew that he was the last thing Bianca had ever seen.

This certainly didn't seem like the same man.

But she also realized that that wasn't really an issue. She had no reason to believe or disbelieve that the man she'd glimpsed and whom Tina Hart had tried vainly to describe to her had anything to do with Bianca's murder.

That's not true of this guy, she thought.

This was a more distinctive personality, a hulking man with well-defined features who sent emails as "rodohorn." Those exchanges with the victim gave them a strong reason to investigate him.

Bruce Clancy lifted his eyes and stared at Lyle. He muttered, "Should I get a lawyer?"

Carly was a bit surprised by the blunt directness of this question. If Lyle was surprised, he didn't show it.

"That depends," Lyle said ambiguously.

"Depends on what?"

"On what you've got to tell us," Lyle said.

Clancy let out a low, rumbling sigh. The man was obviously quite drunk. Judging from the puffiness of his face, Carly suspected that he got that way often. But it wasn't quite noon yet. Was he always this drunk at this time of day? Carly doubted it.

He's got some special reason this morning, she thought. It didn't take any unusual intuitions to see that this man was in pain.

Finally Bruce Clancy took a deep breath and said, "No lawyer. I'll tell you everything."

CHAPTER SIXTEEN

An uncanny silence fell in the room. It seemed to go on forever as Professor Bruce Clancy sat staring numbly into space.

Is he going to tell us anything at all? Carly wondered. The man looked as though he had fallen into a drunken stupor.

She saw that Lyle was scowling silently at Clancy.

That worried Carly a little. She knew that Lyle himself was a recovering alcoholic, although his drinking days had ended long before Carly knew him. Lyle tended to get impatient with people whose drinking was completely out of control, and she could see that this man was definitely getting on her partner's nerves.

She decided that she should do something—at least ask a question. Lyle usually took the lead in interviews, but this time she should play that role. She thought that Clancy probably wasn't going to need a lot of prodding anyhow.

"Tell us all about it," Carly said to the professor. "Take your time."

Clancy slowly crossed his arms and looked up at her with bloodshot eyes. Then he finally began talking.

"I go jogging on Saturday mornings. My route takes me over to the Cheswick campus. This morning I saw some police cars and a crowd of people. I asked somebody to tell me what was going on. They said a girl had been killed. Then I heard other people mentioning her name—a name I knew well. Bianca Voigts. I panicked. I turned around and ran back home. I've been right here ever since."

That's at least one reason why his wife is so worried, Carly realized.

Her husband had come home from jogging, shut himself up, and started drinking.

Lyle shifted uncomfortably in his chair but didn't say anything. Carly sensed that he, too, thought it best that she keep asking the questions.

Just don't rush it, she told herself.

She waited for a moment to find out whether Clancy might go right on talking. He didn't. He just stared into space again.

Finally she asked, "Why did you panic?"

Clancy said nothing.

Then Carly asked, "What was your relationship with Bianca Voigts?"

Clancy groaned aloud and looked at her again.

"Oh, I'm sure you've got a pretty good idea of that already, or you wouldn't be here. In fact, I've more or less been expecting you. All you had to do was check the girl's emails to find out about Rod O'Horn. And it wouldn't have taken any investigative miracle to figure out that that was me. And you've also heard of Lisa Lascivia. Of course, that was Bianca."

"And when did you use those names?"

With a cough of embarrassment he replied, "On RacyChat."

Carly had read about the notorious app.

"That's an online sexting site, isn't it?" she asked.

"That's right," Clancy said. "And of course, you're going to look into our activity there, if you haven't done that already. You'll find all sorts of ... well, let's say steamy messaging that includes some indiscrete photos."

"Does your wife know about RacyChat?" Carly asked.

Clancy took a large swallow of whiskey.

"No, but I guess she soon will," he said. "She's going to have a lot of questions about your visit and whatever else comes out about me in your investigation. Anyway, I'm tired of keeping secrets. I figure it's about time I ... admitted to a few things that ... I'm not exactly proud of."

Carly nodded ever so slightly. Now she understood that the heavy drinking could be both over his shock at Bianca's death and his attempt to summon the courage to talk honestly with his wife.

Unless he's lying about everything.

Her mind raced through the possibilities. If Professor Clancy had actually murdered Bianca Voigts, he could be trying to deal with an emotional backlash and terror at the prospect of capture.

But what about the other girl? Carly wondered.

She asked, "Did you know a young woman named Gentry Chapman?"

"No. Why?"

Lyle put in, "Where were you at 9:30 last night?"

Clancy squinted curiously.

"Right here in my office, preparing for a lecture," he said. "My wife can confirm it. Who was this other woman? Why are you asking me these questions?"

Neither Carly nor Lyle replied. They knew better than to simply tell him that there had been another murder. If he was guilty, they wanted him to dig deeper into his own lies.

Carly studied his face. She found it hard to believe that the man sitting here had killed both Gentry Chapman and Bianca Voigts. He'd have to be a colder character than he seemed to be.

Or a skilled actor, she thought.

And of course, he might have killed neither of them and simply be what he appeared to be, a middle-aged man who had dallied in sexual games with a young woman who turned up dead.

She asked Clancy, "What kind of relationship did you have with Bianca? In real life, I mean. Outside of RacyChat."

A sneer formed on Clancy's lips, an expression Carly recognized as one of self-hatred.

"Let's just say that our 'meet world,' nonvirtual relationship wasn't exactly … symmetrical. If you know what I mean."

He took another swallow of whiskey and added, "And I think you do."

Carly crinkled her brow.

"No, actually I don't," she said.

Clancy turned toward Lyle and said, "What about you? Do you know what I mean?"

Lyle said without looking at him, "Actually, I think I do."

"Well?" Clancy said.

Lyle fell silent for a moment. Carly waited breathlessly for him to speak. She knew from experience that he was a highly observant student of human character, particularly its seamier side.

Finally Lyle said, "You knew her, but she didn't know you."

"Exactly," Clancy said. "I thought maybe you were the kind of guy who would get it."

Lyle frowned more sharply, obviously not flattered by the remark. For Carly's part, she still had no idea what the two men were talking about.

Lyle leaned forward in the chair and said to Clancy, "Yes, you're a bit of a voyeur, aren't you, Clancy? You like to spy on women. It makes you feel powerful to watch them when they've got no idea what you're doing. Isn't that it?"

Clancy nodded ever so slightly and stared at the bottle for a moment.

Finally he said, "She caught my eye around campus—Bianca, I mean. She caught my eye and my … interest. She didn't know me—at least not that I was aware of. Oh, she probably knew my name from hearing it around campus, and maybe she'd been able to put my name with my face. I really don't know."

"So you stalked her," Carly said, starting to understand things better.

"I'm not sure stalking is the right word," Clancy said.

"What *is* the right word?" Carly asked.

Clancy fell silent again, then stroked his chin thoughtfully.

He said, "In my philosophy classes, I teach about a concept called 'consequentialism.'"

"Yeah, I've heard of that," Lyle commented. His voice held a note of disapproval.

"Can you tell me what it means?" Clancy asked, lifting an eyebrow.

Lyle said, "It's got something to do with how you can judge whether an action is right or wrong."

"That's right," Clancy said. "According to consequentialism, the only way to judge the morality of an act is by its consequences. Now, the word stalking implies making a nuisance of oneself. But what were the consequences of my following a girl around without her or anybody else knowing anything about it—consequences to *her* I mean? Nil, as far as I can figure. I don't even see how you can call it stalking."

Lyle scoffed and shuffled his feet. He said, "I hope your thinking isn't this shoddy in the classroom. According to your logic, a peeping tom is innocent as long as he doesn't get caught. That just doesn't wash."

Clancy tilted his head with interest.

"Very good, Agent Ramsey," he said. "You'd make a very good student. I did *follow* her without her knowledge. And I listened in on her conversations with other students whenever I could get near enough to hear. And to those actions … there *were* consequences …"

Clancy drummed his fingers on his desk and continued, "One morning I sat near her table in the coffee shop in the student center. She was talking to her friends about RacyChat. There was a lot of giggling, and they dared each other to join, and Bianca said she would if they could think of a good 'porn name' for her. Finally I heard them come up with the name 'Lisa Lascivia.'"

Things were becoming a lot clearer to Carly now.

"So you joined RacyChat yourself," she said. "And you had no trouble finding Bianca, since you knew the name she was using there. And you took your own fake name …"

"Rod O'Horn," Clancy said with a nod. "I introduced myself to her online and we started our … thing. I suppose you'll wind up reading our texts to each other. You'll also find explicit photos, although none that show either of our faces. She seemed to … enjoy my company."

Lyle let out a sullen growl and said, "Not as much as you enjoyed hers, I'm sure."

"It was all voluntary, remember," Clancy replied. "But I suppose you're right about the … uh …level of pleasure."

"Oh, I'm sure I'm right," Lyle said. "It must have been quite a turn-on, following her around on campus and knowing about your connection when she had no idea about it. Definitely not 'symmetrical.'"

Clancy emptied his glass. He poured himself some more whiskey then took another swallow.

Carly sensed that he was drowning an onslaught of guilt, whether he'd actually killed the girl or not. If he was innocent of the murder, maybe her death had been some sort of final trigger.

She remembered him saying, *"I'm tired of keeping secrets."*

Maybe that was why he was talking to them right now.

So is he really going to tell his wife about the sexting? she wondered.

Then Clancy said, "When I found out what had happened, I knew it would only be a matter of time before you came looking for me. I don't have a very good alibi. I must have been jogging when … whatever happened took place."

"And nobody can confirm that?" Carly asked.

"Probably not," Clancy said. "But I didn't kill her."

"You're acting plenty guilty," Lyle said.

"Yes, I suppose I am," Clancy said. "You can imagine why, can't you?"

"Not really," Lyle muttered. "The truth is, I have trouble understanding what it's like to *be* you."

"Really?" Clancy said, lifting his glass. "Are you telling me you don't know all about *this?"*

Carly's eyes widened with alarm. Clancy seemed to have picked up on Lyle's own history with alcohol.

But how? she wondered.

Lyle's expression darkened.

"You'd better watch your step," he snapped.

"You're right, I'd better," Clancy said.

The two men stared at each other for a moment, and Carly could only hope that some kind of a fight wasn't about to break out between them.

Then Professor Clancy shifted his gaze back to the floor again and he heaved a strange, sob-like sound.

"I didn't kill her," he said yet again, his voice thicker than before.

"So you keep telling us," Lyle said.

Clancy continued, stammering, "But—but there's one thing … maybe you can tell *me* … "

He paused, then said, "Was her getting killed … a *consequence* somehow … of what I did? The way I followed her and manipulated her and … ?"

Lyle said, "I guess that depends on whether you're telling the truth about not killing her."

Clancy's voice hit a higher pitch now.

"I *didn't* kill her. But what I want to know is … did I set events in motion … that might have gotten her killed? Was it … my fault, somehow?"

Carly felt unsettled and confused by the question. But in a way, she could understand how Clancy might feel some sort of nameless, guilty dread. Perhaps it was the same kind of irrational reaction that Denise Holder had about Gentry Chapman's death, or how Tina Hart felt about Bianca's murder.

But in both of those cases, Carly had found it fairly easy to say something reassuring—to tell the two young women that the deaths hadn't been their fault. Somehow, she couldn't bring herself to say the same sort of thing to Bruce Clancy.

Lyle abruptly stood up and said in a tense voice, "We've taken up enough of your time, Professor Clancy. We'll be going now."

Carly was startled at his sudden decision. Clancy, too, seemed to be more than a little surprised.

He stammered again, "Is that … all you need from me?"

"I'm not saying that," Lyle growled. "We expect you to stay put and not leave the area and be available to answer any further questions. Is that all right with you?"

Clancy nodded mutely.

"Good," Lyle said.

Carly followed Lyle out of the office and down the stairs. As the two of them walked back through the townhouse, Betty Clancy stood staring at them with alarmed perplexity.

Lyle stopped and said to her, "Ms. Clancy, could you tell us where your husband was last night?"

"He was right here at home the whole night, and so was I," she said, her voice trembling.

"Can you get more specific?" Lyle asked.

Betty Clancy shrugged and said, "Well, we had guests for dinner, and they didn't leave until quite late. Bruce helped me get everything ready, then helped me clean up afterwards, and that took rather a long time. Then we watched a movie on television and finally went to bed."

"So he wasn't out of your sight that whole time?" Lyle asked.

"No, I'm sure of it. Why do you ask?"

"You might want to ask your husband about that," Lyle said, a little more bluntly than Carly thought appropriate.

The poor woman, Carly thought.

There was a lot about her husband that she didn't know. Carly wondered—was Bruce Clancy really going to do as he said and confess to her about his involvement with the murdered girl?

Carly didn't know, but she did figure it was none of her business. She and her partner still had a murder case to solve.

And we'd better do it before someone else gets killed, she thought. *This guy is moving awfully fast.*

CHAPTER SEVENTEEN

When they left the professor's townhouse and got into their SUV, Carly waited for her partner to say something. Lyle was maintaining a grim silence that she'd seldom seen in him.

After several long moments he asked, "What do you think of our philosophy professor?"

Carly realized that she didn't know how to reply. Certainly they didn't have any hard evidence against him, nothing to suggest they should put him under arrest. But she was awfully tired after the long night and half of a day they'd worked through, and she didn't trust her own judgment right now.

"What do *you* think of him?" Carly asked instead.

"I think he's as manipulative as hell," Lyle growled. "And I let him get the best of me. I'm sorry."

"But how did he know … ?" Carly began.

"About my own problems with the bottle?" Lyle replied. "Sometimes alcoholics can tell, like Geiger counters or something. 'It takes one to know one,' as they say. As for whether he's our killer or not …"

His voice faded for a moment.

Then he said, "A man who would treat a young woman like that, stalk her and spy on her and carry on some kind of weird, lopsided, sneaky sexual thing with her, and then justify it with some pseudointellectual crap … Well, as far as I'm concerned, he might be capable of anything."

Carly shook her head and said, "He seemed genuinely remorseful about all that. Toward the girl and his wife both."

"Remorse can be easy," Lyle said bitterly. "And for all we know, it was an act. Maybe he was just trying to play us. Addicts do that. They're good at it. And psychopaths come in all types, all shapes and sizes, and with all kinds of different styles. Some are cold fish, like Congressman Chapman, and they don't show any human emotion at all. Others know how to fake it. Those are the kinds of psychopaths you've really got to watch out for."

"And you think maybe Clancy is that kind of psychopath?" Carly asked.

"Maybe. At least, I don't think he's a very well-developed human being."

Carly took a long, slow breath, letting impressions run through her mind.

"I don't know, Lyle." she said. "The first murder doesn't seem to have been about sexting or stalking. And Clancy actually seems to have a pretty good alibi for the first one. I really don't think he's our guy."

"Unless his wife is lying for him," Lyle said.

Carly shook his head and said, "I find it easier to imagine Chapman being the killer. Or at least hiring the killer. But the truth is, I've got a feeling the killer is still out there, and we don't have any idea who he is."

"I suppose you're right," Lyle said, finally starting the engine. "So where do you think we should go now?"

Carly was slightly surprised. It was an unusual question for Lyle to ask. He was normally more decisive, more in command of the situation, truly Carly's senior partner.

He's awfully tired too, she realized.

She said, "You mentioned getting Bianca Voigts's address from the local cops. What do you think about taking a look at her apartment?"

After another silence, Lyle shrugged said, "It's as good a plan as any."

He pulled away from the row of townhouses and started to drive.

The apartment building where Bianca Voigts had lived was just a short drive away, close enough to the campus for an easy walk or a brief jaunt by bus. They pulled into an underground parking garage, then walked outside and around the building to the front entrance.

The hulking six-story brick building took up an entire city block. An awkward blend of traditional and postmodern styles, it wasn't a friendly-looking place. In fact, it struck Carly as cold and factory-like. She couldn't guess how many tenants the place must house.

When they walked inside, the bland lobby struck Carly as scarcely more inviting than the building's exterior. A bald man wearing a bowtie and blazer stood at a large marble-topped desk. He didn't even glance up until Lyle produced his badge and introduced himself and Carly.

"I'm Hugo Albanese, the building manager," the man told them. "How can I help the FBI today?"

Lyle said, "Are you aware that one of your residents was a victim of a crime this morning?"

The man behind the desk looked at his watch and stifled a yawn.

"I didn't know that, no," he said in a bored voice.

Lyle glanced at Carly for support. It was always delicate to have to tell a total stranger that somebody they might have felt close to was dead. Lyle generally relied on Carly in such situations.

Carly said, "I'm sorry to have to break the news. A girl was murdered. You probably knew her. Her name was Bianca Voigts."

The man looked utterly unsurprised, as if they'd told him she'd gone on vacation.

"Voigts," he said. "The name rings a bell."

He took out his cellphone and seemed to look over a list.

"Yeah, she lives here—or at least she did. You say she was murdered? Where did it happen?"

"Over on the campus," Lyle said.

"What a shame," the manager said indifferently.

Lyle said, "We were hoping to have a look inside her apartment."

The manager drummed his fingers on the desk and said, "Well, this is kind of a new situation for me. I guess this is where I ought to ask you if you have a search warrant, but ..."

He shrugged and said, "But since she's dead, I guess it doesn't matter, right? OK, then. I'll take you to her apartment."

Lyle and Carly followed Hugo Albanese toward an elevator.

Lyle said to Albanese, "I take it you didn't know the girl very well."

Albanese scoffed, "I don't know *anybody* who lives here very well. I make a point of that. I don't get paid enough to be everybody's friend. People come and go so fast it makes my head spin, especially the college students. They're all a nuisance as far as I'm concerned."

The elevator arrived, and the three of them got inside.

Pushing the button for the third floor, Albanese continued, "Besides, the tenants here have got everything they could possibly want—gyms, a pool, game rooms, the works. But you'd never know it, the way everybody keeps complaining about one thing or another. There's never any letup."

The elevator stopped, and they stepped into a startlingly long hallway lined with apartment doors. The muffled sound of loud music filled the air.

"Do you hear that?" Albanese grumbled. "There's always a party going on here somewhere, 24-seven. I don't know how anybody gets any sleep."

A nearby door opened, and a burst of loud music was accompanied by the strong smell of marijuana. A scruffy man in his 20s stepped out in the hallway

"Turn that music down," Albanese growled. "And what the hell are you smoking in there?"

The young man let out a grunt of laughter as he pulled the door shut. He glared at them with an unmistakably stoned look in his eyes.

"Like it's any of your business, Albanese," he said.

"No?" Albanese said with a gloating laugh. "Well now, I've got a couple of FBI agents right here."

"Yeah, right," the young man scoffed, glaring back and forth between the slender young woman and the tall, graying Black man standing there with the building manager.

We're not what he thinks agents are supposed to look like, Carly thought. It wasn't the first time that she'd realized that neither she nor Lyle fit the popular image of FBI agents as action heroes.

"I'm not kidding," Albanese said.

"No?" the man snorted with palpable disbelief. "Let's see some badges."

Carly wasn't the least bit happy with the introduction, but she produced her badge, and so did Lyle.

A look of panic crossed the stoned man's face. He opened his door again, poked his head inside, and said something inaudible to whoever was inside. The music suddenly got quieter, then he closed the door again.

"What's this all about?" he asked Lyle and Carly.

Carly said, "Did you know another tenant named Bianca Voigts?"

"Bianca?" the man said, scratching his head and pointing at a door across the hall. "Yeah, she lives right over there."

Albanese grunted, *"Lived,* you mean. She's dead."

Carly felt her face redden.

He's really not helping, she thought.

"Huh?" the tenant said.

"She was murdered this morning," Albanese said.

The tenant glanced dazedly back and forth between Carly and Lyle again, but he looked less defiant this time.

Carly's partner spoke up loudly before the building manager could blurt out anything else.

"We're sorry you have to find out this way. Do you know of

anyone who might have meant her any harm?"

"Uh, no," the man said with a shake of his head.

"How well did you know Bianca?" Carly asked.

The man shrugged and said, "Just well enough to put her name and her face together, I guess. I said 'hi' when I saw her, and she said 'hi' back, and she knew my name too. She seemed nice and all. But she didn't hang out with me and my friends. She seemed to keep to herself mostly. Bookish."

"When did you last see her?"

"Not today. Maybe a couple of days ago. She's usually up and out early, and I'm not inclined that way."

Experience told Carly that this man probably didn't have anything else useful to say. She handed him her card.

"Ask around," she said. "If anybody knows anything we should know, have them contact us."

"I'll do that," the young man said, looking considerably more sober now. He took the card and ducked back into his apartment.

Meanwhile, Albanese had already gone to the door across the hall and was unlocking it. He opened the door, and said, "It's a furnished rental. I'll have to inventory it later. Meanwhile, I'll leave the two of you to do your thing."

The building manager strode past them and away down the hall. Carly and Lyle stepped into the room and shut the door behind them.

The first thing that startled Carly was how small the studio apartment was, scarcely any bigger than her own dorm room had been in college. There was a tiny bathroom and a cooking area that hardly qualified as a kitchen. The pinched living area was dominated by an unfolded sofa bed that was neatly made.

Because of the building's location, Carly guessed that the rent must be higher than for her own larger apartment.

I guess it must be worth it to be this close to campus, she thought. *For a college student, anyway.*

What was most telling about the room was its clutter. It wasn't the sort of careless and downright unsanitary slovenliness which Carly herself had been guilty of during her own college years—"mold bait," as her friends had called it. There were no food wrappers anywhere, or any dirty dishes, not even in the sink. There were no signs of anyone else staying there, no different-sized or male clothing in the closet, no extra toothbrush in the bathroom.

Instead, there were books and papers scattered simply everywhere, and most of the books lay open and were heavily marked and highlighted. It was as if the room had been frozen in a moment of intense study.

But Carly didn't get the feeling that desperate cramming had been going on here. She wasn't sure whether her instincts were kicking in, but she got the distinct feeling of excitement and challenge and stimulation.

She loved all this, Carly thought with a twinge of sadness.

It hardly seemed surprising, since one of the few things Carly and Lyle knew about Bianca Voigts was that she'd been a brilliant and promising young scholar.

Looking down at one of the books, Lyle said, "She sure had a thing about Shakespeare."

Indeed, many of the books were editions or collections of plays by Shakespeare and his contemporaries, and many of the others appeared to be history, scholarship, and criticism about the period.

Carly remarked, "And both victims were found with pages with Shakespeare sonnets on them. There must be a connection."

"Maybe, or maybe not," Lyle said turning a page with pencil eraser. "I wouldn't know where to start looking in all this stuff here. And we'd better not spend too much time heading down blind alleys."

A couple of windows opened onto a non-scenic view of the street outside. A desk with a computer and printer on it was pushed up against that wall. An object on the desk caught Carly's eye. It was a paperweight, a little bronze bust of Shakespeare. Something about how prominently it sat next to the computer gave Carly the distinct feeling that it was somehow important to the murdered girl.

She reached out to touch it. As soon as her fingers made contact with the statuette, she felt a sharp vibration all the way through her body.

I'm getting something, she realized.

CHAPTER EIGHTEEN

An electric shiver passed through Carly's body.

She closed her eyes.

The first impression that came to her was a voice—a kindly, nurturing woman's voice.

"Bianca wins this year's prize."

Now Carly glimpsed a whole classroom full of children. She was a little girl sitting at one of its desks and the other students were all looking toward her.

Don't let it overwhelm you, she reminded herself.

A stout, smiling woman was setting the statuette down on the desk in front of her. Shakespeare's bust looked new and shiny now.

The teacher said, *"Bianca read more books than anybody else this summer! In fact, she read more books than any student I can remember. I think she deserves a round of applause as well as the prize."*

The girl blushed with pride as she heard her fellow students clapping for her.

The teacher said, *"I'm so proud of you, Bianca. You're going to do such wonderful things. You're going to have so many wonderful adventures in the world of words and ideas. And I've got a feeling Shakespeare will play a special part in your life."*

The girl smiled through her own tears of delight, and Carly's impressions suddenly faded. She opened her eyes and found herself looking at the bronze bust again—an object that had been a source of pride and inspiration all through Bianca's short life, so much so that she'd kept it right here where she'd always see it when she was at work.

She felt a lump of emotion form in her throat.

Such a terrible waste, she thought.

Then a wave of exhaustion swept over her and she swayed dizzily.

She heard Lyle speaking behind her.

"Carly, are you OK?"

Carly straightened herself up said, "Yeah, I'm fine, Lyle."

Lyle said, "I honestly don't think we're going to find anything here."

Carly heaved a deep, discouraged sigh. Lyle was right, of course. Just now Bianca had communicated her own enthusiasm about reading and learning, but nothing about the murder. And back at the crime scene, all Carly had gotten was a vague impression of a perfectly nondescript man taking her cup away from her and helping her to sit down on an outdoor bench—a man who may or may not have been her killer.

She doesn't know anything about her own murder, she realized.

Carly's gift was of no help at all right now.

She followed Lyle out of the apartment into the hall. As they headed for the elevator, Lyle said, "She must have been one smart girl."

"She must have been," Carly said sadly.

But "smart" didn't seem to Carly nearly the right word for it. She knew that Bianca Voigts was a lot more than smart. She was inspired, a prodigy, filled with excitement for things of the mind. And from early in her life, she'd inspired excitement in others, including a teacher who had done everything she could to encourage her.

Carly remembered something Professor Redfield had said about her back at the crime scene.

"She was so promising, the kind of brilliant young scholar who comes along just once in a very long time."

Carly wondered—had her killer had any idea what sort of life he'd cut short?

Had that been his motive—to destroy a beautiful mind out of spite or envy or some other resentful urge?

Or does he even care about that?

She and Lyle took the elevator down to the foyer and then returned to the underground garage and got into their SUV. Lyle started the engine and drove out of the garage away from the building.

"Where are we going next?" Carly asked.

"I'm driving you back to your apartment," Lyle said. "We've got nothing else to do here right now."

"That's all the way out of town," she protested.

"Just half an hour. Your need some sleep."

"No I don't," Carly snapped. "We need to ..."

Her voice trailed off as she realized she didn't actually know what to do next.

Lyle grunted, "You should get a look at yourself. You look worn out."

Carly couldn't help but laugh as she observed the bags under Lyle's own drooping eyes.

"You should get a look at *yourself,* Lyle," she said. "I can't look any worse than you do. And you're not taking me back to Glensted."

"Yes, I am."

Carly felt a flash of impatience.

"No, you're not," she said. "Stop the car. Let me drive."

"No way," Lyle said.

Carly had to stop herself from really yelling at him.

We're acting like children, she thought. *Get a grip.*

She took a slow breath and said, "It'll be a waste of time. And we're dealing with a killer who's moving fast."

Lyle's shoulders heaved up and down.

"Fast is right," he said with a reluctant tone. "Two murders in less than 24 hours. And for all we know, he's killed again already."

Carly added, "You can't go it alone in your condition, no more than I can."

Lyle growled softly, "I suppose you're right. I hate to think how long it's been since either of us got any sleep. We're neither of us thinking straight. Maybe what we need is to refuel."

"Let's go get some lunch," Carly replied, glad to settle their argument. "Or dinner. Or whatever."

Lyle drove them straight to a café where they'd eaten before because it was conveniently near a parking garage. When they went inside, they saw that the place wasn't crowded because they were between mealtimes, and they found a booth apart from the other customers.

They ordered coffee, of course, although Carly was worried that the caffeine would jangle her rather than wake her up. She'd long since burned through the crude energy boost from her early morning breakfast. Waffles and butter and maple syrup had been a short-term solution to what was turning out to be a long-term problem. In lieu of sleep, what she needed right now was some protein. She ordered a turkey and lettuce sandwich while Lyle ordered a BLT.

As they sipped on their coffee, Lyle said, "OK, we need to think. Where are we at this point? I mean, what are the links between the two murders? And do we have a clue where and how our killer might strike next? Assuming he will strike again."

"I feel sure that he will," Carly said, remembering her vision of a torn page falling out of a book, then another, then another, then another

…

She continued, "And it's all got to do with Shakespeare somehow. Gentry Chapman was an aspiring Shakespearean actress, and she was killed in the middle of a production of *Macbeth.* Bianca Voigts was a Renaissance scholar with a keen interest in Shakespeare."

"The killer is even using Shakespeare sonnets as his calling cards," Lyle added.

Carly took out her cellphone and brought up the photos she'd taken of both of the torn-out pages.

"This new one is Sonnet 19," she said.

Lyle said, "Yeah, and it starts off kind of ominously, if I remember right. How did the beginning go again?"

Carly read the first two lines aloud:

"Devouring Time, blunt thou the lion's paws,
And make the earth devour her own sweet brood ..."

"Do you think it means anything?" Lyle asked.

"If there are any clues here, I ought to be able to find them," she said. "My English-professor mom made me read all 154 of the sonnets when I was eleven, and she taught me a lot more about them than any eleven-year-old could ever want to know."

And she made me miserable in the process, Carly almost added. But she acknowledged to herself that at least she was in familiar territory.

She said to Lyle, "This is another one of the 'Fair Youth' sonnets. In this one the speaker is addressing 'Time' itself, warning it not to ruin the Fair Youth's beauty with age. The speaker ends up promising to keep the Fair Youth eternally young through his poems."

Carly then read the last two lines aloud:

"Yet do thy worst, old time; despite thy wrong,
My love shall in my verse ever live young."

Lyle shook his head and said, "Time definitely cut this girl's life short, in spite of what the poem says. Maybe it's supposed to be ironic."

The sandwiches arrived, and Carly took a bite of hers and tried to shake herself awake.

"So what can you tell me about this sonnet?" Lyle asked.

Carly perused the lines, remembering what she'd learned from

Mom's dreary lesson.

She said, "The idea of time as a destroyer is a really old one, and the first two words are borrowed from some ancient Roman poet—Ovid, if I remember right. Yeah, I'm pretty sure it was Ovid. I think the Latin phrase Mom taught me was *'tempus edax'*—'devouring time.'"

Lyle scratched his chin skeptically.

"'Devouring time,' huh?" he said taking a bite of his sandwich. "What else have you got?"

Carly took a bite of her own sandwich and continued, "The poem then says that Time will blunt even 'the lion's paws' and pluck the teeth out of 'the tiger's jaws.' But the next creature it mentions is really different—'the long-lived phoenix.'"

Lyle squinted at her with a hint of curiosity.

"Isn't the phoenix a kind of bird that lives forever?" he asked.

"In a way, yes, but in a way, no," Carly said, remembering what her mother had taught her. "It lives for a long, long time—several centuries. And then instead of dying, it burns itself to ashes on its own funeral pyre and rises again out of those ashes to live a whole new centuries-long life."

Carly thought as she took another bite.

Then she said to Lyle, "Do you suppose that means anything? I mean, like maybe the killer is thinking of his victims like phoenixes and expects them to come to life again?"

"If so, he's going to be disappointed," Lyle said, sounding more than a little doubtful. "The two women he's killed already aren't likely to come back from the dead."

"Yeah, but maybe that's what he hopes will happen," Carly said.

Lyle scoffed and said, "You mean he's going to keep on killing until he finds a woman who will come back to life again? That sounds like a stretch, Carly."

Carly hastily brought up the other sonnet on her cellphone.

"Maybe so," she said. "But don't forget, the killer left another sonnet in Gentry Chapman's hand—Sonnet 9. Maybe the two poems mean something when you read them together."

She read the opening lines of Sonnet 9 aloud:

"Is it for fear to wet a widow's eye
That thou consum'st thyself in single life?"

Then she said to Lyle, "Like I told you earlier, here the speaker is criticizing the Fair Youth for not marrying and having children. He goes on to say if he doesn't marry and leave a widow, then the *world* will someday be his widow, and it will grieve that he didn't immortalize his beauty by having children."

"I don't see how this is getting us anywhere," Lyle said, taking a bite of his sandwich and finishing his coffee.

Carly drummed her fingers on the table for a moment.

"Both of these poems have to do with the cycle of life and death—how people live on through their children, the same way a phoenix lives by rising out of its own ashes. Do you think that means something?"

"Honestly, I doubt it," Lyle said. "And I don't think we're getting anywhere trying to pry something out of these poems."

Carly felt disappointed at Lyle's words.

"But these sonnets have got to mean something," she said quietly.

"Maybe so, or maybe not," Lyle said. "Could be something about his state of mind. Or maybe the killer just ripped a couple of random pages out of a book he'd never even read and left them with the bodies just to mess with our heads."

"That can't be right, Lyle. He even took the trouble of crossing out the sonnets on the other sides of the pages—Sonnets 10 and 20. He doesn't want us to read those. He wants us to really look hard at 9 and 19."

"Yeah, maybe that's exactly what he wants," Lyle grunted. "I wouldn't be surprised if he's laughing at us right now. I mean, look at how we're using up precious time, treating these poems like some kind of riddle. Meanwhile, he could have moved on to his next victim."

Carly fell silent for a few moments as she finished her lunch.

"I just want to get some kind of break in this case," she said.

"Yeah, and so do I," Lyle said. "But Carly, you're too tired to think straight. We need real-life forensic details."

Carly felt a sudden wave of exhaustion, as if her body was voicing its own agreement with Lyle. Even her vision got jittery, and she had trouble focusing her eyes on her partner's face.

"You've got to get some sleep," Lyle said. "Just a short nap at least."

Carly protested wearily, "Lyle, you're *not* taking me to my apartment. I just won't go."

"Fine," Lyle said getting up from the table. "Let's pay the bill and get out of here. You can sleep in the SUV right there in the garage."

"What about you?" Carly asked, following him to the cash register. "You're tired too."

"You can spell me when you're rested," Lyle said. "Anyway, I've got a few things to take care of."

"Like what?"

"Let me worry about that," Lyle replied.

As they walked out of the café, Carly was surprised to see that dusk was falling. The whole day had passed, and she and her partner had nothing to show for it.

They returned to the parked SUV in the parking garage. Lyle opened the door and Carly crawled into the wide back seat and stretched herself out.

"I'm not sure I can sleep," Carly said.

"Give it a try," Lyle said, shutting her inside the vehicle.

Carly shut her eyes, and sure enough, a surge of exhaustion began to sweep over her. As she slipped off to sleep, she found herself flashing back to that image she'd gotten when touching the statuette—of a kindly teacher promising little Bianca Voigts a bright and exciting future.

"... and I've got a feeling Shakespeare will play a special part in your life," she said.

The thought of it made Carly sad enough to cry, but she was much too tired for that.

All she knew was that two bright young women were dead—and this killer wasn't finished yet.

CHAPTER NINETEEN

As Lyle walked away from the SUV, familiar words rang through his mind.

"You're always watching out for me. What would I do without ... ?"

The memory stopped him in his tracks.

He turned and trotted back to the SUV where he'd left Carly lying in the wide back seat. Looking in through the window, he breathed a sigh of relief to see her sleeping safely and soundly.

But what else did I expect? he wondered.

Of course she would be safe right here for a while in the parking garage while he took a short walk to clear his head. It wasn't like she'd be in any danger.

Even so, as he stood at the SUV window staring at his slumbering partner, he understood the real reason for his spasm of fear. With her mouth hanging open in an unheard snore, she reminded him of a different young partner at the moment of her violent death.

Lyle shuddered, remembering ...

Together with a team of cops and FBI agents, he and Special Agent Dawn Metcalf, were in the middle of a shootout. A small group of murderous bank robbers were holed up in a motel room, firing volley after volley at them through a smashed window and an open doorway. Lyle recognized the sounds of an assault rifle and several other weapons.

Finally the tide turned against the fugitives. He was pretty sure that only one of them was left alive in the motel room, and that one seemed to be running out of ammunition.

Lyle and Dawn crouched behind their parked vehicle, both feeling confident that the last fugitive would soon either be killed or surrender.

Sure enough, the rain of bullets slowed to a trickle and then stopped altogether.

"It's over," Lyle called out to the fugitive. "Come out and surrender. And let's see your hands in the air."

"OK, OK," the fugitive called back. "Just don't kill me, please."

The man stepped out of the motel room with his hands held above his head. Lyle worried for a moment that some trigger-happy local cop would shoot him anyway.

"Don't shoot," Lyle called out sternly to his colleagues. "Let me get him into cuffs."

Lyle and Dawn both stepped out from behind their vehicle, Lyle with a gun in one hand and his handcuffs in the other.

He glimpsed a flash of movement through the smashed motel window.

Someone was still alive in there!

"Get down!" he shouted at Dawn, raising his own weapon to fire.

But somehow Dawn was suddenly between him and the shooter. She took a bullet that had obviously been meant for him.

As Dawn fell at Lyle's feet, the other cops and agents responded with a hail of bullets that struck the shooter dead. Another agent handcuffed the unarmed surviving fugitive while Lyle dropped to his knees beside Dawn's prone body.

To this day Lyle didn't know exactly how Dawn had moved between him and the shooter. But he remembered his own wordless cry of horror.

And her face ...

Dawn's face had worn much the same expression as Carly's did right now, as she lay snoring in the back seat right now. Except for that trickle of blood from the edge of Dawn's lips.

Dawn had blinked several times, trying to focus her gaze.

"Lyle?" she had said with an inquisitive gasp.

"It's me," Lyle had said. *"Stay with me, OK, Dawn? Just stay with me."*

But even as he said those words, he knew that his young partner had taken a fatal bullet to the chest.

Dawn had heaved another gasping breath and said in a delirious voice, *"Lyle, are you OK?"*

The question had caused the blood to drain from Lyle's face.

Why is she asking me that? he'd wondered.

"I'm OK," he'd said.

Then Dawn had managed to twist her dying lips into a semblance of a smile.

"Thanks, Lyle," she had said. *"You're always watching out for me.*

What would I do without ... ?"

Then her eyes had gone dull and her mouth had gaped wide. Lyle had known she was dead.

And now, as he stood watching his current partner sleeping peacefully in the back of the SUV, Lyle shivered deep down in his bones. He murmured a question he'd asked thousands of times during the last few years.

"How did it happen, Dawn?"

And as he always did, he yearned with all his heart to hear Dawn explain everything from beyond the grave. Not being a superstitious man, Lyle knew better than to expect any such thing to happen.

But the mystery remained. How had Dawn wound up in front of him at the exact moment the fatal shot was fired? Had she stumbled there by accident? Or had she deliberately shielded him from the shot by throwing herself in front of him?

The possibility that she had given her life to save his still troubled him. For one thing, it seemed utterly pointless. Surely Dawn's life was at least as valuable as Lyle's—perhaps more so, since she had such a promising career ahead of her, and no history of divorce and alcoholism behind her. It also made those dying words of hers even harder to understand.

"You're always watching out for me."

In her final delirious moments, had she somehow imagined that Lyle had saved her life instead of the other way around? Lyle found that possibility too terrible to contemplate.

He was aware that he'd been very protective of Dawn during her time as his junior agent—maybe excessively so. He'd never had an actual child of his own, but he'd mourned Dawn's death with a father's grief. After that, he'd asked his BAU team chief Preston Voss not to assign him another partner fresh out of the academy.

If Lyle had his way, he'd have gone on working solo for the rest of his career. Barring that, he'd have much preferred to partner with a seasoned, toughened, experienced agent like himself—someone with his own weaknesses and demons who wouldn't stir up his overly keen paternal feelings.

But despite Lyle's protests, Voss had insisted on assigning him to work with Carly, another recent academy graduate.

"She's got talent," Voss had said. *"Something unique. She just needs a good mentor—somebody like you."*

Lyle had to admit, their partnership had worked out exceptionally well. Carly was turning into a superb agent who seemed to be possessed of unusually—even uncannily—keen intuitions.

He didn't really understand how her mind worked, but it hardly seemed to matter. His own analytical skills and Carly's intuitions complemented each other superbly. The trick was to give her space and sometimes a little privacy to do whatever it was she did, as he'd made a point of doing back in the autopsy room.

Standing there by the SUV, his attention returned to the present.

If she wakes up and sees me staring at her, she's going to think this is weird, he realized.

He turned and walked away from the vehicle, listening the clattering echo of his footsteps resound throughout the garage. He reminded himself of what his trauma counselor had told him soon after Dawn's death.

"You can't control everything. Whatever happens is not completely up to you."

He kept trying to live by those words from the Serenity Prayer—*"to accept the things I cannot change."* But even after years of sobriety, that part still didn't come easily.

I guess I'm not the most serene guy in the world, he thought.

Lyle stepped out of the parking garage into the cool night air and took a long, slow breath. When he took out his cellphone, he wasn't surprised to see a couple of unanswered phone calls from his team chief, Special Agent Preston Voss.

He punched in Voss's number. The chief answered quickly and spoke sharply.

"Talk to me, Ramsey."

Lyle gulped hard and said, "Agent See and I think we're dealing with a serial killer. Not a copycat. And definitely not a coincidence."

"I saw the two pages you sent to forensics." Voss said. "The poetry. So that's what connects the murders at the theater and the campus?"

"He seems to have a thing about Shakespeare," Lyle replied. "The first victim was an actress playing Hecate in a production of *Macbeth,* and the second was an up-and-coming Elizabethan scholar. And those poems are Shakespeare sonnets."

"That's all you've got?" Voss asked sharply.

What else can I tell him? Lyle wondered, falling silent for a moment.

He thought back to some of Carly's wild guesses over lunch—that maybe the killer was obsessed with cycles of life and death, as suggested by the phoenix and the issue of procreation, and that maybe he even had some idea that his victims might come back from the dead …

But no, Lyle had dismissed those ideas when Carly had raised them, and he wasn't going to discuss them with the chief.

Voss grumbled, "It doesn't sound like much of a profile. But never mind that for now. I've gotten three phone calls from Congressman Chapman."

Lyle rolled his eyes with frustration. He felt like he should have known he and Carly hadn't heard the last of Gentry Chapman's sociopathic father.

Voss continued, "He wants to know whether your lead panned out."

Lead? Lyle wondered, trying to remember what Voss might be referring to.

Then he remembered the phone call that had interrupted their meeting with Voss—the terrible news that there had been another victim.

"Have you got some sort of lead?" Chapman had asked as they'd headed out the door.

Lyle and Carly had evaded the question. They hadn't even told him there had been another victim.

Lyle said to Voss, "I think that might have been a misunderstanding on Chapman's part."

"Really? Maybe you should tell him that. He thinks his own life is in danger. And he doesn't think that you and your partner and the cops are taking that threat seriously. He doesn't think you're doing enough to protect him."

Lyle put his hand to his forehead. A headache was starting to kick in as he remembered Chapman's obsession with that line in Sonnet 9:

"The world will be thy widow."

"That means me, of course," Chapman had insisted at the time.

And of course, neither Lyle nor Carly had taken the idea seriously. They'd been sure the man was either paranoid or trying to mislead them for some reason. Lyle still hadn't changed his mind about that.

Before Lyle could start to explain this to Voss, the team chief said, "Chapman also told me he handed you a sure-fire suspect on a silver platter. It's a lobbyist from Chapman's home district, a man named Logan Headly. Have you eliminated Headly as a suspect?"

Lyle's teeth clenched and grinded together.

Carly and I really don't need this right now, he thought.

Lyle said, "Sir, we don't consider him a suspect at all."

"In spite of what Chapman said?"

Lyle slowed his breathing to calm himself down, then said, "To put it, uh, politely, Agent See and I are all but sure that Chapman's wrong."

"'All but sure?' Not completely sure?"

"Headly's not on our radar, sir. I think you should trust us about that."

Lyle heard his boss heave a heavy sigh.

"I do trust you, Agent Ramsey. And I don't mean to lean on you. But Chapman's got a lot of power in D.C., and he can cause real trouble for us at the BAU. I need for you and Agent See to pay him another visit, talk to him again, calm him down, put him straight as to facts."

Lyle could hardly believe what he was hearing.

"Sir, we're not going to do that," he said in a sullen voice.

"I'm not giving you a choice. I'm giving you an order."

"And I'm telling you I'm not going to do that," Lyle repeated, a little louder than before. "Chief, we've got an active serial killer on our hands. He's moving fast. Agent See and I don't have time to coddle some paranoid jerk of a congressman."

A silence fell between Lyle and his boss.

Finally Voss said, "Do you need me to send anybody from Quantico?"

The last thing Lyle felt like he needed was more people to coordinate with. In his experience, too many agents tended to lead to more mistakes. He spoke slowly as he said, "The local cops have been helpful. My partner and I just need to head over to the Metro Headquarters and talk logistics with Detective Brown, coordinate our activities. We won't need anyone else out here."

Another silence fell.

Lyle added, "We do need our I.T. guys to look for some connection between the two victims—something aside from an interest in Shakespeare, some hint that they maybe knew each other."

"The guys are already on it," Voss said. "So far they've got nothing."

Another silence fell. Lyle knew that his boss might be feeling a bit guilty for his shortness a moment to go, although it wasn't Voss's style to apologize. He was a fair, ethical man who could be tough to deal with—which of course Lyle knew came with his job.

Finally Voss said, "Ramsey, have you and See gotten any sleep since before the thing over near Middlegate?"

Middlegate? Lyle thought.

Then he remembered their search for Jean Bassman the night before. It seemed like weeks ago now.

Lyle said, "Not really. But Agent See is catching a few winks right now."

"Well, you should do that too. To keep your thinking clear."

"OK. Thanks for the advice."

They ended the call.

Lyle ached all over from exhaustion as he walked back into the garage and returned to the SUV. He saw that Carly was still fast asleep on the back seat, and he hoped she could keep right on sleeping during the drive to Metro Headquarters.

But when he climbed into the car and sat behind the wheel and put the keys in the ignition, Lyle felt a deep spasm of weariness. He was even a bit light-headed, and realized it might actually be dangerous for him to try to drive right now.

Just a minute or two, he said, glancing at his watch.

Then he closed his eyes while sitting upright at the wheel.

As his consciousness flickered, he caught a glimpse of Dawn's dying face and heard her tell him …

"You're always watching out for me."

CHAPTER TWENTY

Maia Stark grew worried as she hurried from her parked car to the Washington Museum of Renaissance Literature. The old building looming behind its courtyard wall looked dark and silent, obviously still locked up for the night.

Where were the two people who were supposed to meet her here?

Maia huffed a little with indignation. Here she was, a volunteer docent, out after hours to make a final check of the new exhibit. Those two paid presenters should at least be responsible enough to get here at the agreed-upon time.

She looked at her watch and thought with a sigh, *Give them just a few minutes.*

Unfortunately, she did have reason to wonder if they were going to show up at all.

She tapped her foot and glanced around at the well-lighted wall, which featured signs advertising the extravaganza that was to open here tomorrow—"Shakespeare & Friends at the Mermaid."

Maia was excited about the show, which promised to be a real crowd-pleaser—an innovative blend of installation, performance art, and scholarly exhibit. Shakespearean scholar Lillis Storer and her actor husband Dennis Ring had planned an exceptional event. Maia was sure that the museum's patrons and trustees were going to love it—if their private opening came off as planned.

Surrounded by authentic-looking facsimile copies of original editions of plays by Shakespeare's contemporaries, Dennis would put on a costume and play the part of Shakespeare himself. Lillis would take the role of a modern-day interviewer, asking him questions before allowing spectators to ask their own questions.

Dennis-as-Shakespeare would regale Lillis and the spectators with wild and rowdy stories about his nights at London's Mermaid Tavern, drinking and exchanging witticisms and sometimes even brawling with his playwright buddies, including Ben Jonson, Christopher Marlowe, Thomas Middleton, and John Webster.

Maia had seen Lillis and Dennis perform "Shakespeare & Friends at the Mermaid" when they'd toured their show at smaller museums, and she'd eagerly signed them to appear here at the museum in Washington. The museum's funding and ticket sales had been slipping during the last year or so, and it needed an infusion of money and excitement.

At tomorrow's gala opening, Maia would greet some of the museum's wealthiest patrons and donors who had promised to attend. She knew that few of the patrons shared her own deep fascination with Renaissance literature. But these openings gave them an A-list opportunity to flaunt their finery, the women looking especially glamorous in designer outfits and decked out with pearls and diamonds.

Jaded though the patrons sometimes were, Maia had been sure this show would excite their interest, loosening purse strings and opening up checkbooks. It was just the kind of event the museum sorely needed right now.

But everything had to be absolutely perfect, which was why she'd insisted that the two presenters meet here tonight to go over everything with her one more time. Tomorrow Maia would have too many other details to check out … the table settings, the refreshments, the servers, the security detail … there were always a dozen last-minute issues to deal with.

And now she also had to worry about the main attraction. Suppose those two didn't get here tonight? Could she count on them being here tomorrow?

What am I *going to do if they don't show?* she worried. *Or if they blow up like they did today?*

A few hours ago, she and Lillis and Dennis had been putting the finishing touches on the exhibit and rehearsing their act when a bitter argument broke out between the couple.

Lillis had accused Dennis of drinking—and judging from the actor's breath, Maia had suspected the same. Dennis retorted that Lillis was exploiting his talents with this "stupid show" and was holding him back from a promising acting career.

After some mutually rancorous comments, Dennis had stormed out of the museum, leaving Maia and Lillis alone among the display stands with the facsimile editions of Renaissance English plays.

Stunned by her actor-husband's behavior, Lillis had apologized to Maia profusely. She'd promised to get Dennis sober and talk him into returning to the show. Lillis had assured Maia that the couple would meet her right here outside the museum entrance at this very hour, ready to make amends and make certain that the exhibit was ready. But neither of them was here.

With a sigh, Maia decided to go on inside the museum and make her own last inspection of the exhibit. She even started considering how she, herself, might improvise some sort of presentation around the books on display. After all, she knew many of the plays well enough to quote some of them at length.

When she got out her key and started to unlock the door to the building's courtyard, she was surprised to discover that it was unlocked already. She swung the door open and saw that the open courtyard and the building beyond were dark.

Dark and silent.

Her worry gave way to a flash of anger. Maia had trusted Lillis with a key so that she could work here at will during these last few days, but if she was here now, some lights would surely be on. Had Lillis, or both she and Dennis, been here and left already, without bothering to lock the building back up? Had they even turned the security system back on?

Even if they were still fighting, there was really no excuse for doing anything so bizarre.

They'll hear about this the next time I see them, she thought.

And surely there would be a next time. Even if the couple bailed on their performance commitment, Maia figured they couldn't avoid her ire for long. They'd have to come back soon to recover those exhibit materials which were their own property.

Even if they didn't, Maia would make sure that pair was never recommended to any other artistic venue. And she'd arrange to have those lovely books added to the museum's collection.

She stepped on into the front courtyard, which was dimly lit by night-lights. In front of her, the central fountain splashed water into the pool as usual. On the other side of the open area, the doors to the building itself were closed as usual. There was still no sign that anybody else was in the place.

As she stepped angrily across the paved courtyard, something in the fountain pool caught her eye—some sort of shadowy shape.

Maia felt a renewed flash of anger. Someone had carelessly dumped something into the fountain—and who could have done such a thing except for Dennis or Lillis?

Was she going to have to find somebody to clean that up in addition to everything else she needed to do?

Maia stormed over to the electric box near the main doors and threw the light switches for the courtyard. As light flooded the area, she was relieved to see that nothing else in the courtyard looked out of place. As she'd feared, the security system hadn't been reset. She thought it sheer luck that no one else had noticed that unlocked door.

She hurried back to the fountain to see what was there in the pool.

The submerged thing in the water was human-shaped.

Familiar words passed through Maia's mind:

But long it could not be
Till that her garments, heavy with their drink,
Pull'd the poor wretch from her melodious lay
To muddy death.

It took Maia a second or two to remember that the lines were from *Hamlet*—and they described Ophelia's death by drowning.

Had Lillis and Dennis decided to stage Ophelia's drowning right here in the courtyard? That didn't strike Maia as a good idea. In fact, it seemed rather vulgar, like a much-too-early Halloween trick.

And what was this piece of paper placed on the rim of the pond?

She picked it up and read:

When I do count the clock that tells the time ...

A Shakespeare sonnet, she realized.

None of this made any sense. Maia leaned closer to the water for a better look at whatever was down there.

What she saw sent a shock of horror coursing through her body. Lillis Storer lay at the bottom of the fountain pool, her eyes closed but her mouth open, and looking deathly pale.

She's drowned, Maia realized.

Then she started screaming.

CHAPTER TWENTY ONE

Carly was looking at a boy's face on her computer screen when she heard a voice beside her.

"Go on. Post something on his page."

Carly turned and saw the freckled face of a girl with curly hair.

"Megan!" she said with surprise.

Carly's younger sister's lips turned into a wry grin that exposed the braces on her teeth.

"What do you mean, 'Megan?'" she said. "You act surprised to see me."

Maybe I am, *Carly thought.*

And yet she really couldn't imagine why, as she and Megan lay stretched out on the floor of Carly's bedroom with its pink wallpaper and posters of pop stars. A brand new laptop computer was open in front of them. They were both middle-schoolers, looking at a site where people could have their very own pages.

It was just that she had an odd feeling of having been somewhere else only a moment or two before.

Carly looked again at Mark Lawson's face on his new page. Although he could definitely use a haircut, she thought he seemed remarkably mature for a high school freshman.

And he was very good-looking.

"I'm not posting anything on his page," Carly said to Megan.

"You know you want to," Megan said.

I guess I kind of do, *Carly thought to herself.*

"What should I say?" Carly said.

"Go with, 'I'm madly in love with you,'" Megan said.

"No!"

"Why not?"

Carly sputtered, "Just ... just ... no!"

"Then just say 'Hi Mark,'" Megan said.

"No."

"Why not?"

"Because he's in high school."

"So? He's just a year ahead of you."

Carly didn't reply. The truth was, she couldn't see any harm in a simple "Hi Mark." Other kids were posting much more personal stuff on his page.

But as she reached out to type the words, the keyboard suddenly started moving away from her, as if deliberately avoiding her touch. She looked around and saw that the pink walls of her room were dissolving into a cloud-like vapor that soon enveloped her and hid everything from sight.

Then the mist began to drift away, and everything around her was different.

Carly was standing on the lighted front stoop of her house with Mark Lawson, who was better-looking than ever, and his hair was better kept. She realized they were both in high school now. And they were sharing a sweet, shy kiss.

"I had a wonderful time," she said to her new boyfriend.

"I did too," Mark said, squeezing her hand. "Thanks."

Mark walked back to his car, and Carly went quietly into her house and headed straight to her bedroom.

Megan was there, bouncing up and down beside the window.

Megan yelped with glee, "You kissed him!"

Carly hissed out a noisy "shhh," then said, "You spied on us!"

"You bet I did! Tell me the details!"

"You're too young," Carly said teasingly.

"Awww ..."

"It was just the one kiss," Carly began.

But before she could tell her sister more about her first date with Mark Lawson, everything changed again. The pink bedroom walls vaporized and swirled around them, erasing the scene from view.

Finally that pink fog seemed to coalesce into a pair of tight bundles.

Cotton candy! *Carly realized.*

She was eating pink cotton candy with Megan, who was taller and no longer wearing braces. They were at a noisy carnival and Mark Lawson was snapping a picture of them.

That picture, *Carly realized.*

Somehow she knew that she'd already looked wistfully at the picture Mark was taking. But that would be during years yet to come.

As young Carly struggled with her confusion, the cotton candy puffed outward into a cloud of vapor again. The thick pink foggy mist swept the whole carnival away and hid her sister from her sight.

Engulfed and lost, Carly stumbled about.

"Megan! Megan!" she called. "Where are you?"

When the vapor finally wafted away, Carly found herself in her house again. She was carrying a suitcase she'd brought home from college, but nobody else seemed to be home.

She called out:

"Megan! Megan! Where are you?"

She walked all through the house.

"Megan! Megan! Where are you?"

But her voice faded as she remembered.

She's gone.

Megan had disappeared last year, and nobody had any idea what had become of her ...

"Carly, wake up!"

Carly's eyes snapped open.

It took her a moment to realize she had fallen asleep in the SUV.

"Huh?" she muttered, still semi-lost in the dream she'd just had.

The alarm in Lyle's face and voice was palpable.

"There's been another murder," he said. "We've got to get going."

Carly felt as though she'd been slapped. She wished she were still dreaming, but she knew she wasn't. She climbed out of the back seat of the SUV, and she and Lyle got into the front seats. Glancing around, she could see that it was quite dark outside the garage where they had parked.

"I guess I was fast asleep," she said, shaking herself awake as Lyle started the engine.

"Not for long enough, believe me. I nodded off for a little bit myself, but Brown woke me up with a phone call."

Lyle shuddered deeply and added in a hoarse voice, "This killer is working fast. Way, way too fast. Three victims in less than 24 hours! I've never been on a serial case that moved like this."

"Who's the victim?" Carly asked.

"I don't know anything about her yet except her name—Lillis Storer. It happened over at the Museum of Renaissance Literature. We can get there in just a couple of minutes."

Carly rubbed her eyes and struggled to get awake. Her dream was still stuck in her head. It had been a long time since she'd dreamed about Megan's disappearance.

Why now? she wondered.

She told herself there was probably no reason except anxiety and exhaustion.

And it was only a dream.

Like all her dreams about Megan, there'd been no feeling at all that she was getting some kind of supernatural message from the beyond. And if it had been only a dream, that didn't mean that Megan was dead. After all, Carly didn't receive messages from *living* people—or at least she hadn't so far.

Besides, if Megan were dead, wouldn't she have communicated with Carly by now?

If only I knew, Carly thought.

But she had no time to ruminate on all that. Before Carly knew it, Lyle was parking the SUV among official vehicles that had already arrived in front of the museum. Detective Brown was waiting for them outside the entrance, next to big signs advertising a show called "Shakespeare & Friends at the Mermaid."

As they walked toward Brown, he said, "This is insane. This is just flat-out crazy. But at least we think we know who the killer is. He's this victim's husband. And we should be able to nail him soon."

"How do you know?" Lyle asked.

"There's a woman inside who can explain it," Brown said. "Come on in."

They passed through the front entrance into a courtyard, where cops were swarming around looking for clues. A fountain in the middle of the courtyard appeared to have been drained of water. Three white-clad forensic technicians were crouched there, around what Carly guessed must be the body.

As they approached the fountain, Carly's eye immediately lighted on a torn page lying on the edge of the fountain pond. A woman's body was lying on the damp tiles inside.

"Another sonnet?" she asked Detective Brown.

Brown nodded and said, "That's how we knew it was our killer."

Lyle peered down at it.

"Has anybody moved or touched it?" he asked Brown.

"Not since I've been here," Brown said. "But our witness said she picked it up and looked at it. She said she put it right down again."

Carly picked up the torn-out page with a pair of tweezers and looked at it.

"It's Sonnet 12 this time," she said, then silently reading the first two lines.

When I do count the clock that tells the time,
And see the brave day sunk in hideous night ...

She turned the page over, and saw Sonnet 13, which began with the words, "O, that you were yourself … …"

As Carly expected, the second sonnet was crossed out with a single line. She dropped the page into a plastic sheath and snapped a couple of pictures of it.

Then she handed it to Detective Brown and said, "Could you have one of your guys take this to Quantico?"

Brown nodded and called to a cop and gave him instructions.

Meanwhile, Lyle was climbing over the over the low wall into the drained pond. He said to the forensic technician in charge, "I take it the cause of death was drowning."

"It looks like it," the technician said. "But I think she was unconscious when it happened. It looks like she took a hard blow to the back of the head. I'll be able to tell the order of things when I get her into the lab. But here's what I think is really interesting …"

Carly leaned over to get a better look as the technician pointed to the woman's face. It was pale except for a bluish bruise on her right cheek.

"She got hit here as well," the technician said. "But this injury happened earlier. It looks like she tried to cover it up with makeup, but the water washed it off."

Detective Brown nodded and added, "Judging from what the witness said, you're liable to find more bruises like that all over her."

"Where is this witness?" Lyle asked.

"I'll take you to her," Brown said.

The three of them passed through a wide doorway into a large exhibit room dominated by a dozen or so podiums with open antique-looking volumes on them. A stunned-looking woman stood over one of the books, turning its pages and perusing them with glazed eyes.

Seated nearby was Officer Heidi Unger, who Carly remembered dealing sensitively with the witness to Bianca Voigts's death this morning.

Brown waved to Unger to join them. Then he nodded toward the woman standing over the podium.

"That's Maia Stark," he said quietly to Lyle and Carly. "She's a docent at the museum, and she found the body when she arrived in the courtyard a little while ago. Officer Unger has been talking to her."

Officer Unger added, "As you can see, she's in a deep state of shock, which waxes and wanes."

Carly asked Unger, "Is she able to answer questions?"

The policewoman said, "Sometimes she's able to talk lucidly. Other times she seems barely to know what's going on. I've requested a social worker to come help her out."

"Did the woman know the victim?" Lyle asked Unger.

Unger nodded and said, "The victim and her husband were scheduled to do a sort of performance thing here tomorrow. Her husband's an actor, and he was supposed to pretend to be William Shakespeare, answering questions from his wife and the spectators."

"Where is the husband now?" Lyle asked.

Detective Brown put in, "We're trying to find out. He's most likely the perp we're looking for."

The docent was clearly detached from reality, a kind of denial Carly had seen many times. Interviewing witnesses in such a state was always tricky, and she knew that Detective Brown didn't have the right touch. Fortunately, the task seemed to have fallen to Officer Unger.

Brown said, "I need to get back to the crime scene. Some of my guys are already out looking for the suspect, and with any luck, we'll have him in custody any time now."

With that, Brown strode out of the exhibit room

Carly and Lyle quietly followed Unger toward the docent, who seemed to be lost in the pages she was perusing.

Unger said to her quietly, "Ms. Stark, I've got a couple of FBI agents here who would like to talk to you about what happened."

Maia Stark turned her eyes toward Lyle and Brown.

"About … what happened?" she stammered, as if she had no idea what the policeman meant.

Officer Unger touched her gently on the shoulder and said, "I mean what happened to Lillis Storer. You remember."

Maia Stark's eyes grew dimmer.

"Yes, I remember," she said.

Then she turned a page in the enormous, antique-looking volume.

"Isn't this beautiful?" she said with a trace of a smile. "It's a facsimile of the first folio edition of the works of Ben Jonson, the Elizabethan playwright. The actual book was published in 1616, the year Shakespeare died. Ben Jonson and Shakespeare were good friends. Doesn't this look real? It's even been weathered to look old. It's kind of magical to be able to touch it like this."

Carly began to worry. This witness's defense mechanisms were in full gear, and she was blocking out the reality of the murder.

The docent began pointing to other books on other podiums.

She said in a distracted voice, "And that book over there is a 1647 edition of the plays of Beaumont and Fletcher. And that one is the original 1623 quarto of John Webster's *The Duchess of Malfi.* And that one …"

Officer Unger interrupted her quietly with a gentle touch on her shoulder.

"Ms. Stark, maybe you'd like to sit down."

Maia Stark nodded blankly and said, "Yes, I think maybe so."

Carly and the policewoman led the docent over to a nearby bench and helped her get seated.

"Now," Officer Unger said to her in a soft voice, "I need for you to tell these agents what you told me about the last time you saw the victim and her husband."

Maia Stark knitted her brow.

"Yes. The three of us were right here in this room. We were all talking about the exhibit … or the performance … whatever you want to call it. I think Dennis—the victim's husband, the actor who was going to play Shakespeare—he seemed to have been out drinking, and he started complaining to Lillis about how she was holding him back from becoming a great Shakespearean actor, that sort of thing …"

The docent's voice faded, and she seemed to be slipping back into shock.

Officer Unger said to the woman, "Tell them what you heard Lillis say to her husband."

Maia Stark tilted her head thoughtfully.

"She said … she was tired of him beating her up. At the time, I hadn't thought she meant it literally …"

Carly and Lyle exchanged glances. She knew they were both remembering the telltale bruise on the victim's face—the one that she had tried to cover with makeup.

No wonder Brown thinks her husband killed her, Carly thought. *But what about the other victims?*

Carly had plenty of questions, but before she could say anything, Detective Brown came back into the room looking discouraged.

"Dead end so far," he grumbled. "We checked the hotel where he and his wife had been staying. Nobody there has seen him."

Lyle scratched his chin for a moment, then a light seemed to come on in his eyes.

He said to Maia Stark, "You said he'd been out drinking."

"That's right," the docent said.

"Did he say where?" Lyle asked.

"No, but his wife said something about ..."

Maia Stark fell silent again, then added, "She said something like, 'You've been boozing it up over at Cutty's, haven't you?' He didn't say no."

Detective Brown's eyes widened.

"That's a bar just a couple of blocks from here," he said. "Think he could be there again?"

"Worth a try," Lyle said. "At least maybe someone there can tell us something."

They thanked Lillis Storer for her help, although she barely seemed to notice. Back in the courtyard, the forensic technicians had strapped the covered corpse to a gurney. As Brown conferred with his other cops, Carly found herself standing right beside the body.

Nobody seemed to be paying any attention to her.

Surreptitiously, she reached over and touched the cloth on top of the murdered woman's wrist. She felt no tingle.

Carly sighed. Her odd ability didn't always work, and this time she was getting nothing at all. She wondered if it would help to reach under the cloth and touch the actual body, but one of the cops was looking at her now, and she thought a move like that would be hard to explain.

As she pulled her hand away, she remembered the shadowy blank-faced man she had visualized back at the scene of Bianca Voigts's murder. That must be who they were looking for, but she had learned nothing about him here.

As she, Lyle, and Brown left the museum, Carly glanced back at the lighted posters advertising "Shakespeare & Friends at the Mermaid." One featured a costumed actor made up as William Shakespeare.

Is it him? she wondered.

Did she dare hope that they were about to catch this killer?

CHAPTER TWENTY TWO

Carly was trying to line up two faces up in her mind—or rather, one face and one mysterious blankness—as she followed her colleagues away from the Museum of Renaissance Literature. Without all that Shakespeare makeup, could the actor from the museum poster be the shadowy man of her vision at a different crime scene early that morning?

It did seem possible.

She felt a surge of excitement as they headed for the bar where that actor might be found.

"Should we just walk there?" Lyle was asking Detective Brown, "If it's just a block or two away, driving could take longer. And on a Saturday night parking might be scarce—"

Brown interrupted, "Nope. There's emergency parking right near Cutty's."

"Then let's take our SUV," Lyle agreed, as they arrived at their vehicle.

The three of them got in and Lyle drove, following Brown's directions a couple of blocks to the designated parking space. But the surrounding area seemed quiet and empty.

"I don't see any bar," Lyle said, turning off the engine. "Are you sure we've got the right place?"

"Yeah, I know my way around these parts," Brown said, opening the SUV door. "Just follow me."

Carly and Lyle scrambled out and followed the police detective along the sidewalk to a dimly-lit stairwell that was practically invisible from the street.

"This is it," he announced cheerfully. "It's set up as a kind of old Prohibition-style speakeasy."

As she leaned over the metal railing, Carly realized that faint music seemed to be bubbling up from below.

Lyle took the lead as they headed down the stairs. At the bottom was a door with a small sign above it that read "Cutty's." The noise from inside was louder now.

When Lyle opened the door, they stepped into a small reception room that was occupied by an enormous, clean-shaven man wearing a bowtie and white dinner jacket. Carly recognized him as the kind of bar employee Lyle liked to refer to as "a gentleman bouncer," a tough guy who managed to look thoroughly respectable when he wasn't tangling with drunken clientele.

They couldn't actually see into the bar from where they were, but the conversation and music told them they must be in the right place. Carly and her two colleagues pulled out their identifications and introduced themselves.

The man's eyes widened with alarm.

"A D.C. detective and the FBI?" he said. "Hey, what's this all about? There's nothing illegal going on here. Honest. You can check with the police commissioner if you need to."

Lyle explained, "We're here to ask about a customer named Dennis Ring."

The man shook his head.

"The name's not familiar," he said.

Carly put in, "Are you sure? He's supposed to appear in a show at the Renaissance Literature Museum just a couple of blocks from here, and we were told—"

The man interrupted with a grin.

"Oh, you mean Shakespeare. That's what everybody here calls him. Yeah, he's been coming in a lot lately. In fact, he's here right now. He came in earlier, and now he's back. The last I heard the bartender's liable to cut him off soon."

The man cracked his knuckles and added, "If he gets cranky about it, that's one reason I'm here."

Carly and her colleagues exchanged hopeful glances.

Then Lyle said, "We want to talk to him."

"What about?" the man asked.

"I'd rather take that up with him," Lyle said, starting toward the wide opening to the bar itself.

The man held up an enormous hand and said, "Now wait a minute, let's show a little finesse here. I don't want there to be some kind of big crazy scene. My main job is to keep things polite and orderly. Lemme go in there and get him. I'll bring him right to you in a peaceable manner."

"Fine," Lyle said.

It seemed like a good idea to Carly as well. There was surely no point in provoking an altercation in an overcrowded bar unless it couldn't be helped.

Carly and her two colleagues stepped into the open doorway and watched the bouncer make his way through the dense, noisy crowd toward the bar.

It was a long narrow room, with an exposed brick wall behind booths on one side and mirrors behind a long dark wooden bar on the other. The bottle and glasses set up along the mirrored wall were well lit, but the overall ambience was dim, crowded, and noisy.

The gentleman bouncer approached a man on a barstool and tapped him on the shoulder. When the patron looked around, Carly almost exclaimed aloud.

Shakespeare!

It was small wonder that people here at Cutty's called Dennis Ring by that name. With his bald domed head skirted with wavy hair, neatly-kept goatee, and mustache that turned up at the ends, he looked exactly like every portrait Carly had ever seen of the Bard. He could play his part in the exhibition without makeup.

The bouncer pointed at Carly and her colleagues, obviously telling him who they were and what they wanted, and Dennis Ring nodded. Looking bleary-eyed and apparently drunk, he got unsteadily up from his barstool and took a step or two in their direction.

The man who looked like Shakespeare hesitated. Then he whirled around and headed for the far end of the long room, flipping his barstool to the floor between himself and the bouncer.

The bouncer tripped over the fallen stool and crashed to the floor among the densely-packed bar patrons, who let out a dissonant chorus of alarmed yelps and screams.

"He's running," Lyle shouted, pushing his own way after the fleeing man.

So much for 'a peaceable manner,' Carly thought as she followed him.

The fugitive seemed awfully spry for a drunk, clawing his way past people and headed for what must be a back exit. Carly wasn't surprised. She knew that even someone who was very inebriated could become downright athletic when a burst of adrenalin hit. He would probably wear out soon, but he might lose them by then.

As she and her colleagues pushed their way through the growing chaos, Detective Brown said, "There's an alley out back. That's where he's going."

Lyle and Carly made their way past the fallen bouncer, but Brown had trouble getting around him.

"Go," Brown yelled. "I'll catch up."

Carly and Lyle pushed on toward the far end of the bar, then passed through a swinging door into a small kitchen where two white-clad short-order cooks were standing with stupefied expressions. They spotted an open back door and charged through it into a stairwell that led up into a dimly-lit alley.

Dennis Ring was nowhere in sight.

Lyle pointed and said, "You go left, and I'll go right."

They split up and ran in opposite directions.

Carly hadn't gotten very far before her eyes adjusted to the darkness and she realized the alley continued a considerable distance in front of her, and the fugitive was nowhere in sight. He couldn't have made it all the way out of the alley before she got there. He hadn't had time. That meant that either he'd run in the opposite direction where Lyle would hopefully catch him or …

He's hiding nearby, she thought.

She slowed her running to a walk and slowed her breathing so she could hear everything around her. The alley was flanked on either side by stairwells that led into basement doorways. She knew the man might be hiding in any one of them.

She peered over a steel railing into one of them, then walked slowly toward the next. Before she could continue any further, she heard a faint scuffling sound.

He's here somewhere.

Carly's eyes lighted on the next stairwell to the right.

There, she decided.

She walked cautiously toward the railing and looked down.

The area below wasn't lit, but there was something dark at the bottom. It was a huddled human form, bent over and not moving. It must be him. Had the alcohol he'd imbibed kicked in again?

She spoke firmly, "Dennis Ring, I'm Special Agent Carly See with the FBI. Come out of there with your hands where I can see them."

The man stood up shakily in the stairwell, with his hands raised. He definitely seemed drunk now.

"Don't shoot," he pleaded. "I'm coming peacefully."

Carly smiled. She hadn't even drawn her gun. Even though FBI agents were required to always be armed, weapons had seldom been involved in her investigations. She'd used the Glock the Bureau had issued her a few times, but drawing a gun wasn't her first automatic reaction to a situation.

She stood at the railing and watched him stagger up the stairs. When he neared the top, he moved before she could react, grabbing hold of the railing and vaulting over it. His feet landed squarely in her abdomen, kicking her violently.

With a cry, Carly fell backwards.

CHAPTER TWENTY THREE

Carly rolled over, gasping for air.

But if the fugitive expected to take her down the same as he had the bouncer and Detective Brown, he was surely disappointed. Carly had never been the strongest fighter in her FBI Academy group, but she was the most agile. Given room to move, she could be a formidable opponent.

She was back on her feet by the time Dennis Ring ran past her, heading farther down the ally. And she wasn't about to let this creep get away. She took a flying leap and tackled him by the legs, laying him flat on his face on the concrete.

Carly scrambled to her feet again, and now she drew her pistol from her shoulder holster.

"Don't move," she snapped at Ring. "I will shoot you this time."

She called out loudly, "Lyle, I've got him."

The fallen man wasn't stirring at all, so she took out her handcuffs with her free hand. When she kneeled on the man with her knee pressing hard into the small of his back, he stayed absolutely still.

Carly put away her gun and handcuffed him then stood up in front of him.

"Dennis Ring, you are under arrest," she snapped.

"For what?" he yelped back at her.

"For resisting arrest and assaulting an officer of the law—but that's just for starters. You have the right to remain silent …"

As she continued to read him his rights, both Lyle and Detective Brown came trotting toward her.

"Wow," Brown said, gazing at the prone, handcuffed man. "Nicely done, Agent See."

Carly didn't thank him for his compliment. Men generally tended to underestimate her skills in a fight, which sometimes worked to her advantage.

When she finished reading Dennis Ring his rights, Brown hauled him to his feet and pushed him against the nearest wall.

Lyle said to Brown, "We need your guys to come around with a vehicle to take him in."

"I've already put in the call," Brown said. "They'll be right here."

"I don't know what this is about," the actor said.

"No?" Brown replied. "Why did you run, then?"

"I don't know what this is about," the man repeated.

He was slurring his words and slumping now. For a moment Carly wondered if it was another act, but she realized that the adrenaline rush of the chase had actually given way to an onslaught of drunken delirium. When he said he didn't know what this was about, it might not be altogether a lie.

"No?" Brown replied to him in a mock-hospitable tone. "Don't worry, we'll get everything sorted out once we get you to headquarters. Meanwhile, you might as well make yourself comfortable."

Detective Brown led Dennis Ring toward a raised doorstep and sat him down on it. The captive gazed wistfully up at the detective. Brown stood squarely facing him, as if about to start an interrogation.

Carly knew what Brown was up to. So far, the suspect hadn't asked for a lawyer, and since Carly had already read him his rights, working on him to talk was fair game—as long as things didn't get out of hand.

"First things first," Brown said. "When was the last time you talked to your wife?"

"Lillis? I dunno. A couple of hours maybe."

"How were things between you when you parted?" Brown said.

Ring shrugged and said, "Fine. Why wouldn't they be fine?"

Of course Carly knew that was a lie. The docent had described their quarrel in some detail.

Then Ring drew himself up out of a deep slouch and said, "Wait a minute. Has something happened to Lillis? Is something wrong with Lillis?"

His speech and manner were so foggy, Carly couldn't tell whether he was dissembling or not. She also began to wonder whether she and Lyle should let Brown continue in this manner.

Brown demanded, "Have you been to the theater lately?"

"Huh?"

"I'm talking about the production of *Macbeth* at the Shaddon Center."

Ring stared at him blearily for a moment.

"Yeah, I might have gone to see it," he said.

"You *might* have?" Brown asked.

"OK, I did go to see it. Last night."

Carly felt her pulse quicken. Was the suspect about to place himself at the scene of one of the murders? If so, she hoped his drunkenness wouldn't make whatever he said inadmissible in court.

"Did your wife go to the play with you?" Brown said.

"No."

"Why not?"

"She just didn't. She had a ticket but she didn't go."

"Why?"

"Just because," Ring said with a clumsy shrug.

Carly heard an unmistakable note of evasiveness in his voice. She wondered—had Lillis decided not to go because she and her husband had an argument?

"Anything about the performance strike you as unusual?" Brown asked.

Ring squinted at him as if trying to remember.

"It got cut short, I guess."

"You guess?"

"Yeah, the whole audience had to leave. Something about somebody getting killed."

"Is that all you know about it?" Brown said.

"Yeah."

"Are you sure?"

Carly sensed that Brown was ratcheting up his questioning. She also sensed that Lyle was getting uneasy about it, as was she. Fortunately, a squad car pulled into the alley before Brown could press the suspect any further. The car came to a stop, and a couple of uniformed cops got out of it and approached the handcuffed suspect. Brown yanked Dennis Ring to his feet and pushed him toward the cops.

"What's going on?" Ring asked, sounding a bit more clear-headed now.

Brown smirked and said, "Just like the lady told you—you're under arrest."

"Don't I get to have a lawyer?" Ring asked.

"Sure," Brown said. "You can give him a call as soon as you get to Metro Headquarters."

The two cops were leading Dennis Ring toward their vehicle, and Brown was walking along with them.

"What about my wife?" Ring said. "I want to call her right now."

Brown let out a snort of cynical laughter.

"Your wife?" he said. "That's a good one."

"What do you mean?" Ring said.

"You know that as well as we do," Brown replied.

"Hold it," Ring snapped. "Tell me what you mean."

"She's dead," Brown snarled.

Carly felt a flash of anger. Brown seemed to have no idea of how to behave.

Ring gasped loudly and almost fell to his knees.

"Dead?" he cried. "Lillis is dead?"

"Get into the car," Brown told him.

"But is Lillis dead?"

"Get in the car, I said," Brown repeated.

"I didn't kill her!" the suspect wailed.

"Yeah, right," Brown said. "You can tell me all about it on the way to headquarters. We'll have a nice chat about it in the car, just the two of us."

Brown was about to climb into the vehicle beside Dennis Ring, but Lyle grabbed the detective's arm and yanked him away from the car.

Lyle snapped, "You're not going with him."

"Like hell I'm not," Brown replied. Even by the low light in the alley, Carly could see that the detective's face had reddened.

"I mean it," Lyle said. "If you keep pushing him like this while he's drunk, you'll blow our whole case against him."

"I know what I'm doing," Brown grumbled.

"Yeah, and so do I," Lyle said. "Nobody's going to talk to this guy until he gets a chance to dry out a little down at Metro. And if he wants a lawyer, he can have one."

"But he's ready to talk!" Brown protested.

"Yeah, and that's exactly the problem," Lyle said. "If he blabs away now, even a lousy lawyer will kill us with it. Intoxicated, under the pressure of painful force. We need to do this by the book, and you know it. My partner and I will drive you back to museum. I assume your vehicle is still there."

Brown was still growling in protest, but he went along as Lyle and Carly escorted him out of the alley and around the block toward their SUV. Then he crossed his arms and fell silent during the drive back to the museum. Lyle pulled up beside the detective's vehicle and told him to get out.

"I'll see you at headquarters," Lyle said irritably. "Lock our guy up. Let him dry out. No questions until I get there."

Brown let loose a stream of mumbled curses and climbed out of the car and slammed the door.

Lyle squinted thoughtfully as he started driving again.

He said to Carly, "Brown seems awfully sure we've got the right guy. How about you?"

"I don't know, Lyle," Carly said. "You saw he way he reacted when Brown told him his wife was dead."

"They all react like that," Lyle said. "And this guy's an actor. He's really good at playing shock and grief. Besides, we couldn't have come up with a profile better suited to these murders. He's a wife beater. And he's mad at the world because he thinks he got cheated out of being a great Shakespearean actor. He was reduced to doing little presentations at high-society gatherings. He was a ticking bomb with all the makings of a serial killer."

"But do you think we can prove—?"

"We also know he was at the performance of Mackers last night. It may not be proof, but I think we're getting there. We've got to connect a few more dots, that's all."

"Lyle, I don't know—"

He interrupted again, "Well, what other conclusions can we come to?"

Carly stared at her partner. She didn't know what to say. Then she noticed that he took a turn that led them away from their route to Metro Headquarters.

"Where are we going?" she asked.

"I'm doing what I should have done hours ago," Lyle said. "I'm taking you home."

"I thought we were going to Metro Headquarters to question the suspect."

"I'm going to question the suspect. You're going to get some sleep."

"But Lyle—"

"Don't argue," Lyle grumbled. "It's for your own good. I'll take things from here. Once I get a chance to question the suspect, we'll know for sure one way or the other."

Carly stared at him in stunned silence. She knew that his exasperation partly stemmed from his irritation with Detective Brown. But she held her tongue.

Besides, maybe he was right. Maybe she just wasn't thinking straight. She was tired, all right. And after all, why couldn't she just agree with him that they'd almost certainly caught their killer?

She could only think of one reason, but it wasn't something she could talk about with Lyle. It had to do with that shadowy, nondescript face she'd visualized in connection with Bianca Voigts's murder. She couldn't help contrasting it with Dennis Ring's striking, Shakespeare-like visage. She was sure that any Shakespeare scholar would have noted that resemblance. And Bianca Voigts's hadn't even registered the face of the man she had seen just before she died.

Carly wanted to believe Lyle was right and that they'd found their killer, but she hadn't been able to throw off that haunting image. Now she just couldn't convince herself that the actor and the faceless man were the same person.

Which meant that a fast-moving serial killer could be still at large.

CHAPTER TWENTY FOUR

Carly positively wanted to be wrong.

At home alone after that long, unsettling day, she really hoped Lyle would call to tell her that Dennis Ring had cracked wide open under tough questioning and confessed to all three killings. It would put her mind at ease to know they'd caught the killer before he'd had a chance to kill again.

As she arranged a plate of crackers and cheese and poured herself a glass of wine, Carly realized that her hands were trembling slightly. It was going to take more than a glass or two of wine to shake off her feeling that they'd arrested the wrong man.

"Get some sleep," Lyle had commanded as she'd gotten out of the SUV.

Still irritable, he'd driven off without saying another word.

Carly scoffed audibly and muttered aloud, "Great advice, Lyle. Maybe you should follow it."

After all, he'd gotten even less sleep than she had—and she'd only napped for a little while lying in the back of the SUV in the parking garage earlier that evening. It wasn't the first time she'd had to wonder what kept her senior partner going. He actually could have retired from the FBI by now with a full pension, although he never seemed to be considering that option.

As she curled up on her sofa to sip and snack, Carly wondered why she was having so much trouble trusting Lyle's judgment. He was a well-seasoned agent. He was her mentor. And his insights were usually right on target.

Besides, she didn't think that her own fleeting visions were being at all helpful.

Taking another sip of wine, she found herself thinking about the murder scene in the theater, when she'd glimpsed a piece of paper that had gone missing from the victim's hand.

At least, that one was a good thing, she thought.

If she hadn't seen that paper and raised the issue with the play director, he might have hung on to the page without ever telling anybody about it. Then Carly and her colleagues might still not know that the first killing was connected to the two that followed.

Then, touching Gentry Chapman's corpse in the autopsy room, she'd gotten an image of torn pages fluttering loose from a book. That was when she'd become sure that she and Lyle were dealing with a serial killer and that there would be more murders. Even so, they hadn't actually needed communications from the dead to tell them that.

Then there had been that vision she'd had while she and Lyle had been in Congressman Chapman's office—a moment from Gentry's childhood when her father had coldly rebuffed her gift of a handmade ashtray. It had told her that Congressman Chapman was a coldhearted man but had not pointed to him as a killer.

At the scene of Bianca Voigts's murder, Carly had been drawn to the victim's gold locket, which had contained information revealing her online sex relationship with an alcoholic philosophy professor who was also not the killer they sought. And finally, in Bianca's apartment, she'd touched a little bronze bust of Shakespeare and had relived a proud moment in the victim's early schooling, when a teacher had praised her for reading so many books.

"You're going to have so many wonderful adventures in the world of words and ideas," the teacher had told Bianca.

Carly shivered at the memory. That vision had been particularly vivid, and particularly poignant, and …

Of no help at all, she admitted to herself.

Finally, she'd gotten no impressions at all from touching Lillis Storer's corpse as it was being carted out of the museum on a gurney.

"What's the point?" Carly muttered, taking a bite of a cracker.

She had some kind of gift for connecting with the dead. But at times like now, she had no idea what possible use it could be. Instead it seemed that the visions were teasing and taunting her and leading the investigation absolutely nowhere.

I can't even find my own sister, she thought.

I don't know whether she's alive or dead.

She told herself, "Just deal with it, Carly. Lyle probably knows what he's doing. And he's probably right about me. I'm too tired to think straight."

As she took another sip of wine, she felt a wave of exhaustion sweep over, and her whole body slumped a little. She welcomed the sensation. Maybe now she could take a shower and climb into bed and really …

Her hopes were interrupted by the sound of her phone ringing.

She picked up the phone and sighed with discouragement to see who was calling.

Mom.

Talking with her mother was about the last thing she wanted to do right now. But she was long overdue for any kind of family contact, and putting off talking to her mother again would lead to trouble on down the line.

She took the call.

"Carly, are you all right?" Mom asked immediately.

Carly was surprised at the question.

"Sure, I'm all right," she said, far from truthfully. "Why wouldn't I be all right?"

"Well, according to the news this afternoon, there's a serial killer at large in Washington. And I caught a glimpse of you and your partner on TV. I didn't call you earlier because I knew you must be frantically busy, but I've been worried all evening."

Carly stifled a weary groan, remembering the reporters who had approached her and Lyle at the scene of Bianca Voigts's murder.

I should have known Mom would find out, she thought.

"There's nothing to worry about, Mom," she said.

"But I *am* worried, Carly. This case sounds dangerous. Have you caught the killer yet?"

Carly rubbed her forehead, unsure of how to answer the question.

"We think maybe so," she said.

"Well, that doesn't sound very reassuring. Just tell me you're being very careful."

"I always am," Carly said. "And I've got my partner to watch out for me. Lyle's the best, Mom."

"Maybe so, but I keep telling you, you've got to get out of that awful line of work. You're not a youngster anymore, and you need to find something safe and secure and non-life-threatening to do for a living."

Carly hoped Mom couldn't hear her teeth grinding.

Let's not have this conversation again, she thought.

Mom had some idea that Carly might yet go back to college and go into academia and become a university professor somewhere and become esteemed in the world of scholarship.

It wasn't going to happen, of course—in no small part because Mom had soured Carly on that kind of lifestyle and second-hand learning from a very early age.

"How's Dad?" Carly asked.

"You're changing the subject," Mom said.

Yes, I am, she thought.

"No, I'm not," she said. "I miss Dad. How is he? Could you maybe put him on the phone?"

"You know perfectly well I can't pry him away from the TV," Mom said.

Carly knew that was true. Dad worked as a dentist during the day, chatting loquaciously to patients who usually couldn't even reply. He always clammed up when he came home and refused to budge from watching television.

Carly couldn't really blame him. She knew that Mom never let him forget that she gave up a promising career as a literary scholar to stay with him in Currie, Illinois, frittering away her once-enormous talents teaching English at a Podunk two-year community college.

Small wonder Dad had shut himself off from life at home. That was why Mom had always vented to her daughters, as if her life's disappointments were all their fault. Small wonder, too, that Carly's sister had fled such seething resentment.

Did Megan run away? Carly wondered, as always.

Or did something awful happen to her?

Carly didn't know, and she all but given up hope of ever finding out. She found it comfortable to believe that her sister was still alive somewhere, living her own life. After all, she'd never had a message from Megan that would mean she was dead.

"Say hi to Dad for me," she said, hoping to end the conversation.

"I'll do that, although he probably won't listen to me," Mom said. "But before you hang up on me—is there anything I can do to help?"

Carly squinted with surprise. Mom didn't often ask such a question. Anyway, how could Mom possibly help in this investigation?

Then Carly silently mouthed the word "oh."

She remembered all those dreary childhood lessons Mom had given her about Shakespeare, especially the sonnets.

She said cautiously, "Uh, the killer has a thing about Shakespeare."

"Really?" Mom replied, sounding almost pleased.

"Yeah. The first victim was a Shakespearean actress in a production of *Macbeth.* The second was a budding Shakespearean scholar. So was the last one. She was preparing a museum show of works by Shakespeare's contemporaries."

"You mean Ben Jonson, and Christopher Marlowe, and Thomas

Middleton, and … ?"

"Yes, those guys," Carly said, interrupting lest Mom recite an entire lengthy list. "And he's left a torn-out page from a book of Shakespeare sonnets with each of the victims. Can you think of any reason why a serial killer might be obsessed with the sonnets?"

Mom thought for a moment, then said, "Well, there's a lot of anger and resentment in some of the later sonnets. The speaker gets jealous of a rival poet who writes poems for his beloved 'Fair Youth.' Then the speaker falls in love with a so-called 'Dark Lady,' who treats him badly and cheats on him with a friend—"

Carly gently interrupted, "These aren't late sonnets, Mom. These are early ones in the sequence. So far he's left the ninth, the nineteenth, and the twelfth."

"In that order?"

"That's right."

"How odd …"

Mom fell quiet again.

Finally Mom asked, "How did the victims die?"

Carly rolled her eyes at the thought of going into all that.

"Oh, Mom—" she began.

"You don't have to go into all the grisly details. Just give me the basics."

Carly took a deep breath, then said, "The first victim was stabbed to death. The second was drugged to death."

"Poisoned, then?"

"I guess you could put it that way," Carly said. "And the third one drowned."

"Well," Mom said with a cluck of her tongue. "Then I can certainly tell you what to expect next."

CHAPTER TWENTY FIVE

Is she serious? Carly wondered.

How could her mother, of all people, have any idea of what the killer was going to do next?

Mom continued, "Of course, if you've already caught the killer, it's all a moot point. I certainly hope you've got the right man, dear. I have to say that you didn't sound very positive about that."

"I'm not completely convinced," Carly said. "Although everybody else seems to be. But just in case, what's your theory about his next method?"

At that, Carly heard her mother slipping into teaching mode.

"Isn't it obvious, dear?" Professor See asked. "Those are all Shakespeare-style murders. There are lots of stabbings in Shakespeare, from Polonius in *Hamlet* to almost everybody in *Julius Caesar,* especially Caesar himself. There are also several poisonings, including the murder of Regan in *King Lear* and, of course, Romeo's suicide. And then there are some drownings, most notably Ophelia in *Hamlet.* Although that last one is generally believed to have been a suicide as well, or possibly just an accident. It's a matter of some discussion in the play and even among a few scholars."

Mom stopped her mini-lecture and said, "But I gather that your drowning victim was neither a suicide nor an accident."

"No, it was definitely a murder. And the work of a serial killer."

"Well, there are multiple deaths in Shakespeare. Aside from stabbings, poisonings, and drownings, you've got hangings, like Cordelia in *King Lear,* or suffocations, like Desdemona in *Othello.* A few are more exotic—getting beheaded like Macbeth, or eaten by a bear, like in *The Winter's Tale,* or getting baked into a pie and eaten, like in *Titus Andronicus."*

Mom paused again, then said, "Based on those texts and the information you've given me, I have a strong feeling that your killer would choose suffocation or hanging for his next murder. It's certainly simpler than beheading or baking."

Then Mom added in a less formal tone, "Still, it's just a hunch, I guess."

Carly's eyes widened.

Not a bad hunch, she thought, but she couldn't quite bring herself to say so.

"Anyway," Mom said, "I hope your cohorts are right, and you've caught the evildoer and the whole unpleasant matter is over."

"I hope so too, Mom."

"Well, I shouldn't keep you. You sound tired. Maybe you can get some sleep."

"I'll try."

"Do phone me when you've decided on a better choice of careers," Mom added.

"You'll be the first to know," Carly promised.

They said goodbye and ended the call.

Carly sat staring at the phone for a moment. She hadn't stopped to consider that the killer might be choosing his methods of killing from the Bard himself. If Lyle had thought about it, he hadn't mentioned it.

Suffocating or hanging, she thought.

If the killer was still at large, did he have either of those methods in mind? So far, she hadn't been able to anticipate any of his moves. And each of his murders had happened very soon after the last one. If he was still free, would he hold off for a while now that someone had been arrested, or would that just drive him to move faster?

She knew she could only be sure of one thing.

There's nothing I can do about it right now.

It was time to take a shower and try to get some sleep.

But before she could get up from her chair, Carly's phone rang again. Her heart quickened as she saw that the call was from Lyle.

Lyle's voice sounded excited.

"Hey, kid, were you watching the TV news just now?"

"No. Why?"

"I was just on TV, making a joint announcement with Detective Brown and the Chief of Police on the steps at Metro Headquarters. I'm sorry you weren't there. I was a celebrity for a few minutes there, and you could have been too. But don't worry, Brown and I both gave you plenty of credit."

"What are you talking about?" Carly asked, rubbing her eyes.

"We've nailed Dennis Ring but good, kid. And we went public about bringing charges against him. Officially he's just a suspect, but he's definitely our guy."

Carly sat sharply upright.

"Do you mean he confessed?" she asked.

"No, but he didn't need to. He did plenty of talking when I questioned him."

"Didn't he lawyer up?"

"Sure, but he wound up with a public defender who wasn't too finicky about letting him answer questions. And guess what. I connected Ring to the second victim, Bianca Voigts."

Carly's eyes widened.

"How?" she asked.

"Turns out he liked to hang out on college campus wherever he and his wife toured with their exhibition/performance thing. It was research, he says. He'd sit in on Shakespeare classes, talk to professors, visit libraries, pick scholarly brains for details he could use in his act. And as it happens, he sat in on Professor Redfield's seminar on Renaissance literature a couple of mornings ago."

"The seminar Bianca Voigts was taking," Carly said, remembering her conversation with Neal Redfield.

"That's right. That puts him in the same room with the victim. He knew her, Carly."

Carly almost said aloud, *Is that all?*

Instead she fell silent for a moment.

Finally Lyle grumbled, "Well, don't go all crazy congratulating me."

Carly stammered, "I—I'm sorry, Lyle. I'm just not sure what to say."

"There's nothing *to* say. He doesn't have alibis for any of the killings, not even at the bar.. Some of Brown's guys talked with the bartender, and although Dennis Ring was there a lot during the day, he wasn't there when his wife was killed."

"What about the theater the night before?"

"He says he changed seats a couple of times during the show just to get a better view, so the people in the seats around him can't account for him at the exact moment of the murder. And with his wife dead, he's got no one to account for his whereabouts at any time."

"But what about motive?"

Lyle scoffed aloud.

"Come on, kid. You know better than to get hung-up about motive with serial killers. They don't murder for the regular reasons. They're psychopaths, and I'd be willing to bet that this guy is paranoid schizophrenic. We'll soon find more about what makes him tick. Let's just hope he's not crazy enough to sell a jury on an insanity plea."

"I don't know, Lyle ...," Carly began.

"You don't know what?"

"I just—I don't know. Maybe if I'd been there in the room with you when you questioned him ..."

"Are you telling me you think his connection to Bianca Voigts is just a coincidence?"

Possibly, Carly thought. *Quite possibly.*

Lyle himself had taught her to always consider the possibility of coincidences.

Instead she said, "Probably not, Lyle. You're probably right."

"You bet I'm right."

"OK, then."

A silence fell.

Finally Lyle said in a tight voice, "You don't buy it yet. That's OK. You're just worn out, that's all. You'll see it my way after a good night's sleep. Go ahead and sleep late. You could use it. I'll talk to you tomorrow."

Lyle ended the call, and Carly sat staring at the phone.

Maybe he's right, she thought. *Maybe I'll believe it in the morning. Maybe it just* seems *too good to be true.*

But was Lyle himself really thinking straight? She could easily imagine Detective Brown jumping to conclusions. But it didn't seem like Lyle to ignore the possibility of a coincidence. Was Lyle letting his own exhaustion affect his judgment?

She turned toward her blank TV screen and briefly considered turning it on to see if there was any further reporting about the case. Maybe she could even catch a replay of Lyle's announcement.

But she felt her eyeballs jerk, and the room seemed to shift under her.

I've got to get some sleep, she told herself.

She got up from her chair and headed to the bathroom to take a shower. Then she went straight to bed.

Carly found herself in a deep, impenetrable fog. She heard a woman's voice whispering, and the sound seemed to come from all around her.

"It's all my fault."

Carly looked around but didn't see who was whispering.

"What's all your fault?" she asked.

The voice simply repeated, "It's all my fault."

"Who are you?" Carly asked.

"It's all my fault," the voice repeated again—and then again, and then again.

Carly realized she was dreaming. She also sensed that this dream was extremely meaningful. She had to do whatever she could to understand it.

She began to step carefully through the fog, hoping to catch sight of the whisperer, who kept on saying "It's all my fault" *in an increasingly tearful voice.*

Carly's head filled up with questions.

She and Lyle seemed to have had an unspoken agreement that their killer was probably male. It was a safe assumption with serial killers, the overwhelming number of whom were male.

But were we wrong? *Carly wondered.*

She took a deep breath and spoke through the fog.

"Did you kill those women?" she asked.

"No."

Of course not, *Carly thought.*

Typically such visitations came to her only from the dead. As far as she knew, the killer was still alive.

"Then why—?" Carly began.

"It's all my fault. Please help me."

"How can I help you?"

A shape started to appear in the fog—a shadowy woman. Carly couldn't make out her features.

Carly wondered—was it one of the victims?

Carly asked, "Are you Gentry Chapman?"

"No," the figure said with a sad shake of the head.

"Are you Bianca Voigts?"

"No."

"Are you Lillis Storer?"

"No."

"Then who are you?" Carly asked with growing despair. "And why is everything your fault?"

"Please help me."

"But how?"

Then came a fluttering in the foggy air, and smaller shapes flitting bat-like around Carly and the woman.

"Look," the woman said, pointing to shapes as they darted about.

"I'm looking," Carly said.

"Look," the woman repeated again and again.

Struggling to focus her eyes on the shapes, Carly began to see that they were apparently random numbers and letters ...

Z ... 5 ... B ... 4 ... R ... 9 ... F ... 7 ... M ... 3 ...

"Order," the figure said, pointing.

"I don't understand," Carly said.

"Order," the figure said.

The figure turned and walked away from Carly, and the swirl of letters followed her into the mist until they all disappeared.

Then the whole scene dissolved into whiteness.

Carly's eyes snapped open, and she saw morning light streaming in through a window. She'd been dreaming, all right—and it had been no ordinary dream.

It was a visitation, she realized.

A dead person was reaching out to her from the other side—someone who felt deeply responsible for the murders, and who wanted Carly's help. But like many such visions and visitations, the message wasn't clear.

Carly believed that it was a struggle for the dead to communicate anything at all through the barrier between them, just as she herself had to struggle to understand what they were saying. The resulting message often came through much like a riddle.

But she was sure this visit from this alarmed spirit meant that the killer was still at large, not in a jail cell. Of course she still had no way to convince Lyle of that. It was up to her—and only her—to solve the riddle of the dream.

And Carly had an idea how she could do that. There was one trick she had used before to open up the communications she needed to hear.

But the last time she had tried it, Carly had found herself in terrifying danger.

CHAPTER TWENTY SIX

Carly sat up in bed and frowned at the sunshine glowing in her window. It was a beautiful bright day, and here she was contemplating going into a very dark place.

But I've really got to do it, she told herself.

She scrambled out of bed and pulled on a robe.

It was a Sunday morning, and she wouldn't be expected to turn up for work unless she and her partner were in the middle of an investigation that couldn't wait. She checked her phone and saw that she'd gotten a text message from Lyle that confirmed her freedom for the day.

I'm heading to Metro Headquarters to wrap things up. Don't worry about joining me there. Get as much rest as you can today and report in on Monday. I'm sorry I barked at you last night.

Carly smiled as she read the message. She wondered whether she should reply.

And tell Lyle what? she thought.

He certainly wouldn't understand what she had in mind to do. It was probably just as well if he thought she was sleeping soundly all morning. If she got any new insights, she could figure out how to share them with him later on.

I just hope I can get an appointment, she thought anxiously. She knew that the place she wanted to go to never really closed. Its owner lived in an apartment upstairs from the business, and she was always ready to come downstairs and deal with clients at all hours and on all days. But some of those days got heavily booked.

Carly logged into the website and pulled up the appointment calendar. Several slots were open today, and one was just over an hour from now.

Perfect, she thought. *I can get there in time.*

She signed up for the opening that she wanted, and then sat down with a cup of coffee and a slice of toast with cream cheese. To prepare herself for the experience, she opened a notepad, and thought back to the dream she'd awakened from.

She remembered all too well the distraught figure saying the same thing over and over again.

"It's all my fault ... It's all my fault ... It's all my fault."

If the spirit somehow felt guilty about the murders, it was up to Carly to find out why. Then there had been that mysterious swirl of numbers and letters fluttering through the foggy air.

"Look," the figure had said, pointing to them. *"Look ... Look ... Look ..."*

And now Carly could see those numbers and letters in her mind.

But what did they mean?

Suddenly Carly remembered an idle remark her mother had made when she'd told her the numbers of the sonnets that had been left with the bodies—nine, nineteen, and twelve.

"In that order?" Mom had asked.

"That's right," Carly had said.

"How odd ...," Mom had said.

Now that Carly thought about it, it *was* odd—and probably important. And the woman had tried in her helplessly obscure way to give her a hint as to what it meant.

"Order," she had said. *"Order."*

Then a possibility began to dawn on Carly.

She had found no useful messages in the poems themselves. Could those particular sonnets have been left with the bodies because of their numbers rather than their words?

If the numbers were important, what could they be? A phone number? An address? Carly jotted them down.

9-19-12

But there weren't enough of them to be a complete phone number.

At least not yet, she thought glumly.

Could it be an address—say, 919 12th Street?

She knew that the east-west streets in D.C. were numbered, and the numbers ran up into the 60s. A quick look at a digital map showed her that there was no number 919 on 12th Street Northwest. That number on 12th Southeast was a nice townhouse. Although she told herself she should look into that, the image of the house didn't stir any response from her intuitions.

She looked at the numbers again.

9-19-12

Could those digits be a code? She remembered that the numbers had danced around with letters from the alphabet. In the simplest of all codes, numbers equaled letters.

Even kids know that trick, she thought.

For some reason the idea felt right to Carly.

She counted through the alphabet to nine, then jotted down the corresponding letter "I."

Then she counted through the alphabet to 19, then jotted down the letter "S."

Finally she jotted down an "L" to correspond with the number 12.

She scratched her head to see that she had jotted down "ISL."

Not exactly a word, she thought.

Maybe it's the beginning of "island," she thought.

But if that was true, what could the word *island* possibly signify?

And maybe it wasn't supposed to be a word at all.

Initials, maybe? she wondered.

She didn't know. And even if she was right about the code, this could be just the beginning of a set of initials or a word—or even a sentence. It could take another murder or several or even many more for the killer to complete the thought. Carly had to crack the message long before that happened.

And right now she had to get going if she was going to make her appointment.

Carly swallowed the remains of her coffee, grabbed a jacket, and left her apartment. She took the elevator downstairs, got into her car, and drove the short distance to her destination.

*

The Full Lotus Health Center was housed in a large residential house painted a soothing bluish-green. Carly walked into the familiar reception room with its comfortable furniture and plush carpet, all in pastel colors. Abstract paintings with swirling soft colors hung on pale blue walls. The glass counter case featured candles, incense, inspirational cards and books, organic supplements, and other New Age merchandise. A woman wearing a full-length sari-like dress stood waiting behind the counter with her hands clasped.

"Hi, Carly," the woman said with a welcoming smile.

"Hi, Cornflower," Carly replied.

The woman went by the name Cornflower Blue, and she never looked other than cheerful.

"So what will it be this morning?" Cornflower asked. "A massage? The sauna?"

Carly took a slow, deep breath and said, "I want to use the tank."

A flicker of worry crossed Cornflower's beatific features.

"Are you sure?" she said. "I mean after last time …"

Cornflower's words faded away, but of course Carly knew exactly what she meant. Her last isolation tank session had ended abruptly with a fierce panic attack, the sort of reaction Cornflower had probably never seen before among her clients for such a calming form of therapy.

"Yes, I'm sure," Carly said, producing her own credit card. This wasn't the sort of expense she could charge to the agency's account.

"All right, then," Cornflower said, running the card. "How about some soft music."

"No, I want silence."

"Complete sensory deprivation?"

"Yes."

Cornflower tilted her head earnestly.

"All right, if you're sure that's what you want. But remember, I'll be right here if you need me. You just need to press the alarm button that's inside the tank."

Carly nodded. She knew the alarm was there, but she hadn't used it before and didn't want to now.

Then with a sigh, the woman stepped out from behind the counter and led her into a small, softly-lit, tiled private room. With a final reassuring smile, Cornflower left, closing the door behind her. The little room had a closet for clothing, a bench, a shower stall, a shelf full of soft towels, and an open doorway into an adjoining darkened area.

Carly undressed, showered, and then walked naked through the doorway into the comfortably warm float room, feeling vulnerable and worried.

In front of her stood a large, smooth, clamshell-shaped tank. She pushed a button and it opened, yawning wide as the top half tilted upward, revealing shallow water inside. Carly climbed into the salty water and stretched out, floating easily, her loose hair extending in all directions. The water was comfortable, and she was well aware that it wasn't possible to drown in this tank. Even if she somehow dozed and flipped over, the sharp salts would force her back to full consciousness.

You need to close the top now, she told herself.

Still she hesitated.

She knew that this device had been invented back in the 1950s by a physician and neuropsychiatrist named John Lilly, who had carried his own personal experiments to quite an extreme, using psychedelic drugs to enhance his experiences.

Other famous and important people had found floatation tanks beneficial for a variety of reasons. The physicist Richard Feynman had written about his own experiences and insights in his memoirs, and John Lennon had used the sessions as therapy to help recover from heroin addiction. Even star athletes had found a variety of uses for the tanks.

These sensory deprivation tanks, called floatation tanks, were used by hundreds of people every day to achieve relaxation, healing, and sometimes for insights. People often experienced hallucinations, although typically in benign and pleasant ways.

Without telling Lyle about it, she'd used this float tank several times to help her get insights into cases. It plunged her into such a deep meditative state that she found it easy to connect with the dead, often in the form of vivid hallucinations that had revealed useful information.

Your last time was only an anomaly, she tried to convince herself.

But what if it happened again? That time only some animal-level instinct for survival had led her to push the button that ended the session and opened the tank. She had emerged shaken, crying, barely able to crawl her way out of the water. Eventually Cornflower Blue had come looking for her and found her sitting on the floor of the tiled room, half-dressed and dizzy.

Of course Carly had tried to make light of the experience, and she had certainly never told anyone else about it. She hadn't been sure she'd ever try the isolation tank again, but now she was baffled by this case and didn't know where else to turn for help.

I've got to try, she told herself.

She finally pushed a nearby button to close the pod and found herself lying in complete darkness and silence.

The relaxing effect of the tank was immediate, and her muscles began to loosen throughout her body. Only now did she really appreciate how tensed up she'd gotten during the last couple of days. Under normal circumstances, the tank would be exactly the therapy she needed right now to calm her nerves and get herself rested.

In the darkness, she tried to visualize the shadowy figure she'd seen in her dream, remembering that haunting voice.

"Please help me," the spirit had pleaded with her.

Floating weightlessly in the darkness, Carly spoke in a soft whisper.

"I'm here to help. Tell me. Help me to help you."

But then the thing she feared began. The spirits surrounding her were angry and dangerous.

"Bitch!" a faint angry whisper cried.

"How dare you come back here!" another voice challenged her.

These were the spirits that had made her last session so traumatic, hallucinations that always lurked in the background of even her successful sessions. Just like last time, they ruthlessly violated the peacefulness of this solitary place.

She didn't know who they all were, but she recognized one as a criminal who had been killed in one of her few gun battles, another who had eventually been executed in a case she's helped solve in another state. Just as they had before, the voices grew stronger, overwhelming any other thoughts or images.

But this time the hallucinations were even more aggressive. Now she felt fingers plucking at her body, and then hands clutching at her throat.

"You can't hurt me," Carly said aloud. "You're not real."

But the physical threat felt very real. Nevertheless Carly was determined that they would not overpower her this time.

Never again, she thought, gathering all her internal strength and pushing back mentally against the angry voices. She had to defeat them herself, without pushing that alarm to call for help.

And she heard their cries grow weaker.

Although she could still feel the dark spirits reaching for her, she ignored the one that threatened, *"You'll regret ..."* and firmly focused her mind on the contact she wanted to make.

I have to be stronger than they are, Carly told herself.

I am *stronger than they are.*

She wrenched her focus away from the angry dead, and reached again for the spirit who had asked for her help. To her relief, those ugly voices faded as Carly glimpsed the figure from last night's dream and heard her whispering inaudibly. There was no fog surrounding the woman this time, and as she came nearer, Carly could clearly see her kindly, inquisitive face, which was streaming with tears.

Then the woman spoke softly.

From fairest creatures we desire increase,
That thereby beauty's rose might never die ...

Those words were so familiar. Carly wondered, where had she heard or read them? Then she realized, it was a famous Shakespeare sonnet—the very first of the entire sequence.

"Sonnet number one," she said to the woman.

"Yes," the woman whispered.

And if Carly's theory of letters matching the numbers was right, number one was simply the letter *a.*

"Yes," the figure whispered again when Carly spoke the letter aloud.

So the letters would spell *isla.*

"Iz-la?" Carly said aloud

"ILE-lah" came the reply, gently correcting her. Then the figure spoke three words clearly: "*Fortune's Dearest Spite.*"

Carly found the words dimly familiar.

Probably from one of the sonnets, she told herself.

"What does that mean?" Carly asked.

The woman opened her mouth to speak and made a desperate gasping sound, as if she couldn't force any words out of her throat. More tears poured down her cheeks.

Finally she managed to say, "I—I can't. That's all I can ..."

She held out her arms and rolled up her sleeves.

Carly was stunned to see blood pouring out of long gashes in her wrists.

Then she rolled down her sleeves again and there was no sign of blood.

Her voice faded, but Carly knew what she was trying to say.

"That's all I can do."

Then the woman said, *"Find him. Stop him. It's up to you."*

And then the figure evaporated like a billow of mist

Carly was floating alone in her float tank, surrounded by darkness and silence, feeling relaxed now but baffled by her experience. She punched the button to open the tank.

As she showered and dressed, she kept wondering, *Did I succeed?*

She had connected with the spirit she'd hoped to find, but she still didn't know who the woman was. Nevertheless, she felt almost giddy, and triumphant at having fought down the angry dead and seeing the task through as well as she could. She also felt more hopeful than she'd felt for quite some time.

But what had the spirit been trying to tell her?

She remembered the spirit saying, *"It's up to you."*

Carly knew she had to get right to work.

CHAPTER TWENTY SEVEN

Suppose it didn't mean anything at all, Carly worried as she walked toward her car. She couldn't entirely dismiss the possibility that some of her visions came from nowhere except her own troubled imagination, and that the whole isolation-tank experience was quite meaningless.

Deep down, she didn't believe that. She'd faced such qualms before, and she knew that although she couldn't completely explain the source, the messages she got actually helped her solve murders.

And this communication from the unidentified woman had felt powerful.

It was real, she told herself firmly. *It just must have been real.*

She just had to figure out what the spirit's words meant.

When Carly reached her car, she thought better of driving anywhere right now. For one thing, she was so relaxed that she wasn't sure she could drive safely. Besides, she didn't want to go home. She didn't want to go anywhere. She needed to sit down and process the vision she had just experienced.

Fortunately, there was a coffeeshop just next door to the Full Lotus Health Center. That would do. She walked back and went inside, bought a scone and a cappuccino, and sat alone at a small table.

Although her body felt relaxed, her brain seemed electrically charged—keenly alert and ready for action. She took a few deep, long breaths to slow down her thoughts. Now she was going to have to make more sense of the riddling clues she'd just received.

Then it occurred to her that first she'd better check on something else.

She took out her cellphone and brought up the morning newsfeed. Sure enough, there was a story about the arrest of a suspect in the recent murders of three women. And sure enough, Lyle and Detective Brown and the Chief of Police were quoted as having made the announcement. And just as Lyle had said, Carly herself had gotten credit for helping to apprehend the suspect.

But Carly wasn't in a self-congratulatory mood right now. She was more certain than ever that Dennis Ring was not the killer, and that the true murderer was probably getting ready to strike again at the very moment, if he hadn't done so already.

She wondered—should she call Lyle and … ?

And tell him what? she asked herself.

That they'd definitely arrested the wrong man, and she'd just gotten a vision in a floatation tank that might just lead directly to the killer? No, that wasn't an option. She was on her own, at least for the time being, at least until she had more solid information to share.

What she needed to do first was a bit of online research.

She took out her cellphone, opened a search engine, then typed in the letters "ISLA," and found that it was a not-uncommon woman's name. And it was pronounced just as the vision had said.

"ILE-lah."

But her search brought up a list of countless women with that first name. How could she possibly narrow it down?

As she sat there thinking, an eerie chill swept over her forehead, and she heard a woman's voice whispering in her ear.

"Fortune's Dearest Spite."

Carly turned toward the voice, but no one was there, and that chill in the air dissipated. But the voice was unmistakably familiar. It was the woman in her vision, saying three of the words Carly had heard her say during her time in the floatation tank.

Whoever she is, Carly thought, *she hasn't left me.*

Carly felt suddenly grateful and less alone.

"Thank you," she murmured aloud.

There was no reply, nor did Carly really expect any. She needed to make the best of those words she had just heard, needed to discover their significance.

She typed the word ISLA again in the search space, followed by "fortune's dearest spite."

The first item that appeared made her gasp aloud.

Fortune's Dearest Spite was the title of a scholarly book about Shakespeare's sonnets.

And its author's name was Isla Broughton.

Carly's heart was beating rapidly now, and her fingers were shaking.

Who is Isla Broughton? she wondered.

Or who was *she?*

After all, if the woman in her vision was Isla Broughton herself, she must be dead, as her suicidal wrist wounds would indicate.

Carly ran another search for "Isla Broughton" and immediately ran across an obituary from about a year ago for a 38-year-old woman of that name. Broughton had been a respected professor at Schor University in the D.C. area. The cause of the death was "apparent suicide," and the text remarked that Broughton's friends were shocked and surprised and hadn't expected her to take her own life.

Most of the article was about Broughton's considerable accomplishments in Shakespeare studies, especially her critically praised book about Shakespeare's sonnets, *Fortune's Dearest Spite.* Broughton had never married and had no children.

Carly clicked through a handful of news stories about Professor Broughton's suicide, but they offered little information beyond fond statements and memories of grieving friends, colleagues, and students. There had obviously been no police investigation of the woman's death, since foul play had clearly not been involved.

The exact cause of death was tactfully not mentioned, but of course Carly already knew how it had happened. She shuddered as she remembered again the apparition of those slashed wrists. She realized she knew something that Broughton's closest friends and colleagues apparently hadn't known—that she had killed herself out of despair and guilt over unleashing a killer into the world.

What do I do now? Carly wondered.

She still knew next to nothing about the killer—not even his relationship to the deceased woman. But Broughton's spirit was doing everything she could to help Carly bring him to justice. Alas, the dead woman had to struggle to communicate even the vaguest clues.

And one of those clues seemed to be that book itself:

"Fortune's Dearest Spite."

Carly quickly decided to try to track down a copy. Turning her attention to her computer, she searched for the title among online booksellers. It wasn't exactly a rare book, but it wasn't a common one either—not the sort of thing that became a runaway best seller, but was of niche interest. Nevertheless, a few booksellers had it, and some of them guaranteed shipping in one to three business days.

Too long to wait, Carly thought with a groan.

But surely she could find a copy locally that she could simply buy right off the shelf. Was there a bookstore anywhere in the area that might stock that particular kind of title?

She ran another search:

This time she found a bookstore called Sea Change Books, which specialized in Renaissance literature. It was located in Foggy Bottom not far from Cheswick College, where Bianca Voigts had been murdered.

Carly called the number and immediately heard a professional but cheery woman's voice.

"Sea Change Books, this is Becky. How can I help you?"

Carly asked, "Do you happen to have a copy of *Fortune's Dearest Spite ... ?"*

Before Carly could finish her sentence, Becky said, "Oh, by Isla Broughton! Yes, I think we might have one copy left. Let me check."

Carly could hear the woman's fingers rattle across a keyboard.

"Yes, we do have it. I can go get it off the shelf. Do you want me to ship it to you?"

"No, I'll come and pick it up. That is if you're open on Sunday."

"We open five minutes from now."

"Perfect. I'll be there in about half an hour to pick it up."

"Very well. I'll keep it at the front counter for you. Just tell me your name."

Carly gave Becky her name and ended the phone call.

As she finished her scone and her cappuccino, she realized that some of the deep relaxation from her floatation tank experiment was ebbing away. Between the caffeine and thinking about the case, she could feel her adrenaline levels start to rise.

It's just as well, she thought. *I need to be at the top of my game.*

But as she stood up to walk out of the coffeeshop, she felt another eerie chill across her forehead and heard that whispering voice again.

"Be careful. He's dangerous. He doesn't know who he is. He thinks he's someone else. He's quite insane."

Carly felt another wave of gratitude, mingled with a touch of frustration. She wished the spirit of Isla Broughton could tell her more. But she knew perfectly well that her gift didn't work like that, and that the spirit was doing the best she possibly could.

She left the coffeeshop and hurried to her car. The city was just 20 minutes away, and on a Sunday like this it would only take a few minutes more to reach Foggy Bottom.

*

Carly parked in a small lot just a few doors away from Sea Change Books, a little store squeezed between two larger businesses in the same brick building. As she walked up to the entrance, she stopped for a moment to read an ornate text painted on the front window—a passage from Shakespeare's *Tempest* and the source of the bookstore's name:

Full fathom five thy father lies;
Of his bones are coral made;
Those are pearls that were his eyes:
Nothing of him that doth fade
But doth suffer a sea-change
Into something rich and strange.
Sea-nymphs hourly ring his knell
Hark! Now I hear them – Ding-dong, bell.

When Carly pushed the door open, a little bell rang to announce her arrival. The narrow store was charming and intimate, with bookcases featuring new titles and others that seemed to contain antique volumes. A stairway led up to a little balcony crowded with more bookcases.

Carly heard a cheerful voice call out, "You must be Carly See."

She turned and saw a tall woman with short black hair and an enormous, sparkling smile standing behind the counter.

Carly smiled back at her.

"That's right," she said.

"It wasn't hard to guess," the woman said with a giggle and a glance at her wristwatch. "You're the first and only customer we've had today, and you're here exactly when you said you'd be. I'm Becky Delaney, the owner of the store."

"I'm pleased to meet you," Carly said.

"We've got your book ready," Becky said, reaching under the counter. She took out a medium-sized hardback book with a dustjacket collage of Renaissance portraits that Carly assumed were of people associated with Shakespeare's sonnets. The book appeared to be brand new.

Becky added as she slid the book toward Carly, "It's been quite a while since anyone came looking for this one. A terrible shame what happened to the author. She killed herself, you know. I met Isla, oh, just a few times. She did a book signing here when *Fortune's Dearest*

Spite came out, and came around two or three more times just to browse."

Carly's curiosity was piqued.

She asked, "Does anybody who knew her have any idea why she took her own life?"

"I don't believe so, no. I've spoken to a few of her colleagues at Schor University, and they were stunned by it. They said she was happy and outgoing and not the type of person who would do something like that. They also said that she was ... well, very frightened of something during the last few days of her life. Terribly, terribly afraid. But she wouldn't say about what, and they had no idea what it might be."

Becky tilted her head and looked at Carly with interest.

"Fortune's Dearest Spite is a marvelous book, but hardly of interest to most people. If you don't mind my asking, why are you so eager to find it?"

Carly swallowed down a lump of uncertainty.

Should I tell her what I'm doing? she wondered.

She quickly decided that wasn't a good idea, nor was identifying herself as a BAU agent. Rumors might run rampant if word got out that whoever had killed those women the night before last and yesterday might still be at large. Carly was already treading on shaky ground by going it alone.

Instead she stammered, "I—I, uh, guess I'm just interested in this sort of thing. I read all of Shakespeare's sonnets when I was eleven."

No point in telling her it was a miserable experience, Carly thought.

Becky let out a chuckle.

"Wow, you got an early start!" she said. "Well, I promise you'll love this book. It's the best one I know about the sonnets. And I've read a lot of them."

Becky opened up a leather-bound book—a ledger full of names and addresses.

"Care to sign up on our contact list?" she asked. Then with a wink she added, "I like to send notes and postcards about our events. I know, it's kind of a low-tech way of keeping in touch with people. But I still like to do some things the old-fashioned way."

Carly wasn't particularly interested in being on a Renaissance literature mailing list, but she wrote down her name and address just to be polite. As she took out a credit card of her own to pay for the book, she felt that strange chill across her forehead again, and thought she heard a voice whisper in her ear.

"Look!"

CHAPTER TWENTY EIGHT

At the whispered command *"Look!"* Carly glanced all around the bookstore. A flash of motion on the balcony caught her attention, and she was sure that someone had just stepped out of sight behind some shelves.

Odd, Carly thought.

Looking up at the balcony, she said to Becky, "I thought I was the only customer here today."

Becky said, "Oh, that's just my guy stocking shelves. On a slow day like this, he's the only help I need."

Sure enough, the man came into view again, going about his business and putting books on the shelves. There was nothing the least bit suspicious about him. But for some reason, that peculiar chill stayed with Carly as she finished her purchase and carried the book away in a bag.

It must have something to do with the book itself, she thought. *And what I might find out from it.*

As she started toward her car, she found herself thinking about Lyle, who surely believed she was still at home sleeping late. According to the message he'd sent this morning, he could be right here in D.C., still working at police headquarters. But he'd told her not to bother joining him, and she really was anxious to get home and read the book.

She couldn't even tell her partner why she had looked for this book and bought it. She never revealed to anyone that messages from the dead helped her solve mysteries, and right now she was at a loss for an alternate explanation for even being in the city.

So why was she still feeling a bit guilty for just rushing on home?

She reminded herself that Lyle was her partner, after all, and he deserved to know she was nearby if he wanted her help.

As Carly sat down in her car, she took out her cellphone and called him.

She was relieved when she got his answering machine. Speaking hesitantly, she left a message.

"Hi, Lyle, this is Carly. Listen, don't get mad, but I'm still checking out a few things about … well, you know what. I know you're probably wrapping up the case and you think I'm being stupid, but … there are still some things I think are important. I'd like to talk through them with you. Let's do that soon, OK?"

She ended the call and started the engine.

At least I tried, she told herself. If the book revealed anything new about the case, she would be more persistent about telling Lyle. Her senior partner usually did at least listen to her odd theories, because so many of them had proved helpful in one way or another. Yesterday he had been uncharacteristically impatient, but of course both of them had been exhausted.

As she started to drive, Carly recalled that odd moment back at the bookstore when she'd felt a chill and heard a voice whispering the word, *"Look!"*

She'd looked, but had seen nothing really. So what could the command have meant?

Did it mean anything at all?

At least she didn't feel that chill anymore. What she needed to do right now was get back to her apartment and pore over the book and see if it contained any clues. If she was right that the killer was still out there, she had no time to lose.

*

The man listened as he heard the entrance bell ring again.

That's her leaving, he thought.

He stepped from out of behind the bookshelf in time to see the woman through the front window heading away from the store down the sidewalk. He suddenly felt a bit foolish for bothering to conceal himself from her.

So what if she'd spotted me? he thought. *Why would that matter?*

Even if she'd seen him before—and as far as he knew, she hadn't—she probably wouldn't have recognized him. He seemed to have that effect on people—or rather that *lack* of effect. For all his unacclaimed, unacknowledged, neglected brilliance as an actor as well as an author, few people ever seemed to remember his face.

Of course, Isla had been the one great exception.

She had treated him as if he were the most beautiful and brilliant man in the world, and he had her to thank for revealing to him who he really was.

I miss her, he thought.

Why did she have to leave like that?

It still didn't make sense to him.

He remembered how she'd cried and kept saying, *"You're wrong, you're not who you think you are."*

And then …

She was gone.

It was so wrong. *She* was so wrong. If she could only have been with him during the last couple of days. If only she could have seen the fruits of his dramatic genius. She'd have believed in him again, just as she had before.

Now he had no one to believe in him except himself.

But soon that would change. Soon the world would believe in him.

In fact, it was already beginning to happen. The news was abuzz with his accomplishments. Of course no one yet knew who he was or had grasped the meaning behind his artistry.

But they would.

He had recognized the importance of certain sonnets and created the brilliant script. He had written the stage directions and allowed the first three women to cast themselves in his tragic drama.

Reaching for a specific book of sonnets on the bookshelf, he thought back to how beautifully his scenario had worked. One by one, they had come into the store and just happened to pick up this book to look at it, oblivious to the fact that they'd sealed their fates. He was sure they'd all noticed the torn-out pages.

But now the situation had changed.

This morning, a woman had come in looking for a different book, one that she had no business even knowing about.

How dare she buy Isla's book. That wasn't in the script.

But he was up to the challenge. Now he was going to prove himself a master at improvisation as well as a master tragedian. This new woman had unknowingly sealed her own fate just by being who she was—an FBI Agent in pursuit of him.

For of that fact there could be no doubt. Last night on the news, he'd heard the investigator—Special Agent Lyle Ramsey was his name—foolishly boast about capturing the killer of the three women.

Such idiots, to think that some other author could have conceived murders of such genius! Because of course, they had arrested some fool who had stumbled onto the set.

It was really quite infuriating.

A smirk formed on his face as he mimicked something else Detective Ramsey had said on TV, capturing his voice as flawlessly and perfectly as a recording machine:

"Credit must also go to my brilliant partner, Special Agent Carly See."

Yes, he had the man's voice down perfectly.

And he would put his skill to good use very soon—for now was the time to act.

"Carly See," he murmured with pleasure.

He'd recognized the name as soon as he'd heard his boss repeat it over the phone. Carly See had ordered Isla's book. She wanted to pick it up today.

He'd personally found it on the shelf and brought it down to Becky.

It occurred to him, not for the first time, that Becky Delaney probably also had a role in this play. Somehow or other, she would surely become part of the tragedy—because the story had to continue beyond the few scenes he had already written. He was just waiting for the muses to help him work out that part of the story.

He tucked the book of sonnets into his jacket, walked down the balcony stairs, and stepped behind the counter where Becky was standing in wait of a customer.

"What are you doing, Bill?" his boss asked as he opened the ledger with the customer contacts in it.

He didn't reply, just turned to the page where Carly See had written down her information. He read her address, which was instantly imprinted on his memory. Then he turned and strode toward the store entrance.

"Where are you going?" Becky called after him.

"Just out for a breath of fresh air," he said with a smile. "I'll be back in a minute or two."

"Oh. OK."

He opened the door, causing the bell to jangle, then continued on his way to his parked car.

CHAPTER TWENTY NINE

Any remaining anodyne effects of the floatation tank session had thoroughly worn off by the time Carly pulled into the parking garage below her apartment building in Glensted. She parked and hurried toward the elevator, her whole body buzzing with excitement.

I'm going to crack this case, she thought. *I can feel it in my gut.*

She was certain that the book she'd just bought at Sea Change Books—*Fortune's Dearest Spite,* by Isla Broughton—held some sort of key to the case. Isla's very spirit had signaled as much to her in her vision. Even if the secret of the book was vague, that hardly mattered. If she just got a hint, she could surely solve the rest of the mystery through her own deductive skills.

Carly went into her apartment and hung up her jacket. She took off her gun and put it in its case in the closet. Then she sat down on her sofa and placed the book in front of her. It was a hardcover with a dust jacket, and it looked brand new.

When she picked the book up and opened it, a folded piece of paper slipped out from under the dust jacket. Carly put the book down and picked up the paper.

She unfolded it, and gasped aloud.

The paper was a page torn from a different book.

A Shakespeare sonnet was printed on it.

Carly gasped aloud. She couldn't believe what she was seeing.

But there it was, right in front of her—a page with Shakespeare's Sonnet number one on it.

She read the opening lines.

From fairest creatures we desire increase,
That thereby beauty's rose might never die ...

Those were the words she'd heard Isla Broughton say so tearfully in her isolation tank vision. And the page she held in her hand had obviously been torn from the same book as those found with the bodies of three murdered women.

The killer put this here, she thought.

But who was it intended for? Could he have put the sonnet in this book especially for Carly herself to find?

How was that even possible?

Surely her finding this sonnet hadn't been merely random.

Carly was swept by dizziness and confusion as the telltale tingling began. A voice from the dead was reaching out to her, and for a moment she felt lost in unintelligible whispers and flickers of unrecognized images.

None of this is real, she told herself.

This is another vision.

Did that mean she was still in that isolation tank, imagining going to the bookstore … imagining bringing a book home?

Carly forced her eyes to focus on her surroundings and saw that she was definitely in her own apartment. Everything was where it ought to be, nothing was melting or shifting or …

She shook herself hard, trying to clear her head. Real or not, she had to make sense of the experience she felt coming on.

She dropped the sonnet on the coffee table and picked up the book that was there, half expecting it to have become some completely different volume, perhaps one of the cozy mysteries she read for fun.

But the book was still *Fortune's Dearest Spite* by Isla Broughton

She turned the first of pages until she came to the preface written by the author, which consisted mostly of acknowledgements and thanks. Then her eyes fell onto the last paragraph of the preface.

Finally, I must reserve my fondest and deepest thanks for my research assistant, Bill Davenant—one of the most talented young scholarly minds I have ever encountered, with a vast range of talents too numerous to list. Since we first began working together, Bill has become much more than an assistant to me, or even a colleague, but a beloved friend and companion.

This book is dedicated to him.

"Bill Davenant," she murmured.

Then she heard the woman's voice repeating the name in her ear.

"Bill Davenant."

The name meant something to the spirit who had been reaching out to Carly.

I've got to understand why, she thought.

She closed her eyes and let herself slip into a reverie.

Before she knew it, Carly found herself in vivid surroundings—a comfortable, well-furnished living room lit only by a friendly roaring fireplace.

She was gazing at a young man with a remarkably nondescript face who was gazing at the fire with a glass of wine in his hand. Carly lifted a glass of wine to her own lips and sipped it …

But ...

She knew she wasn't Carly.

She was reliving a memory of Isla Broughton herself.

"William Davenant," Isla murmured with a slight chuckle, clicking her glass against his. "What an extraordinary name."

The young man turned toward her. A twinkle in his eye suggested that he was much more remarkable than he appeared.

"How so?" he asked.

"Don't you know?" she replied. "William Davenant was a famous 17th-century poet and playwright who was also supposedly William Shakespeare's godson."

"I've never heard of him," the young man said.

She chuckled again, more heartily this time.

"Well, I didn't say he was famous anymore. But in his own day, Bill Davenant was something of the stuff of lore and legend. Rumor had it that he claimed to be more than Shakespeare's godson. He said he was Shakespeare's illegitimate son—the true natural heir to the Bard's genius."

The young man's tilted his head with interest.

He asked, "Did Davenant himself have any children?"

"Well, none that anybody knows of," Isla said. "But who can really say?"

"But my name ..."

"Just a coincidence, of course."

The vision faded, and Carly opened her eyes. She was amazed and fascinated. Outside of the floatation tank, she'd never had a vision so detailed and vivid and lengthy. This morning's isolation session had definitely triggered something profound and important and powerful. And it was somehow connected with the book she'd just bought.

She stared the dedication again. She knew she had just learned something important. Isla Broughton had known the killer. More than that, she'd mentored him, and he'd been her protégé, and then …

They'd become lovers.

She closed her eyes again, and this time she found herself handing a book to the young man …

"I've got a little gift for you, Bill. It's nothing really valuable, except maybe to me. It's an edition of Shakespeare sonnets, not rare or anything like that. It's just that my father gave it to me when I was a girl, so it means a lot to me. And I hope it will mean a lot to you."

The voice and vision faded, and Carly opened her eyes again.

So that's how that particular book of sonnets came into his possession, Carly realized.

Then she flashed back to what Isla's spirit had said to her repeatedly.

"It's all my fault."

Carly had no doubt that Isla blamed herself for the murders her lover had committed.

But why does she think they're her fault?

She felt a renewed vision taking form and closed her eyes again. Again, she found herself witnessing an event through Isla's eyes.

Isla stood helplessly by while Bill stormed around her office, knocking objects off her desk and books off their shelves.

"You don't believe me!" he shouted at her.

"Bill, please just listen—"

"You think I'm making it up."

"You're not *making it up. It's just ... it's just not ..."*

Bill stepped toward her menacingly.

"It's just not what?"

Isla gathered up her courage and said, "It's just not true."

A silence fell between them.

Then she said, "You are not *Shakespeare's heir, descended from him through the original William Davenant. I wish I'd never have told you that story. Your name is just a coincidence."*

"You're wrong," Bill snarled.

"Perhaps you could get a DNA test—"

"That's impossible, and you know it. There are no other descendants, no other samples to compare mine to. Besides, I can feel it in my blood. It's more than just his DNA. It's his spirit coursing through his veins. Although the world doesn't know it, I am

Shakespeare himself, come back to humankind to create anew."

A sob burst from Isla's throat.

"If only I hadn't told you that story," she said. "This is all my fault. You're no longer the man I love. I destroyed that man, and I can't live without him. My heart is broken."

Bill struck her hard against the cheek.

Carly's eyes snapped open again and she gasped aloud.

Things were beginning to make horrifying sense.

For all his apparent brilliance, young Bill Davenant had carried within himself the seeds of madness—of murderous, psychopathic paranoid schizophrenia. Poor Isla had been devastated to see his scholarly and literary brilliance give way to hopeless insanity.

She'd killed herself out of guilt and despair.

Carly shook her head and spoke aloud in a soft voice.

"Isla, it wasn't your fault. You mustn't blame yourself. His illness is his own. You were not the cause."

Carly jerked upright at the sound of a knock at the door.

"Who is it?" she called out.

A familiar voice replied, "It's me, Lyle. Let me in, OK?"

Carly breathed a sigh of relief. But then she felt uneasy. She knew she needed to talk to Lyle, but …

How can I tell him about … all this?

She knew she had to do her best. She rushed toward the door. Just as she unlatched it and turned the knob, she thought she heard a voice.

"Don't!"

But the warning came too late. The door burst open, smashing against Carly's head and sending her reeling. The pain was blinding. She could only see stars and sparks all around her. It took a fraction of a second for her to gather her wits and understand what had just happened.

The intruder's face looked almost remarkably plain.

It's him, she realized.

It's Bill Davenant.

It's the killer.

He'd placed the sonnet in the book she'd called about and bought.

He'd been marking her as his next victim.

And now he was standing in front of her, holding a dagger that looked like a prop for a play. But like the one that had killed Gentry Chapman, this blade was obviously sharp and real.

CHAPTER THIRTY

The man who had burst into Carly's apartment slammed the door shut behind him.

"Carly See," he said, holding the shining blade out toward her, "I've looked forward to this moment. You don't know me, but I know a few things about you."

I know more about you than you might suspect, Carly thought.

This was surely the man that the spirit of Isla Broughton had been concerned about.

Still stunned from the blow to her head, Carly found herself seeing double as she tried to focus her eyes on the dagger in his hand. She didn't dare try to disarm the man, not in her dazed condition. He was handling the blade quite capably—which Carly didn't find surprising, since he had already murdered one woman with a similar weapon.

Carly didn't dare strike out against him, not until her head cleared.

Meanwhile, she had to keep him from fatally attacking her.

Maybe if I can keep him talking ...

Carly said, "But—but when you knocked—I thought you were my partner."

Davenant's lips shaped into a sneer, and he spoke in a voice that sounded uncannily like Lyle's.

"'Credit must also go to my brilliant partner, Carly See. Her hard work and insights made it possible to apprehend this suspect.'"

Carly was amazed by his skill at mimicry. He was doubtless repeating verbatim something he had heard Lyle say on the TV news last night when he'd spoken about Dennis Ring's arrest.

Davenant took a step toward her, and she took a step backward.

Then he said in a voice that sounded eerily like Carly's own, *"'I read all of Shakespeare's sonnets when I was eleven.'"*

Carly could hardly believe her ears.

Then she realized, *He overheard me say that at the bookstore.*

He swung the dagger back and forth in a swaggering manner.

"I am a master of my art, no? Oh, you have no idea of the skills at my command. This is theater, you see. Your death is to be a magnificent dramatic act, conceived and staged by the greatest dramatic genius the world has seen in centuries."

He took another step toward her and continued, "Theater is a synthesis of all the arts—painting, sculpture, music, poetry, oratory. Only a universal creative genius can master all of them, a mind that comes along once in 400 years."

"A mind like Shakespeare's?" Carly asked, feeling her head just starting to clear.

Stay cool, she told herself.

Just keep him talking.

Davenant squinted with surprise.

"Yes, exactly, like Shakespeare's."

"And you have that kind of mind, eh?" Carly said. "You are Shakespeare's heir."

Davenant chuckled darkly.

"I *am* Shakespeare—reborn, incarnate. You are remarkably discerning, Carly See. A truly exceptional soul."

Carly shook her head and said, "Whatever talents I have are not my own. They are courtesy of you. After all, aren't I just a character in your play? Your own creation? The same as Gentry, and Bianca, and Lillis?"

Davenant's eyes widened.

"You understand!" he said with pleased amazement. "At last, someone who understands. It seems a shame …"

His voice faded.

Carly said, "To have to kill me? Well, if the script is written, aren't you powerless to change it?"

A cloud fell over the man's features. Carly knew why.

I used the word "powerless."

It was a word that he dreaded in his very bones. And now his eyes were darting back and forth with indecision. She knew what he was thinking. Maybe he shouldn't kill her after all, just to prove that he wasn't powerless over the story he was telling.

Carly's equilibrium was coming back to her now. She shifted back and forth from one foot to the other, calculating what move would catch him most off guard.

Then everything happened fast.

Just as she decided on her move, he drew his arm far back.

She felt a now-familiar tingle, and a woman's voice in her mind whispered *"dodge."*

And the man's arm whipped forward, expertly hurling the dagger through the air toward her chest.

Even though she had jerked to one side at that warning, the blade struck Carly with full force. But instead of plunging into her chest, it hit just below her left shoulder blade and stuck there.

Carly let out a cry of terrible pain and almost fell to the floor of her living room. In a flash, Davenant was upon her, straddling her, pinning her on her back by her right wrist. The pain in her left arm was searing, all the way from her shoulder to her fingertips, and she couldn't move it. She simply couldn't fight him off.

Through the haze of agony, she heard him say, "Of course that wasn't the way you were supposed to die."

He yanked the knife out of her flesh, and she almost blacked out from the pain. Then he reached toward her sofa with his free hand and lifted up one of the big soft pillows. He raised it above her head and declaimed in a startlingly powerful voice.

Thou mak'st me call what I intend to do
A murder, which I thought a sacrifice.

Carly recognized the lines. They were spoken by Othello before he murdered Desdemona by smothering her with a pillow.

As the pillow came down upon her face, Carly flashed back to her mother's words.

"I have a strong feeling that your killer would choose suffocation or hanging for his next murder."

Carly couldn't breathe now. But as her consciousness began to fade, she realized that her mother was right—Davenant had planned exactly this death for his fourth victim, just as he had the stabbing, the poisoning, and the drowning for the other three.

She realized angrily that she hadn't psyched him out at all.

She'd given him the chance to get the best of her.

Carly's helpless writhing was using up her lungs' last ounces of oxygen.

Soon the world went black …

… and then everything was bright again, an infinite-seeming expanse of white light.

Standing in front of her in the midst of the light was Isla Broughton. Tears were in her eyes again.

"I'm sorry," she said. "I tried to stop it. I tried to save you."

Carly felt her own tears well up in sympathy for the distraught spirit.

"It wasn't your fault," she said. "I blundered. You couldn't have done anything to stop it."

Carly studied Isla's eyes, hoping to find some trace of comprehension there. But the spirit still didn't seem to understand.

Then Carly said, "It was him, *Isla. He was responsible for his own actions. No one is responsible for what other people do."*

Isla said in a choked voice, "Then ... then you forgive me?"

"There's nothing to forgive," Carly said.

"And the others ... who died ... do you think they ...?"

"They don't blame you. I'm sure of it. They want you to let it go. So do I."

Isla's lips exploded into a glittering smile.

"Thank you," she said. "I needed to hear that. Oh, thank you."

Isla turned and began to walk toward what appeared to be the source of the light. Carly took a few steps to follow her, but Isla turned back and waved her away.

"No, you can't come yet," she said. "You've still got work to do."

Isla turned again and dissolved into the light ...

... and Carly found herself conscious again, with something still mashed against her face.

The pillow, she realized. He was smothering her.

The words she'd just heard echoed through her mind.

I've got more work to do, she thought.

I've got to live.

She heard muffled noises—a pounding followed by a loud crash. Despite the searing pain from the slash in her shoulder, Carly struggled with renewed energy and pushed the pillow violently away, sending her assailant reeling.

Out of the corner of her eye, she glimpsed someone else charging into the room through the broken front door.

Davenant lunged at her, and for a moment he and Carly were clutched in each other's arms in a fierce struggle. In spite of her dizziness, she kept wrestling with all her remaining strength.

Suddenly her assailant's body lurched away from her and Carly fell to the floor.

Through her blurred vision she saw someone else struggling with her assailant.

Lyle, she realized.

It was her partner who had burst into the room. Lyle had grabbed the man from behind and yanked him backwards. Then she saw her partner draw back his fist and slam it into Davenant's face. The man fell crashing to the floor, completely unconscious.

"Are you all right?" Lyle said to Carly as he handcuffed Davenant to a radiator.

"I'm—I'm—"

The word "fine" couldn't escape from Carly's lips. She sank to the floor, reeling from the blow to her head, and also from the pain and the loss of blood from her knife wound. She was dimly aware of Lyle using his cellphone to call for emergency help. Then her partner knelt down beside her.

"You're badly hurt," he said. "You've got to lie down."

He helped Carly get prone on her back on the floor.

She sputtered weakly, "But how … did you … ?"

Lyle chuckled and said, "How did I get here when I did? Hey, you told me to come, remember? You left me a message saying you wanted to talk. Well, I was driving from Metro Headquarters to Quantico, and of course your place is right on the way, so I thought I'd drop in. I heard a commotion inside, so I forced my way in."

Carly forced out a single-syllable laugh.

"I'm glad," she said.

Lyle glanced over at the still-unconscious man cuffed to the radiator.

"So that's the real killer, huh?" he said.

"Yeah," Carly said.

Lyle's eyes darkened with sadness and regret.

"I'm sorry, I was wrong. I should have listened to you."

Carly managed to smile.

"Well, you'll do better next time," she said.

"Yeah, next time."

Then Carly heard the sound of approaching sirens.

Lyle remarked, "That must be the ambulance, or police backup, or both."

"I don't need an ambulance," Carly said deliriously.

"Like hell you don't," Lyle said. "Lie still."

Carly shifted her elbows, trying to raise herself up again, but the pain and the dizziness were too much for her.

She lost consciousness.

CHAPTER THIRTY ONE

Several hours later, after medics had whisked her away and doctors finished patching up her wound, she tried her best to explain everything that had happened to her partner.

Lyle had just come into her little hospital room carrying flowers, his dark features creased with concern. She heard him draw an audible sigh of relief when she looked up at him and smiled.

Then she struggled to think what she had already told him, and what she could say to him now. Her shoulder was well-bandaged, and her left arm was in a sling, and the pain medications she'd been given were making her more than a little woozy. She began stumbling through parts of her story, trying to remember what she could reveal without him thinking she had gone mad

Fortunately, Lyle assured her as soon as he sat down by her bedside that Bill Davenant was doing a lot of talking of his own now that he was in custody, and he was spilling out the whole strange story of his murderous delusions. So Carly felt as though she could skip over a few parts of her own story—especially her floatation tank session and her subsequent communications with the deceased Isla Broughton.

"He followed me home," she said. "I didn't even notice. And I was even dumber to fall for his imitation of you."

"Of me?" Lyle barked. "He didn't tell me anything about that."

"Well he's a good mimic. He'd heard you on TV and he was good enough to convince me it was you at the door."

"That explains why you let him in," Lyle muttered. "But he won't have a chance to pull that trick again."

Carly found herself getting tired much too quickly. Her voice was fading, and she could feel her eyelids drooping.

"I wasn't worried at first," she said weakly. "I thought I could take him."

"We'll work on that," Lyle commented.

Then he patted her hand and said, "You've had quite a day, haven't you? There's just one thing I'm not sure I understand. Why did you go to … ?"

Lyle fell silent, but Carly was pretty sure what he was about to ask.

Why had she gone to the bookstore, and why had she bought that particular book—*Fortune's Dearest Spite* by Isla Broughton, the very book that had a torn page from the poetry book tucked in its dust jacket?

Lyle peered into her eyes for a moment.

Then he looked away and said with a smile, "Well, I guess you don't have to explain every last little detail. Some stuff just doesn't matter, as long as you got the job done."

"Thanks for understanding," Carly whispered.

And she meant it in ways that she figured Lyle might or might not fully comprehend.

"Well, I've kept you awake way more than I should have," he told her, rising from his chair. "You need to get some sleep."

"I guess so," she agreed. "Don't worry, though. I'll be back at work in a day or two."

Lyle wagged his finger at her and said, "You'll do no such thing. The doctor told me that knife barely missed your lung, and it was in the general neighborhood of your heart. You're lucky to be alive. And I want you to stay that way."

Lyle's voice tightened with emotion as he added, "I'm sorry."

"Sorry for what?" Carly asked. "You probably saved my life."

"But if I hadn't been so thick-skulled about the case, if I'd just listened to what you were trying to tell me, you might not have gotten into any danger."

Carly felt a lump of emotion in her own throat. She knew that he was thinking about Dawn Metcalf, his partner who had been killed before Carly even knew him.

I must have given him a terrible scare, she thought sadly.

Carly smiled a little and said, "What do we always tell people who go blaming themselves for things they can't help?"

Lyle nodded and said, "We say, 'It's not your fault. Don't blame yourself.'"

"And that's what I'm telling you right now. You're the most wonderful partner in the world. You have nothing to feel guilty about."

With her last gasp of energy, she added, "And stop worrying about me."

Lyle chuckled ironically and put his hat on and said, "Yeah, fat chance of that."

He left the hospital room, and Carly found herself alone and very sleepy. She closed her eyes and actually heard herself emit a snore.

Then an image took shape in her mind's eye. It was that little pinwheel toy she kept at her apartment in memory of Tyler Glick, her childhood friend who had been murdered.

She murmured half-asleep, *"Tyler, I'm sorry. I wish I could have …"*

But then she remembered her own words to Isla Broughton when she'd been on the brink of death.

"It wasn't your fault."

"No one is responsible for what other people do."

And of course, she had said much the same thing to Lyle just now. Carly figured she should take her own advice.

She watched the pinwheel as she let go of her spasm of guilt.

Then, to her surprise, the pinwheel started turning, as if struck by a breeze.

Carly asked, "Tyler—are you there?"

She heard a little boy's voice whisper, "I'm here, Carly."

"I've missed you, Tyler," she said.

"I've missed you," Tyler whispered. "But I came here just to show you something. Come with me."

She followed after the voice into a deep fog. For a short time, Carly had no idea where she was, although she didn't find that frightening. Finally she emerged onto a beautiful sparkling beach. She saw a woman standing at the edge of the surf looking out over the ocean at a golden sunset.

At the sight, Carly felt a great, strange emotion swelling up in her chest.

"Megan?" she called. "Is that you?"

The woman didn't reply.

Carly moved across the beach until she could see the woman's profile. She let out a gasp of ecstasy.

This was not the 18-year-old who had gone missing long ago. This was a woman nearly Carly's age—as Megan would be if she were still alive.

But there was no mistaking that face.

It was her sister.

"Megan, are you alive?" Carly asked. "Where are you now?"

Megan didn't reply.

Instead she heard Tyler whisper, "She can't hear you."

"Why not?"

The boy's voice laughed slightly.

"Why do you think?" Tyler asked.

Carly couldn't bring herself to say the words aloud.

Because I can't communicate this way with the living.

Which means Megan isn't dead.

She must be still alive!

The sun dipped below the waves, and the scene grew rapidly dark.

Carly murmured, "I'll find you, Megan. Wherever you are, I'll find you."

Then Carly slipped away into a comfortable dreamless sleep.

NOW AVAILABLE!

NO WAY BACK
(A Carly See FBI Suspense Thriller —Book 2)

Women are disappearing on their walk home at night, their bodies are turning up the next day staged as famous sculptures. FBI Special Agent (and psychic medium) Carly See must decode the mystery, and finds herself in the race of her life to find the killer—and save the next victim—before it's too late.

NO WAY BACK (A Carly See Suspense Thriller) is book #2 in a chilling new series by mystery and suspense author Rylie Dark, which begins with NO WAY OUT (book #1).

FBI Special Agent Carly See, a star in the elite BAU unit, hides a terrible secret: she can speak with the dead. The murder of her sister, still unsolved, plunged her life into grief and awakened a new power within her. Sometimes messages come from direct contact, other times in dreams. All of it feels like a curse—until Carly realizes she can harness her new skills to solve cases. But her abilities are unreliable, and Carly must use her brilliant mind to complete the puzzle—all while struggling to keep her secret from her colleagues.

With her vision leading Carly to dark and irrational places, she finds herself in a cat and mouse game with a diabolical killer—who always seems to be one step ahead of her. Why is he staging these bodies? What is he trying to create?

A page-turning thriller packed with twists and turns, secrets, and harrowing surprises you won't see the CARLY SEE series is a mystery series that will have you on the edge of your seat, endearing you to a brilliant and unique new character and having you turning pages, bleary-eyed, late into the night.

Book #3 in the series—NO WAY HOME—is now also available.

Rylie Dark

Debut author Rylie Dark is author of the SADIE PRICE FBI SUSPENSE THRILLER series, comprising six books (and counting); the MIA NORTH FBI SUSPENSE THRILLER series, comprising three books (and counting); and the CARLY SEE FBI SUSPENSE THRILLER, comprising three books (and counting).

An avid reader and lifelong fan of the mystery and thriller genres, Rylie loves to hear from you, so please feel free to visit www.ryliedark.com to learn more and stay in touch.

BOOKS BY RYLIE DARK

SADIE PRICE FBI SUSPENSE THRILLER

ONLY MURDER (Book #1)
ONLY RAGE (Book #2)
ONLY HIS (Book #3)
ONLY ONCE (Book #4)
ONLY SPITE (Book #5)
ONLY MADNESS (Book #6)

MIA NORTH FBI SUSPENSE THRILLER

SEE HER RUN (Book #1)
SEE HER HIDE (Book #2)
SEE HER SCREAM (Book #3)

CARLY SEE FBI SUSPENSE THRILLER

NO WAY OUT (Book #1)
NO WAY BACK (Book #2)
NO WAY HOME (Book #3)

www.ingramcontent.com/pod-product-compliance
Lightning Source LLC
Chambersburg PA
CBHW030617310726
48979CB00003B/756

* 9 7 8 1 0 9 4 3 9 3 5 8 2 *